# KC KEAN

Ruthless Rebel
*Ruthless Brothers MC #2*
Copyright © 2023 KC Kean

www.authorkckean.com
Published by Featherstone Publishing Ltd

Cover Design: BellaLuna
Editing: Zainab M. - Heart Full of Edits
Proofreader: Sassi's Editing Services
Interior Formatting & Design: Wild Elegance Formatting

Ruthless Rebel/KC Kean– 1st ed.
ISBN-13 - 978-1-915203-38-0

*To You,*
*My beautiful reader, thank you for always trusting in me*
*to create a world for us all to escape in.*
*You complete my soul, and warm my heart.*
*Thank you.*

*In a world of suffering and pain, choose hope and kindness.*
*It will conquer all.*

# PROLOGUE

## Scarlett
### Eleven Years Ago

A mottle of purples, blues, and blacks cover my skin from head to toe. Each bruise is a different shape as one blends into another. Yellow frames the edges of the older marks on my legs, which only serves as a reminder that they'll be targeting there next.

Swamped in a room of filth, the once white walls now stained with dried blood and smoke stains, I cower in the corner. My bare feet are backed right up to the wall as I try to make myself impossibly invisible.

Shadows flicker over me. My body's sore and aching, but I don't sob, cry, or scream for mercy. I've done that before, and it doesn't change anything, doesn't make me stronger or braver, and it definitely doesn't encourage anyone to come to my aid.

I'm alone in this world; I learned that a long time ago. Blood isn't thicker than water; it's venomous, seeped in poison and able to sink its claws into you. Water cleanses and feeds my wilted bones, cradling me in this God forsaken world, when all blood does is destroy me again and again.

The man tied to the chair in the middle of the basement grunts as another fist comes hurtling toward his face, splattering a fresh spray of blood across the floor. Despite his pain, he still doesn't talk. My father will stop at nothing until he gets what he wants. No one will cross him, especially not when they're in that chair, and if they have the gall to defy him, he ends them. It's as simple as that. At least on the surface it is.

I know better.

One victim, three bikers looming above him, and me cowering in the corner in nothing but a long t-shirt. It's as dirty as the walls I'm pressed against, but no one cares. I can't imagine what I look like to anyone who sees me, but deep down, that's not something *I* care about.

Survival.

That's it. Nothing more, nothing less, just my next breath.

"I'd recommend giving him what he wants, Gusto, otherwise the Grim Reaper is going to come calling," Billy says with a sneer, a wicked gleam in his eyes as his gaze flashes in my direction.

I will my racing heart to calm, praying Gusto does as he asks, but to my disappointment, he spits at Billy's feet instead. My breath lodges, and a sinking feeling washes over me as dread mingles with the grime that coats my skin.

"Scarlett, come."

My body aches with every breath I take. I can stay and hide in the corner, pretending like he can't see me, or I can get this over with. My chest clenches as I take a small step toward them.

When I'm within arm's reach, my father spins me on the spot, gripping my chin and forcing me to look at Gusto. Thick bushy eyebrows, jet-black eyes, and a hooked nose look up at me. There's a hint of surprise in his eyes over my presence. He knows just as much as I do that this shouldn't be a place for me, but here I am, right along with him.

"Gusto won't talk, Scarlett. He's been given plenty of chances. Now, it's time for you." I attempt to shake my head in his grasp, but it only tightens, bruising my jaw as he presses his nose into my cheek and growls, "It's almost cute that you think you have a choice, runt. I made you ruthless, but you keep acting reckless. Would you like to take Gusto's seat instead?"

I almost scream yes. *Almost*. The thought of putting an end to all of this, ending my pain and misery is tempting, real tempting, but it doesn't give me the end result I want.

Survival.

"What are you doing, man? She's just a kid," Gusto says, and I glance at the leather cut he's wearing, searching his name tag as I swallow harshly.

A Scorpion.

There have been a lot of them down here lately.

"It's time Gusto met the Grim Reaper, Scarlett. Don't disappoint me."

My hands clench at my sides as he loosens his hold on my face and dangles a blade in front of me. My eyelids flutter, my jaw tightening as I speak through clenched teeth.

"I don't want to." My voice sounds so weak, especially in comparison to his.

"I. Said. Kill. Him."

I want to be bratty and confirm those weren't actually his exact words, but that would only earn me another bruise. I want to scream in his face, take the blade from his hands and stab him with it instead, but before I can really consider it, he continues.

"You either kill him, Scarlett, or I let Billy here have his way with you."

I glance at the predator, and every inch of my body screams in protest as he looks at me hungrily with a sneer curling his lip. Gulping, I wrap my hand around the hilt of the blade. I don't want to do this, but I don't want Billy to touch me either.

"Shame, I was excited to have some fun, runt," Billy murmurs, stealing my father's nickname for me. It makes the bile burn the back of my throat even more.

Trying my best to ignore him, I inch closer to Gusto. I want to say I'm sorry, I want to say that I really don't want to do this, but nothing comes out as I bite my bottom lip so hard the taste of copper floods my mouth.

He's smirking at me, like it's laughable, like he doesn't believe I have the guts to bring a man to his demise, but that's where he's mistaken. Didn't he hear my father? This is all I've been trained for, all I exist for.

"Now, Scarlett," my father grunts. He doesn't need to follow up with a warning, I know one will come, and that knowledge alone spurs me on.

"What—"

Gusto's words cut off as I drive the knife into his chest with a level of precision I shouldn't have. His eyes widen as the tip of the blade pierces his skin, and I slice between his rib cage, piercing his organs, before tearing the blade out and tearing at his abdomen, watching as his guts spill out.

Anger and pain consume my breaths as I lunge the blade into his stomach a few times, too. I don't stop until I feel a hand on my shoulder—a silent order that my job is done.

As I stumble back, the blade clatters to the floor. My father grabs the neckline of my t-shirt and pulls me toward him until we're face to face. "Next time I tell you to do something, I don't want to have to repeat myself. Do you hear me?" His eyes blaze at me. "I've kept you a secret, made you my scapegoat so there's no blood on my hands. Your actions will determine how soon you meet your maker."

My hands ball into fists at my side, my nostrils flaring as tears prick my eyes, but I force them back. This man loves nothing more than seeing my emotions, feasting on them like it's his favorite pastime.

"When the police come for you, runt, and they will, you better be ready because if you think what I'm about to do to you is bad, you have no idea."

I frown at Billy's voice as my father releases me, and I tumble straight into Billy.

"Just bring her back in one piece. She's our most prized possession." My father turns away from us as an arm bands around my waist and I'm lifted off the ground.

I don't wriggle; I don't scream; and I definitely don't fight back.

He likes it too much when I do that.

# ONE

## *Scarlett*

Unfaltering, I stand my ground as five men dominate the room. Hitting Kronkz's arm, or Shift as everyone calls him, I sigh, rolling my eyes at the turn of events I was really hoping to escape.

I should have known better. I should have gone for this option to begin with, but I thought running was the answer to everything. Washing all emotion from my face, I roll my shoulders back and speak. "My last assignment was to kill the Ruthless Brothers' Prez. A transaction set up by my contact, Kronkz, aka Shift."

His eyes widen, but his jaw doesn't tighten with anger, like he half expected me to throw him under the bus, yet clearly hoped I wouldn't. *Well, screw you, motherfucker.* I should have been halfway to hell by now, the wind in my hair and my bike vibrating beneath me as I hightailed it away from the madness that is the Ruthless Brother's MC.

Ryker, Axel, Gray, and Emmett are gaping at both Shift and I, before Ryker finally steps toward me. It's not me he wags his finger at though; it's Shift.

"Wait, *you* put the job out for someone to take out *our* Prez and profit from it? Who the fuck ordered that, and why the hell did you allow it?" A vein in his forehead pulses with anger, as the scrape of a chair distracts my attention.

"I did."

My jaw drops so low it almost smashes into the floor as everyone turns to face Axel. Silence descends over the room at this unexpected revelation.

*Well, this is a drop in this rollercoaster of life that I wasn't expecting.*

"You did?" Ryker echoes, looking at Axel like he's never seen him before.

"I didn't fucking stutter, did I?" Axel gives him a pointed look and runs his tongue along his teeth in irritation.

Ryker presses his palms into the back of the chair. "Don't give me that bullshit, Axel. Like you're not dropping fucking bombs on the club right now. Don't look at me like *I'm* the one inconveniencing *you*."

Rubbing my lips together, my eyebrows practically reach my hairline as I watch the back and forth. *Fuck, pull up a stool, Maury is about to get saucy. Find out who the real daddy is after the break.*

"How about everyone calms the fuck down and takes a seat." Emmett's gruff voice cuts through the room, putting a small crack in the tension escalating around us as each of the men drop into their assigned seats.

Ryker takes his spot at the head of the table, occupying the President's seat, with Emmett to his left, his VP badge sitting proud on his chest as he leans back in his chair. Axel grunts as he drops to Ryker's right, while Shift takes the seat next to the gruff asshole who deserves his tag as sergeant at arms, leaving Gray to sit opposite his brother.

Axel's confession is definitely taking the limelight off me. Inching toward the door, I barely get two steps before my name bursts from Ryker's lips.

"Take a seat, Scarlett. This involves you too."

Pursing my lips, I fight back an eye roll as I turn back to the other end of the table, cursing each of them in my mind with every step I take. My ass hits the seat and Ryker doesn't waste a second before diving in.

"Please explain to me why you decided it was your call to turn your back on your brothers, Axel?"

I really don't need to be here for this. I come in, get the job done, and leave, none of this matters to me. I didn't know the club before, I didn't care for it, and I shouldn't now, but the way my heart clenches tells me I'm far more invested than I want to admit.

Fuck.

"I'd rather hear all about these skills that our Miss Scarlett Reeves has," Gray interjects, cocking a brow at me.

Asshole.

I was in the clear, then.

"And the connection she seems to have to your brother," Axel adds, like I didn't complete the job *he* set.

Annoyed, I shake my head with a downcast gaze.

Shift clears his throat. I'm literally the killer here because of both of them, yet they're more than happy to keep all of the attention on me.

Pussies.

"I don't feel like hashing out my life story right now, but thanks," I murmur. Shards of ice cut through my veins at the reality that the man I thought was a friend holds all of my personal details. My pain, my torture, my twisted past.

This is why I shouldn't have any friends, not even in a moment of weakness, and especially not over a video game chat when I think they'll never learn who I am in real life. Now he's somebody else with leverage over me. Fuck that.

"Scar," he murmurs, almost soothingly, and I snicker.

"Don't fucking *Scar* me," I hiss through bared teeth as I glance at him, but he doesn't wilt under my deathly gaze. Instead, he leans closer.

"Don't downplay the fact that you took out our Prez, and in response, they wiped out the entirety of the Ice Reapers—the club I didn't know the name of when you told me the story. A club that has continued to pull your strings, control your every move, dictating your life while holding you captive all at once."

My teeth clench together at his words, hating the way they set my veins on fire. I'm heartless, a killer, but admitting the vulnerable state I've balanced my life on fucking hurts.

I hate it.

I hate it. I hate it. I hate it.

Stabbing my fingernails into my palms, I exhale harshly, trying to piece together some kind of response, when Axel's voice cuts through the air instead.

"They were doing what?"

My gaze cuts to his, but he's not looking at me, he's staring directly at Shift who opens his mouth so easily to respond, but I cut in before Shifts gets the chance. "I. Said. Don't."

"I think you need to, Scar, because despite the fact that this was a paid job on your end, you still did something that benefited the Reapers," Emmett states, his tone calm, like he's trying to be the voice of reason, but he doesn't understand the can of worms he's threatening to open.

Slapping my palms on the table, I rise from my seat

with a grunt. "I'm done."

"We haven't even started," Ryker retorts, tilting his head at me. He's mad, raging inside, like a bubbling volcano yet to erupt, but he doesn't know who to aim it at.

Me. Axel. Shift?

"You're right. We haven't even started and you're already drawing up your own conclusions, assuming you can know every little thing about me when you don't have the right." *Continue to push me, Ryker, and I'll happily push back.*

"Then explain to us so we don't have to assume, Sweet Cheeks."

My chest tightens at Gray's nickname. It's an attempt to lure me into a false sense of protection, but I fucking grew up in a club like this, and I know far too well that men will say and do whatever they please to get what they want. My jaw tenses, my pulse ringing in my ears as I try to come up with an escape.

"We didn't find anything on Scarlett when I searched, for the exact same reason I couldn't find any information on Gamer Scar Nine either. I don't even know how I didn't piece the two together, but I never imagined she would be so close to home," Shift explains.

"Kronkz," I warn again, using the name *I* know him by and not the one gifted to him by the club, but the solemn look in his eyes tells me I'm going unheard because he thinks he knows better.

"She doesn't exist."

*I hate him right now.* I hate him so fucking hard I'm considering reaching for the gun at his hip and putting one of his own bullets through his stupid skull.

"What do you mean, she doesn't exist? She's standing right in front of us," Gray asks, confused.

Shift sighs, swiping a hand down his face. "It means—"

"It means I was born to a drugged-up club whore who died giving birth to me. Some might say I've been a killer since birth." I shrug, pushing up off the table as I glance at each of them. "So, if that's all you need to know..." I trail off, praying for an end to this goddamn conversation. The concern flashing in Shift's gaze only deepens.

"You're not helping yourself right now, Scar."

"I'm not trying to," I bite, annoyed.

"Well, I am," he retorts quickly.

I try to calm the rage inside of me by taking a deep breath that feels more like a heavy pant as I struggle to exhale through my nose. "I told you things in confidence, *not* for you to use against me."

"I'm not using it against you, Scar, and it's a good fucking thing that I know because right now, that's pretty much the only thing stopping a bullet from going through your skull," Shift states, and I pound my fist into the table.

"Please try, I dare you." There's not a drop of humor in my tone, not a single hint that I'm playing it off, because I'm fucking not. My hands are trembling, my fingers unable to remain still, and it's not because I'm scared. It's because I really want to end this conversation by any means possible. It's playing on a loop in my head, all I can think, all I can seek, all I can taste.

Axel clears his throat, leaning back in his chair as he eyes me. "I will go against you, dove, happily and willingly, but I want to hear it first."

Dove? What the fuck does that mean? Before I can press the matter, Shift jumps straight in.

"When she was born, they decided not to register her birth."

The four men at the table gape at me.

"Why?" Ryker's forehead crinkles in confusion as he scrubs at the back of his neck.

"Because her mother was a whore, and…"

Shift glances at me, knowing he's about to go too fucking far, but I know the information is going to come whether I like it or not, so I take control into my own hands and lay the truth out there.

"My father is, or *was,* Freddie Bartlett."

I hear Gray's sharp intake of breath over my own whirling thoughts. Shift gapes at me, not realizing that my father was prez so close to home.

"As in the Reaper's old prez?" Ryker clarifies. "The one who died ten years ago?"

The memory of that night comes flooding back to me. Bile burns at the back of my throat as my eyes close of their own accord.

"Why the fuck didn't he register you?" I shake my head at Emmett's question, trying to calm the wave of emotion that filters through my veins.

"Because he was angry I existed. Not registering me meant not accepting my existence as a blood relative to him." My words start out firm and strong, but end weak and pained. Even if they only sound like that to my own ears, it's enough to make my knees wobble.

"Why don't I like where this is going?" Gray's soft voice cuts through the struggles inside of me, but I don't drop my walls and let him in; instead, I double down.

"Because you have a soul?" I scoff, acting unfazed and uncaring about it all, but I can't shield the way my foot taps uncontrollably. Is it getting hotter in here? It feels like I can't fucking breathe. Blackness threatens to blind my vision, but I try to focus the best I can. "I need to breathe," I murmur, my mouth failing me and my bravado.

"You're not going anywhere," Axel says.

It's fight or flight time, and I'm feeling a bit of both.

Put me in a state of panic like this and my body will

take over, leaving logic as an afterthought.

Nobody moves as I cut the distance toward Shift. His eyes widen as I linger over him. "Don't make me."

"I wouldn't dare," he replies, lifting his arms in the air while his gaze remains fixed on mine.

Before he can change his mind, I reach for the gun at his hip, flick the safety off, and aim at them.

"What the fuck, Scar?" Gray grunts when I aim it in his direction. The hurt is evident in his blue eyes, but I can't offer sympathy right now. I have to put myself first, and to do that, I need to escape these four walls.

"When the Reapers were burned to ash, I vowed to never take orders from anyone else again. That includes you. You're not my Prez or my VP, or anything in between. If I say I need to breathe, then I need to fucking breathe." My head pounds as I push each word through my lips, my eyes scanning each of them.

"Fine." My eyes widen ever so slightly as I look at Ryker, that one word offering the first gulp of oxygen to my lungs. "Go, but don't go far, Scarlett. This isn't over."

I nod and move toward the door. When I have the handle in my free hand, I place the gun down on the table, and run from the room in a flash. Stepping into the bar area, I instantly become overwhelmed with the men filling the space, each looking in my direction with a new hint of curiosity after the little gun display I put on for everyone earlier.

Fuck.

It's no easier to breathe out here either.

"Hey, Scarlett, everything okay?"

Maggie stands behind the bar, shoulders tense and eyebrows pinched as she looks at me, and I shake my head.

"I… uh…" At a loss for words, I struggle to piece anything together, but she seems to understand.

"Get out of here, girlie. Get some fresh air," she says with a wave of her hand, and I nod a few seconds longer than necessary as her words process in my head, before I turn and race for the door.

I push the double doors open, gasping for breath. Planting my hands on my knees, I heave one lungful of air after another. When I feel a little calmer, I wet my lips, failing to quench the thirst taking over me, before heading toward the garage.

My bare feet hurt against the ground, and I realize I'm still only wearing a long t-shirt and panties. Reaching the bush I stashed my bag in earlier, I quickly step into a pair of leggings.

I hope like hell when I step into the garage my shoes are there from earlier, but none of my belongings are. One of the guys must have moved them when Gray carried me inside.

Fuck.

It doesn't matter. I've ridden my bike barefoot before; I can do it again.

My eyes fall to my bike, my Harley, my most prized possession.

I don't have a lot of time to consider my next option, but one thing is for certain, the confines of this compound are restricting my every breath and I need to get out of here.

All I can do is try and escape. If it doesn't work, then so be it, but at least I didn't go down without a fight.

Rolling my shoulders back, I almost cry with relief when I see my key in the ignition, and then I wheel it out. My heart thunders in my chest, the hairs on the back of my neck standing on end as I watch for any of the Ruthless Brothers, but it's a clear shot all the way to the entrance.

The gate is still slightly open and only has one person manning it. I'm willing to take my chances. Making sure my duffel is secured in the saddle bag, I climb on and turn the engine over. My body vibrates as it comes alive beneath me.

Inching closer to the only barrier standing between me and freedom, I let the adrenaline take over. The Ruthless Brother at the entry station looks up, eyes wide as I near, but it's too little, too fucking late.

# TWO

*Gray*

The door slams shut in Scarlett's wake, and a silence descends around Church like I've never felt before. My head is still whirling from the massacre she left behind earlier. To protect our club, our women and children, us.

It was the hottest moment of my entire life and my dick is still swollen because of it. She fucking dominated. I can't decide if the facts that followed, that stained the walls of Church, make me even needier for her or more pissed off.

Our former Prez died at the hands of the woman I'm infatuated with, but it's hard to be mad about it when we were plotting his demise anyway. She just kept the blood off our hands, and that decision was made by Axel and Shift, who orchestrated the entire thing.

Adjusting my dick, trying to alleviate the strain against

my jeans, I sigh. "What the fuck is going on?"

Ryker folds his arms over his chest and shakes his head. "Don't ask me, Gray. I'm only the president of this fucking MC, with two members working behind my back." His eyes darken as he glances at my brother and Axel across the table.

A ghost of a smile crosses Axel's face for a brief second, before he bites it back. "*For* your back, Ryker. We were working for your back."

Shift leans back in his seat, nodding in agreement, while Ryker's stare turns into a glare. "Right now, without all the fucking facts, it doesn't feel like it."

Feelings are hurt, pain is clearly being poured over the wood table between us, adding to the layers that have settled previously, but this isn't our downfall. I know it.

Axel casually adjusts his brown hair into a fresh bun on top of his head as he keeps his gaze fixed on Ryker. "Open your eyes, man. Sit here in front of me as Ryker, my best friend, and not Ryker, the president of this club."

Ryker sighs, but drops back in his seat as he nods for Axel to continue.

"Vengeance was clawing at you, driven by the need to prevail for your father, right the wrongs that were made and bring justice to the MC. If it was you and I that brought the destruction to the table, the five of us that laid the Prez out on the table and stained it with his blood, then the club

30

would look very different right now because there's no way in hell everyone would have understood."

My legs bounce, understanding settling in my stomach as I watch the annoyance and reluctance in Ryker's gaze. He's not wrong, not one bit. It was more than easy to slip into our new roles with the old prez being taken out by a different hand.

"We killed an entire club in retaliation. An. Entire. Club. Not only that, but we brought the one responsible into our own and made her comfortable," Ryker says, scrubbing a hand down his face.

"That club deserved it, Ryker. For what they've put her through… shit, if I had known who they were when I first found out, I would have marched us over there and done it in her honor." My brother's words catch me by surprise. He feels just as strongly about her as I do. Does he…

"Have you fucked her?" The question shoots from my mouth before I can even consider whether to bite it back or not, earning me a frown from my brother.

"Gray, did you even hear the part where I knew nothing about her? Not where she lives, not where she grew up, nothing. I heard the deeper shit, the weight on her shoulders, but I've never even seen so much as a photo of her. The only reason I knew she was actually a girl is because we played some video games from time to time."

I tap my finger on the table as I stare him dead in the

eyes. "Do you want to?"

"I'm quite sure she has her hands full with the four of you, huh?" He raises a brow at me, but I don't give up, that's still not an answer. He sighs eventually when I continue to stare at him. "No, Gray. My heart already belongs to another."

Uh, that's the first I'm hearing of it. Who does he have feelings for enough to not even see Scarlett as the stunner she is? Not that I need another fucking guy in the mix; I already want to steal her all for myself as it is.

It's on the tip of my tongue to press him more when Axel beats me. "Three, there's only three of them," he murmurs, waving his hand at us.

I glance at Ryker and Emmett out of the corner of my eye, ready to call bullshit on this guy, but Ryker shakes his head ever so slightly, telling me to keep my damn mouth shut. Since there's already enough being debated at the table, I bite my tongue.

"Why would you assign jobs to someone you didn't have a full background on? Especially an in-house hit?" Emmett asks, bracing his elbows on the table as he changes the subject.

"Specifically because there was no background. She's completely off the grid and it works entirely in our favor."

"Did you add Bill to the kill sheet as well?" Emmett considers, and my brother shakes his head.

"No, that's a mystery to me, but I can't say I'm sad about it."

Bill was a dick. The meanest cunt around when it came to women and children. Everyone was beneath him, but because he had a higher place at the table than us, there was nothing we could do about it.

"She did us a fucking favor," I grumble, ready to get a beer and lose myself in my thoughts or Scarlett. Possibly both.

"Didn't you ask her about it?" Ryker asks, a lingering hint of confusion in his eyes.

"Since I've been with the other chapter and she's unknowingly been hiding in my home, we haven't been online."

"You're her one gaming friend? That's how you figured out who she was."

He nods, confirming my realization. My jaw tightens and my heart races. Of all the things to bring it all to light, it was that.

"If she's off the grid, then that's probably why she panicked when the cops showed up and arrested Emmett and Euro."

"That and trauma," Axel adds, and I frown.

"Trauma?"

"You know it when you have it. I was an ass in the moment, but when I thought about it afterward, she was sinking in trauma, panic, and fear. That's why I got the bike. Something to ground her, or try to at least, despite the mess that was likely consuming her."

And this motherfucker thinks he doesn't have feelings for her? I hate that Ryker had already given me the signal to keep my mouth shut, but I hate it even more that I'm slightly glad he was the one to give her the Harley back. I don't like it, not one bit, but it makes fucking sense.

Asshole.

"Everything we've said in here today doesn't leave this room, doesn't feel the weight of the gavel hitting the wood, and doesn't change anything," Emmett announces, running his fingers over his beard as he meets each of our gazes.

"I can't lie to the club," Ryker says, indecision getting the better of him.

"You're not," I quickly interject. "Look at us, Ryker, look at this fucking club. Despite all the bullshit we're dealing with from the Devil's Brutes, we're still fucking thriving. We're in sync, united, and solidified together for what feels like the first time in forever. I refuse to let both your father and Eric die for nothing. We're making something of this place. Tainting others' judgment when they don't see the bigger picture is pointless."

He assesses me, his eyes crinkling as he thinks, but the moment is broken as the door swings open and Duffer sticks his head in. "Uh… she's gone."

Rearing my head back, I wait for more to come. The panicked expression on his face makes me confused. Emmett rises to his feet.

"Emily?"

*Oh, shit.*

"Fuck no," Duffer rushes out. "Scarlett. *She's* gone."

What the fuck?

"How?" I grunt, not bothering with the politeness of walking around the table as I clamber over it and rush to follow him out into the bar area.

"Literally through the fucking gate," he calls out, pushing his way through the unaware crowd as I chase after him.

The double doors ricochet against the walls as I slam them open, coming to a stop in the middle of the yard as I hear the telltale sound of a Harley Davidson driving off in the distance.

Despite the anger and frustration warring inside of me, a smirk teases my lips as my cock stands at full attention. My body craves her even as she runs, putting unnecessary miles between us.

*You can have a head start, Sweet Cheeks, but you won't get far. You're mine now.*

# THREE

*Scarlett*

A ripple of excitement courses through my veins, the wind whipping through my hair as I put more and more road between myself and the Ruthless Brothers. It's exhilarating and heart-clenching all at once. The rubber on the handlebars bites into my palms as I hold on for dear life.

This is exactly how it should have been. Me, my Harley, and the open road. So why does it feel… wrong? Why does it feel like I've left a part of myself at the compound?

I hit the pedal even harder, refusing to let the thoughts consume me and lead me down a dark path. My focus needs to be on where I'm going. I don't have any kind of safe haven to offer me shelter, no secret corners to escape to. Nothing.

The windy roads turn into the town's busier streets as I

blast through Jasperville. Darkness casts over me, the soft glow of the lamps guiding the way as I head toward the highway. The arrows point ahead, but I somehow lean to the right, heading deeper into the outskirts of town instead of rushing for the next state.

I know the roads I'm taking without even considering it, my heart galloping in my chest as I worry whether they will follow me here or not, but it doesn't make me turn around. Instead, I slow, despite the urgency inside of me, appreciating the roads that are only lit by the moon, without another soul in sight.

The trees rustle with the night's breeze as the sound of the water cascading before me grows louder, but still dim under the rev of my engine. Rolling to a stop, my bare feet scrape across the stone path, before I knock the kick stand down and release a heavy sigh.

The sound of the water lulls me into a sense of calmness that I don't seem to get anywhere else but here. If I'm leaving, then I'm leaving with this feeling in my soul. I tuck the loose tendrils of hair behind my ear as I climb off my bike, moving closer to the boulders framing the small pool of water that holds all of my hopes and dreams.

I stumbled across this place when I was younger, maybe ten years old, when my sperm donor threw me out of a moving vehicle, giving me a three-hour window to find my way home. Another one of his training methods that I detested, but was forced to endure regardless.

I hadn't made it home in time, but I did manage to dip my cut toes in the crystal clear water and hide my sobs in the sound of the waterfall as it cascaded from the rock formation above. To my left, it trickles off and swirls into a river, joining the bigger creeks in town. But this little spot, hidden behind trees and unworn paths, was like a sliver of heaven.

Ever since then, when I've been out on an assignment or offered even an ounce of freedom, this is where I've come to. My favorite part of Jasperville. I never told another soul about it, not even the whores who cared for me in secret when the president of the Ice Reapers wasn't looking.

This was for me and only me.

Taking a seat on the same boulder that I occupied the first time I came, I dip my toes into the icy water and focus on my breathing for a moment, making a conscious effort to calm my heart rate and the trembling of my bones.

The moon reflects in the water. I can't look away from it as I lose myself in my thoughts. Some old, some new, some full of wonder for the future.

What did that look like for me? What did my future hold?

I let myself get comfortable with the Ruthless Brothers and that's my own fault. I strayed from the plan that kept me going all my life.

Survival.

Faking my role as a whore wasn't my best move, it just locked me in another club despite my longing for freedom. The uncertainty and surprise of the Ice Reaper's fall from grace caught me off guard, rendering me helpless. I should have grown a backbone then, put up a fight and used the skills and abilities I was taught so I could have fled on my bike, leaving that life behind me without a backward glance.

I should have… but what would that have really looked like for me?

Minutes turn into hours as I ponder the moves I've made so far. I never excelled at games as a child. I wasn't raised with the tact and strategy to succeed. I was taught the brutality and blood-staining horrors that crept through the dark and claimed those in its path.

If I hadn't let the Ruthless Brothers believe I was a whore, what would they have done with me? Would they have put up a fight against a woman? Showed me the error of my ways like the Reapers enjoyed so much? I don't know, but what I do know is if I hadn't gone with them, then I'm not sure how else I would have survived. Besides, I would never have experienced anything with the Ruthless Brothers that enjoy consuming me either, and I don't think I could pass that up.

How would life be if I didn't hear Gray call me 'Sweet Cheeks'? If he hadn't shared his pizza with me and let me lose myself in video games with him? If he hadn't been the one to claim me as part of the damn rite of passage, only to refuse to go through with it and lead me down the hall to privacy instead?

Would it hurt to never meet the gaze of the blond Viking that bears a scar down his chest? To hear him mutter those sweet words about how I'm his *good girl*, or feel the stretch of his huge length as he claimed me again and again?

My thighs clench as I recall dropping to my knees in the shower for Ryker, a promise of more to come, and it did, in the form of both him and Emmett taking me in the garage, while I had the most perfect view of Gray and Axel.

To never experience that again?

Fuck.

And Axel... he's a complicated, cocksucking asshole who looks like sin with his man bun and his abs on display. He's enticing, making me want to touch him, but I know that trauma lurks there too, so I've never been given the chance. I never will if I run either. Not that my chances were actually high to begin with, but I never got the opportunity to say thank you for rescuing my Harley and bringing it back to me.

Swirling my feet in the water, my chest tightens as despair and confusion war inside of me. Why the hell do

I feel so torn? It should be as simple as it's always been.

Survival.

Nothing more, nothing less. It has been my mantra all this time, but it means nothing when I need it the most.

My gut knows the answer, even when my head refuses to. The sliver of life that I've lived alongside the Ruthless Brothers offered me a taste of something new, something different, altering my path like I never thought was possible. I was too blinded by their presence, the sex, and the intoxicating need that filled me, instead of focusing on putting one foot in front of the other like it's always been.

The truth washes over me. Maybe survival alone just isn't enough anymore.

What if I want more? What if I finally fucking deserve more than to just exist? What if I want it with them?

Shit, they're likely glad to see the back of me. Either that or they want my head on a pike for smearing the blood of their former prez on my hands. How I left things is completely unclear.

Is that how it will remain forever? Am I happy with that?

Sinking my head into my hands, I pull my feet from the water, crossing them under me as I will my thoughts to find an answer rather than tumbling through the questions that flit through my mind. I tilt my head to the moon, the want and need to scream up at it all-consuming, but instead I grab a small rock from beside me and toss it into the water. The splash echoes around me in the otherwise silent night, offering no sense of relief to my pent-up feelings.

Any thought of getting on my bike right now and taking off for somewhere new makes my heart hurt. That's an answer in itself. I know that. Sitting here alone without the craziness of a club around me, the clarity is palpable.

I can't leave it like this.

I could walk back in there and meet my end, but my heart refuses to let me leave without finding out. The overwhelming feeling I get when I think of any of them is indescribable, leaving me desperate for more and confused as hell.

Even knowing that the Devil's Brutes are raining havoc around the Ruthless Brothers, the pain they put me through lingering over my skin and making the hairs on the back of my neck stand on end, it still doesn't feel like enough of a reason for me to climb back onto my bike and never look back.

How long am I supposed to run for? The blood on my hands isn't going to disappear no matter where I go, but those it has affected... shit, that's enough to leave me looking over my shoulder for the rest of my life.

Rising to my feet, I stretch my arms above my head, groaning as my tired body relaxes a little. The moon starts to disappear as dawn brings the world back to life once more.

Have they realized I've left? Do they care? Are they mad or relieved?

There's only one way to find out.

My stomach grumbles as I move back toward my bike, but before I can lift my leg over the leather seat, the sound of an engine revving in the distance makes me pause. Uncertainty washes over me as the noise gets louder until a Harley Davidson appears. The cut on the back could be anyone's, but the long blond hair beneath the small black helmet is unmistakable.

Enraptured, I'm frozen in place as he rolls to a stop beside me, his face void of any emotion that may give him away. He unclips his helmet before hanging it off his handlebar. My heart hammers in my chest as he climbs off his seat, turning to face me head-on.

"Hey, Snowflake."

RUTHLESS BROTHERS MC

# FOUR

*Emmett*

Snowflake… fucking snowflake? I don't even know where that came from, but the second it falls from my tongue, I love it. It's fitting for her, considering her porcelain skin, especially with how her jet-black hair only makes it glow like a snowflake shimmering under the light.

She's unique, like no one else I've ever met before, a mysterious queen of her own design.

My snowflake eyes me cautiously, skimming over me from head to toe.

"How did you find me?" Her husky voice sets my soul on fire as I bask in her presence. The worry and confusion I felt when Duffer declared she left is long forgotten as she stands right in front of me.

Smirking at her, I forget to answer for a second, more than happy to just gape at her like a kid in a candy store.

"Are you upset about it?"

"I'm undecided. Your answer might help with that." She quirks a brow at me, softening the snark in her tone, but I love it regardless.

Nodding, I run my hand over my beard. "Axel placed a tracker on it before he gave it to you."

Her eyes widen in surprise, then crinkle in annoyance, which feels like it's aimed more at herself for not considering that fact. "Of course he did." She turns away, folding her arms across her chest as she looks out over a small waterfall that glistens in the early morning sun. "It took you a while to get here, then. If you've known where I've been this whole time."

I shrug despite her not even looking in my direction. "It took us a while to decide which one of us would come here to you."

A snicker falls from her lips as she glances over her shoulder at me. "Out of choice or reluctance?"

"Does it matter?" I bite back a grin, sensing the irritation bubbling inside of her at the fact that I keep answering her questions with one of my own.

"Maybe," she breathes, a nervous hint to her tone that catches me by surprise. At least she's being honest with me.

Folding my arms over my chest, I adjust my stance so my feet are planted shoulder width apart like I'm preparing for battle. "We vetoed Ryker being the one to come out here since everything is going to shit with the Brutes. It made sense for the prez to stay and focus on that. Much to his reluctance, I might add." She nods slightly, digesting the information without giving her thoughts. "Axel got declined because we thought you would be pissed when you learned he put a tracker on your bike, and we didn't want you two talking with weapons instead of words."

She bites her lip adorably. "And Gray?" She turns to face me now, and I drop my arms to my sides.

"I arm-wrestled the fuck out of him," I reply with a shrug, feeling just as victorious now as I did then.

"No, you didn't." A ghost of a smile threatens to stretch her lips as she blinks at me.

Showing off the bicep of my right arm, I point at it as I flex my muscles. "Snowflake, don't underestimate me. You're not the only one who can handle guns."

A giggle bursts from her lips, her eyes dancing with amusement like she's forgotten to be guarded with me, and I'm desperate to hear it again. The sound of her stomach grumbling stops me from making her do it again, and I remember what I have packed away in the bag on my bike.

Reluctantly moving away from her, I dive into the bag I brought from the club, keeping my eyes fixed on her. "Maggie promised me you would appreciate this," I explain, sandwiches in hand.

She peers inside the brown paper bag before glancing up at me. "Maggie was right, thank you."

Wordlessly, we sit side by side on a large boulder that frames the pool of water, enjoying the chicken and bacon subs that Maggie made for us. I feel like a teenager when our thighs touch and it warms my skin, but I like it too much to try and play it cool.

"So, are you here to drag me back?" My gaze lifts from where we're touching, my mind taking a moment to catch up.

"That depends on whether it will take much convincing or not…"

My words trail off as I raise a brow at her, but she sighs, her shoulders slumping in defeat.

"So I don't have a choice."

"We always have a choice, Snowflake."

"No, I fucking don't, and if I do, it's forced or a threat in order for them to have the upper hand over me. They want to play me like a puppet and drain my soul, so I never know right from wrong unless it's in their best interests."

Wow.

That's heavy for six in the morning. It seems like someone has been out here contemplating life. I can't tell if she means someone specific or the old club in general, but I don't want to force her to delve deeper when she's slowly becoming forthcoming with me.

"You're an enigma, Scarlett."

"Hmm."

She stares out over the water, her eyelids hooded as she wraps her arms around her legs. The glow from the sun frames her beautifully. She's tired, completely exhausted, but still manages to look like a fucking angel, basking in the rays of sunlight breaking through the clouds.

"Is it true? That you weren't registered as a child?" The question that's been plaguing my mind since last night tumbles past my lips, but before I can backtrack, she nods.

Fuck.

"Why would they do that? I mean, Freddie seemed to earn a name for being a dollar grabber. The fact that he didn't register you and get the income from it blows my mind." It sounds like a low fucking blow, but it's the reality of the world we live in. I watched whores try and get pregnant simply for the increased income it would get them.

"So I would be what they raised me to be."

My brows furrow as she continues to look out over the water. "Which is what?"

"A killer."

She says it so casually, like it's a mundane word that holds no weight behind it, but I'm a killer too. There's blood on my hands, but it's really not as simple as that.

"That doesn't make any sense," I say, more to myself

than her.

"Maybe that's because you have a heart, Emmett." She snickers, but there's no humor to it. I might have been the one to lead the conversation in this direction, but shit, I feel like it's only leading to more questions rather than answers. Scarlett must sense my confusion because she nudges her knee against mine. "I was never registered so I was never placed in the database, which means I can kill anyone and everyone without leaving a trace of identity behind."

I grasp her chin and tilt her head back. "Who the fuck taught you to kill?"

"My father."

Scrubbing a hand down my face, I stare at her in disbelief. "I've heard stories about Freddie, but that sounds extreme, even for him."

"I'm sure you didn't come all the way out here to discuss my bad childhood, Emmett." Her attempt to change the subject falls flat as I quirk a brow at her.

"What do you think I came all the way out here for, then?" I push, and this time, she quirks her brow at me.

"That's what I'm waiting for you to get to."

*At least her sass is still going strong.*

"I came out here because I care, Scarlett." My heart thuds in my chest at the truth, while she assesses me.

"Are they mad that I killed Banner and Billy?"

"You can keep trying to steer the conversation in a

different direction, Snowflake, but I'm going to keep bringing it right back around," I declare, loosening my hold on her chin as I stroke my fingertip down her throat. "They're mad because you left without a word." Her eyebrows raise in surprise. "Is that surprising to you?"

"Yes," she breathes without missing a beat.

"Why?"

"I don't know, maybe because it's not something I'm used to. People don't care about me. They simply decide what purpose I serve for them, then get disappointed when I don't follow through with precision, and respond with anger and violence toward me. This... this is nothing like that, and it scares the hell out of me."

"Anyone that's still currently breathing that caused you any kind of pain will die at our hands. You just have to tell us who." The words are firm as I grit them out, not in anger toward her, but those that thought they could hurt her in any way, shape, or form.

"I can do it myself, remember?" Her eyes soften slightly, her face so expressive when she drops the walls she strategically places around her. It's intoxicating.

"You could, but you don't have to. It doesn't have to be your hands dripping in blood when there are people ready to slaughter motherfuckers on your behalf."

A ghost of a smile touches the corner of her mouth as her eyes meet mine properly for the first time in what feels like an eternity. "It's all I know."

"Not on my watch, it isn't," I grunt, inching closer to her. So close my nose skims over her collarbone.

"And what does your watch look like?" Her voice is breathier, hitting me straight in the dick and leaving me needy as fuck. Talking like this, delving into her tainted past, feels more intimate than anything else we've already done together.

Cupping the back of her head, I make sure her eyes are fixated on mine, before pressing my lips to hers. She groans instantly at the touch, her hand rising to my chest, but I reluctantly pull back.

"It looks like you, laid out for me, legs spread and tits on display, as I feast on you."

Her breath hitches as she hums in response. "That sounds tempting."

"You like that, huh?"

"I'd like to see it in action before I give you my honest answer."

*Fuck*, this woman.

"Understood, Snowflake."

Cutting the breath of air between us, I kiss her again, harder and more demanding than before. We're not close enough. I want to feel every inch of her skin against mine, every breath that leaves her lips, and every single ripple of her orgasm that I'm going to draw from her.

As if sensing my thoughts, she climbs into my lap without breaking our kiss. She plants one knee on either side of my thighs and sinks her fingers into my hair.

"Fuck, Snowflake."

"I like it when you call me that."

*Shit, me too.*

Finding the hem of her t-shirt, she lifts her arms in the air as I discard it, only to reveal no bra underneath, and I almost come on the spot. I capture her nipple, sucking gently on the taut nub as I engulf her other tit in my hand, strumming my thumb over her needy peak.

"All of you. I want to see all of you."

Scarlett groans at my plea, her head tilting back to the morning sky, as I kiss from her breast, over her chest, ghosting her collarbone, and feeling the thrum of her pulse at her neck.

Grabbing her waist, I switch our positions on the boulder, letting her hair down from the bun and watching it cascade over the side, dipping into the pool of water slightly. She looks up at me through her lashes as I grab the waistband of her leggings and slowly peel them down her thighs along with her panties. When she's completely bare before me, I take my time running my eyes over the length of her, appreciating my view with the perfect backdrop and the sound of the waterfall cascading in the background.

I reach for her ankle, positioning myself between her

spread thighs before lifting it to my lips. I graze my mouth over her in soft kisses, all the way to the apex of her thigh, before retreating and repeating the same languid presses of my lips up her other leg. Every time she clenches her thighs, desperate for friction, I almost consider restarting, dragging this out even more, but that would mean being selfish to myself as well, and I'm far too desperate for her right now.

When I hover my mouth over her core, her clit like a beacon as I lightly blow against her heated skin, she groans, "Please, Emmett." One breathy moan and I'm back under her command, swiping my tongue from her entrance to her needy button as her back arches and her moans turn to raspy cries. "Let me see you too."

It takes a second for her words to process through my foggy mind, and I swipe my tongue once more for good measure before I lean back, shucking off my cut and tee. Her teeth sink into her bottom lip as she reaches out for me, but I quickly jump to my feet, kicking off my boots and jeans along with my boxers.

A chill runs down my spine, but the more I bask in her heat, her presence, the warmer I get.

The moment I'm back between her thighs, she reaches up and gently runs her fingertip over my jagged scar from surgery years ago. My breath lodges in my throat as I remember the words she spoke to me about how selfish it was for me to not continue to get it checked.

Apart from protecting Emily and representing the MC, I've never felt like there was anything else that warranted me breathing. *Is she worth living for?* My gut twists, confirming what I already know is true. The answer to that very question not leaving me half as paralyzed with fear as I thought it would.

She's worth more than living for. She's worth everything, but something tells me she's not quite ready to hear that yet. Locking away my newfound knowledge, I grab her thighs, hiking her legs up in the air and wrapping them around my head, before I feast on her sweet pussy.

Her cries of pleasure are like a symphony to my ears, placing me as the conductor, *her* conductor. With her clit nestled between my teeth, I thrust two fingers into her core, stretching her out in anticipation for my cock, but the second her pussy clenches deathly tight around me, I know she's ready to tumble over the edge.

"Emmett... Fuck, Emm—" My name drops off her tongue as a groan starts in her toes, rippling through her entire body, before she climaxes with a scream that sounds across the waters next to us.

Making sure to drag out every drop of her pleasure, I only stop when her limbs turn to jelly beneath me, my name on her tongue once more. "Emmett, God, Emmett." She reaches for me blindly, one hand knitted in my hair, while the other tucks under my arm as she tries to lift me up to her. "I need you."

Three sweet words and I'm moving at her encouragement, dragging my tongue over the goosebumps that coat her skin, until I can press my lips to hers again. "I need you too, Snowflake."

"Then take me."

I use every ounce of control I have to lean up and search in my jeans pocket to find a condom. Twirling it in my hand, I look at Scarlett before tearing the foil open. "This is the last one I have, Snowflake. I won't be buying more and I won't be using another. This is your fair warning. If you don't want my seed deep inside of you, then we'll need to figure out an alternative."

I've never been more sure of my words. I've never fucked without a condom, a level of safety and protection that I'm certain of, but I mean it. I want to feel every inch of her, inside and out.

"Fuck, Emmett," she groans in response, her hands falling to her tits as she squeezes them, her thighs nudging further open.

Rolling the rubber down my length, I lower myself over her again, glancing around us to make sure there's no fuckers watching me claim my girl, but all I'm greeted with is the sway of the trees and the constant flow of the waterfall. With my pulse hammering through me, I line my cock up with her core and take what's mine.

Inch by inch, my heart rate accelerates as her pussy warms my dick, transporting me to fucking heaven as my hips become flush with hers. I give her a moment to adjust, but probably not long enough as the need and desire scorching through my veins have me retreating, only to slam straight back inside her.

Scarlett's nails dig into my arms, claiming me as hers, as she holds on for dear life. With every thrust of my hips, we inch along the boulder, and I worry she might be hurting her back, but the second I slow to check, she digs her nails in and pleads for me not to stop.

Planting one hand on the rock and gripping her waist with the other, I do as I'm ordered and fuck her like my life depends on it. It does. Every breath I take is for this. This feeling of pleasure and life that I've never felt anywhere else but with her.

My snowflake.

Every slam of my cock inside her has more and more of her hair dipping into the water until her head hangs over the side. There's a hint of a smile on her lips, her back arched, and her telltale flush creeping over her skin.

Moving my hand to her throat, I attempt to hold her in place as I chase my own release.

"Fuck, Emmett," she grinds out, her throat bobbing beneath my palm as her pussy clenches around me once more and she finds her release, shattering beneath me as wave after wave of ecstasy washes over her.

The second I feel my own tingling through my body, my movements become more jagged, more forceful, and we both edge closer to the water, when I explode inside her just as her head starts to go underwater.

A groan vibrates in my chest, but I don't hear it over the pulse ringing in my ears as I look at her perfect body. Scarlett's nose and mouth fall under the surface of the water, my hand feeling the icy liquid for the briefest moment, before I pull her head up. I don't miss the way her pussy clenches around me again though, or the awe in her eyes as she looks up at me.

Fuck.

I pull her by the waist so I can place her in my lap. Her arms lazily wrap around my neck as she looks deep into my eyes. "Come home with me." My heart thunders with apprehension, waiting on bated breath for her response as she smiles serenely at me.

She nods, sending such relief rushing through my veins that I think I'm going to climax all over again.

This woman was made for me, for us, and whether she sees that now or in time to come, I'm going to make her, no matter the pace. If anyone or anything tries to get in the way of that, then I'll be more than happy to slay every single one of them.

RUTHLESS BROTHERS MC

# FIVE

*Ryker*

The feel of Scarlett's soft skin and parted lips are ripped from my mind as someone shakes my shoulder. "Prez? Ryker, you've got to wake up."

I groan at the sound of Shift's voice as he interrupts my dream and brings me right back to reality. "Fuck off, man," I grumble, but he doesn't stop shaking my shoulder until I glare at him.

There's no chance of me drifting back into the dream world now, and I was so damn close to filling her cunt with my cock.

"No can do, Prez. The guns are coming in early like we asked, which means we need to get a move on."

Fuck. I hate it when he talks sense.

Shoving him off the bed, I sit, swiping a hand down my face as I let the last tendrils of sleep escape me. "Fine, give me five minutes and I'll be good to go."

He nods, rubbing at the back of his neck as he heads for the door. We haven't really spoken since we left Church yesterday. I've been focused on the club and my own hurt feelings, while he likely waits for my anger and the repercussions for the truth that was revealed yesterday. I call out his name and he pauses by the door. "Is Emmett back yet?"

A quick glance at my cell confirms it's almost noon, so I'm hoping he is.

"Yeah, he came back about two hours ago." There's a knowing sparkle in Shift's eyes. He fucking knows what I'm hinting at, but if I want my answer I'm going to have to be more specific.

"Alone?"

His lips spread into a smirk as he shakes his head. "No, Prez."

*Thank fuck for that.*

My shoulders sag in relief as I wave him out the door. Once it clicks shut, I grab my stiff dick and groan. He brought her home, he fucking did it. Maybe my hot dream can become a reality sooner rather than later, but I'm not a complete fool. I know there's a lot of heavy shit we need to wade through first.

We clearly knew nothing about her when we brought her back to the compound, but shit, she let me get far too addicted before the truth spiraled. Now, I don't know how to cope without her presence.

It's bizarre as hell. This woman took away what I had been working toward for the past twelve months; what consumed my every waking breath. She killed Banner. There was no remorse in her eyes, no apology on the tip of her tongue, nothing. It was simply a job that she took, a job my brothers contracted her to complete.

If there was anything in the world that declared someone was made for me and my brothers, it's that. Her ability to survive, to smear blood on her hands without blinking, yet remaining so… humble? Fuck, I don't know if that's the right word to describe her, but it suits her all the same.

With one final tug of my cock, I jump from the bed, leaving the sheets in a tangled mess before I quickly dress in my usual jeans and tee with my cut. Stepping into my boots, I don't even consider the laces as I leave in search of her. I want to see her with my eyes before we leave.

Staring at Emmett's door for a moment, I don't bother knocking and step inside to find them both curled up together. Emmett's on his back, Scarlett's draped across his chest with her black hair fanned out around them. A peek of her pretty pink nipples call to me as I inch closer to them.

Emmett's eyes open, but he doesn't move as I lean

over the mystical woman beside him. I tuck a loose tendril of hair behind her ear, prepared for her to startle awake and chew my ear off for disturbing her, but she's completely out of it. If the smug grin on Emmett's face is anything to go by, then he has something to do with her exhaustion and he's fucking proud of it. Rightly so, but I'd rather it had been me.

"We're on guns, we need to ride out." Emmett grunts in response, pressing his lips to Scarlett's forehead before climbing out from under the sheets.

This is fucked up as hell. I've never shared anyone before, never been interested in someone that also holds the attention of my brothers, but this is different. Even when he kisses her, it doesn't fill me with rage. It has me wanting to slip my fingers between her thighs and see how easily she gets wet from his touch.

Dragging a hand down my face, I lean back, putting some much-needed distance between us before I abandon the gun run and give all of my time and attention to her.

"I'll be two minutes," Emmett murmurs, trying not to wake Scarlett. I nod, reluctantly heading for the door.

"Ryker?" Her raspy voice calls out my name, and I pause, clutching the handle as I glance back at her. "Where are you going?"

"We have a run to do." My heart races in my chest, wonder filling my veins as I track my eyes over every inch of her. If she asks me to stay, what will I say? Will I stutter? Will it anger me that she doesn't see the importance of the club to me?

"Be safe," she breathes, a soft smile on her face as she blinks slowly. Sleep pulls her back into its grasp as she yawns.

I nod even though she's not looking.

There's no anger that I'm pulling Emmett from her or that we're leaving without more information. There's nothing but understanding with a hint of worry in her eyes. She was made for us, made for my brothers, and I've never been more sure of anything in my life.

I've also never had a reason to 'be safe' before, but it seems I do now.

My bike rumbles as we cut across town, putting more and more distance between us and the girl who is filling my every waking thought. The quicker we get this over with, the quicker I can get back.

Gray, Axel, Emmett, Shift, Euro, and Dax, a newly promoted prospect, ride behind me. Once this gun run is done with, we can head back, put our game faces on, and put our heads together to formulate a plan in response to the Devil's Brutes. Those fuckers swarmed our compound just hours after taking out our men at the shipment yard.

They need to pay. In blood.

My grip on the handlebars tightens as anger consumes me once more. The smoother this goes, the quicker I can figure out a way to rid my mind and body of my rage.

As we take the next right, our other depot comes into view. We're closer to the water's edge here and further away from the bigger yard. We don't use this location often as we don't have an in with the operators, but it's smaller and draws less attention, so I'm hopeful this goes as planned.

A glance in the mirror shows Axel pulling out of line and speeding up beside me, and I slow once he's close so he can take the lead. As my sergeant at arms, it's his job to be armed and ready at all times, making our safety paramount to him. He's going to be the first to go into any burning building and I'll be right on his tail whether he likes it or not.

Once we're through the metal gates, he signals to the left, rolling to a stop and taking his helmet off. I exhale sharply as I do the same, making sure to shake off any lingering thoughts distracting me.

"Let's split up and come at the cargo from both sides," Axel murmurs, glancing at me, and I nod.

"Shift, Euro, and Dax can come with me," I reply, waving for them to follow, and I take off to the left without waiting for a response.

Am I being short and pissy with him? Fuck yeah, I am, but he shouldn't expect anything else after what he revealed yesterday. I know I need to talk to him, but I'll do it on my terms, not his. Placing him with Gray and Emmett will leave them all worrying over where my head is at. I would usually keep our closer knit group together, but they deserve a little unnerving anyway.

"You ready for the big leagues now, Dax?" Euro asks, clapping him on the shoulder. I don't miss the slight flush to his cheeks. It's exhilarating and nerve-wracking all at once to go from prospect to a fully fledged member, but he'll get into the swing of it soon.

"I'm ready for whatever the prez needs from me," he responds, shaking Euro off. I smirk, but don't say anything until I see our storage unit ahead.

"Euro and Dax, take the next left so you can come at the container from behind. Shift and I will push this way." Nodding, they move, leaving me with Shift at my side. The second he clears his throat, I know he's going to bring up yesterday's events. "Whatever you have to say can wait, Shift. Yesterday was a lot to take in, and right now, all of our focus needs to be on the delivery."

"Yes, Prez."

It's always a little crazy to me that Gray and Shift are brothers, Shift being eighteen months his senior, but my connection with him is completely different. I think it's because what Axel, Gray, Emmett, and I have been through and faced together brought us closer. There are things we had to see and do that didn't put Shift at the scene so he doesn't feel things like us. We've been friends for as long as I can remember, attending school together, pledging as prospects at the same time, and everything in between.

That's not to say I don't love the guy. But after yesterday, I'm unsure whether that makes me want to draw him in closer or shut the fucking door on him altogether.

Sighing, I swipe my hand down my face, irritated with the fact that he's distracted me again. Axel appears in front of us and reaches for the container lock. My heart slows as I come to a stop beside him, glancing in every direction as he pulls the door open. With my nerves on edge, I almost drop to my knees in relief when I see our crates loaded up and ready to go.

Emmett and Gray step inside, confirming the contents, and I'm practically bouncing on my feet with adrenaline and victory as we finally get a fucking win, or a brief second of reprieve. Whichever way we look at it, today is positive.

Splitting the contents up between the seven of us, I give the orders of who needs to take what and where, before heading toward Hunter Springs, our neighboring town, to make my delivery. Axel joins me. These are our biggest dealers, but also our most chaotic, which means we have to show up, take no shit, and get the fuck out of there.

We ride side by side down the highway, cutting in and out of the cars on the road as we pass the sign confirming we're now in their territory. An old rundown church sits on the outskirts of town, serving as the Iron Scorpions' hub. I roll to a stop when Paisley, their leader, steps out onto the lawn with a smoke in his hand.

Axel does the same, exhaling heavily after each pull on his cigarette before finally grabbing the goods. We would usually do this kind of thing in our SUVs, but that just felt like we were drawing attention to ourselves after everything we've already been through, so carrying this way is going to have to work for the time being.

"Ryker, it's been too long." There's a smirk to his lips and a glimmer of something I can't quite put my finger on in his eyes, but I still shake his outstretched hand.

"It always is," I reply.

Axel carries the shipment inside to trade off.

"Heard you've had the pleasure of the Devil's Brutes at your door."

I don't turn to look at him right away, keeping my surprise in check at the mention of them. "They've definitely made their presence known." I plaster a grin as I shrug, tilting my head to meet his gaze. "Have you had any dealings with them?"

He chuckles, patting me on the shoulder as he takes another drag of his cigarette. "Our club, like most others, have always opted to do as we're told with them. Pay our dues and be left the fuck alone. I want to say it's almost refreshing to see someone stand their ground."

I raise a brow at his comment, looking at him properly for the first time in years. Paisley is old enough to be my father, shit, I'm quite sure before MC life became all they knew, they were friends once. His peppered hair and gray stubble age him even more as the wrinkles around his eyes deepen with his smile.

It's surprising that the Iron Scorpions are under the thumb of the Devil's Brutes. Am I the one being foolish for not following suit?

I almost ask it out loud when Axel steps out of the church doors, cigarette still burning, and heads toward us. "Always a pleasure doing business, Paisley," he murmurs, not waiting around for a response as he moves toward our bikes.

"Always, Axel," Paisley hollers before offering me his hand once more. "I'd love to offer our assistance in the current turmoil you find yourself in, but I gotta do what's right for my club just as you have to do for yours. You get me?"

Is it pride or admiration that's in his eyes? Is that what I can't quite place? Fuck, I don't know.

"I get you. Take care of Belinda," I reply, referencing his old lady, and he grins at me. It isn't until I'm standing beside Axel that he calls out my name, and I turn to look back at him.

"Congratulations, Ryker. Prez looks good on you."

Yeah… it really fucking does.

RUTHLESS BROTHERS MC

# SIX

## Axel

Ryker takes the lead as we head back to the compound. The usual euphoria and sense of calmness I get while I'm riding my Harley is nonexistent with all the stress that surrounds us. It's palpable. I could pull my blade from my boot and slice it with jagged edges and it still wouldn't move.

I barely fucking slept, so when Shift popped his head around the door to tell me there was a run, I was ready to go. Wearing my same clothes from yesterday, sitting in the same position I placed myself in last night.

I rev up the engine, but it does nothing to calm my bubbling veins. I'm angry at myself. The truth of Banner's death shouldn't have come out like that, but I was foolish to think it wouldn't. I should have worded it better, but as I watched everything come to light, there was nothing more to say than those two words. *I did.*

I fucking did and I don't regret it, but hurting my best friend, my brother, my goddamn family, wasn't what I intended. There's never been this level of awkward tension between us before, and even though it's my own doing, I don't know how to fix it.

The compound comes into view, I don't know whether to be relieved or irritated by its presence. The solitude I usually find at the club isn't there. That's because it comes from Ryker.

*Fuck.*

I follow Ryker as he heads straight into the garage, knocking down the kickstand when we come to a stop. I need to speak to him, say something to mend this between us, but I can't apologize. There's nothing to apologize *for*.

With a heavy sigh, I tug my helmet off and rise from my bike, turning to face him as he does the same. "Ryker," I start, but he shakes his head at me.

"I need you to give me a minute, Axel," he says, raking his fingers through his hair.

Balling my hands into fists, my nostrils flare as I attempt to remain as calm as possible. "I haven't got a minute to wait, Ryker."

Ryker grunts, shaking his head at me again before he settles his gaze on me. "This isn't going to be on your terms, Ax. You know very well I wanted to handle things myself."

Swiping my sunglasses from the bridge of my nose, I toss them across the room before scrubbing a hand over my face. "Fuck, I know that, Ryker. I. Fucking. Know. But I was trying to protect you, protect our future." My muscles tense as I force my arms back to my side, locking eyes with him. "I watched you carry all the pain, stress, and anger of your father's death for twelve months. Twelve. Months. And I was done watching you destroy yourself over someone else's actions." I pace, arms flapping down at my side in frustration. "I couldn't bring your father back for you, none of us could, so this was the next best thing."

The sound of my boots hitting the floor echoes around us. My chest heaves with every breath while Ryker's gaze turns downcast.

"In doing that, Axel, you also took away the one thing I wanted more than anything. The one thing I was living and breathing for."

"You didn't need the weight of Banner's blood on your hands." My frown furrows, a sharp pain jabbing my temple as frustration gets the better of me.

"Maybe you're right, maybe you're wrong, but I'm too fucking pissed off right now and this conversation isn't helping," he hisses, jaw clenching with annoyance flashing in his eyes.

Fuck. I was supposed to be making this better, not worse.

"Ryker," I start, calming my tone quickly, but just as I called his name before, he waves me off with a shake of his head.

"Not now, Axel. Not fucking now," he bites, storming from the garage and slamming the door shut behind him.

With my head in my hands, I fail to calm my ragged breaths, my fingers curling into my hair as anger, pain, and a sense of loss overwhelms me.

Noise from outside of the garage doors captures my attention and I notice that the entryway for the vehicles is still open. Stomping over to the button, I slam it with my fist before the sound of the garage door dropping rings in my ear.

I need to be away from everyone right now, myself more than anyone, but since that isn't an option, the only choice I have is to get very fucking lost so I can forget. Need consumes my limbs, and before I know it, I'm moving toward my stash. The brown liquor calls to me as I pull the drawer open, the bourbon screaming my name as I untwist the lid of the almost full bottle and take a large gulp.

One.

Two.

Three.

Four.

Every time, it burns a little less and warms my soul even more.

This isn't the game I was set on playing today, but it's familiar. It's where I know exactly what is expected of me. A wasted Axel has no feelings, no emotions, and certainly no fucking guilt for letting his brother down.

I take another swig and wipe my mouth with the back of my hand. My eyelids fall closed, darkness surrounding me. I exhale, relaxing my hold on the shadows that haunt me all the time except when I'm drinking.

Bourbon makes me feel invincible and trauma-free, like I don't carry a twisted world on my shoulders. It alleviates the weight of my past that I feel every single day without fail. My lips twist as I consider how to loosen myself up further and forget. Opening my eyes, my gaze instantly lands on the small tool box in the far corner, and I move toward it in the next breath.

Lifting the lid, I dig deep inside until I feel the small plastic bag against my fingertips, and a smile creeps over my face. *Fucking gold.*

Retrieving my little bag of joy, I trudge back over to my bike and sit beside the pile of tires, leaning back against them as I eye my usual drug—Cocaine.

Fuck.

Every nerve-ending inside of me is desperate for a taste, even if it's just a line, but something at the back of my mind nags at me. Last time was bad, last time was *real* bad, but this time… I can't find a solution to my problems.

It's usually my trauma that brings me here, powder lodged in the tiny ridges of my callused fingertips, and my past disappearing until it no longer haunts me anymore. She can't get me anymore, none of them can, and the cocaine helps me forget. Now, though, there's no way past the sudden barrier between Ryker and I, whether I like it or not it's still going to be there in the morning.

Shit.

My chin hits my chest as the alcohol wanes, the pain bubbling in my chest once more as my eyes close. Pressing the rim of the bottle to my lips, I chug the bourbon like it's water. My muscles slowly loosen, the tension dissolving as minutes morph into an infinity of time. The world continues to circle around me as I stay holed up in the garage, my eyes barely able to open as I tap at the cocaine in the plastic bag, willing it to give me a decision on whether or not I should indulge.

It's never been a question before, the answer is always simply a yes, but something still remains between me and the blackout waiting with my name on it.

The creaking of the garage door opening pulls me from my thoughts, the foggy cloud still resting over me as I try to blink through the confusion. The confusion which turns into anger and irritation the second I see her face.

"Fuck off, Scarlett," I grunt, turning away from her as I take another swig of bourbon.

She doesn't reply at first, and when I hear her footsteps, I'm almost granted relief at the fact that she's leaving, but it doesn't last long as the steps get louder and she gets closer.

"Axel." My name falls from her lips like a heady breath, making my body tense for the briefest moment before the alcohol continues to work its magic.

"I said, fuck off, whore," I bite, desperate to get a rise out of her for interrupting my serene drinking session, but the scoff that greets my ears is the complete opposite.

"Please, that little word bullet doesn't hurt me, Axel. You should know that after yesterday's revelations."

I blink up at Scarlett to see her standing with her arms crossed, but the concern in her eyes is the complete opposite of the stance she's trying to give off.

*How was that only yesterday?*

I lift the bottle to my lips again when she speaks. "Fuck if I know."

Wait, what?

*Did I say that out loud?*

"You're saying a lot out loud," she clarifies, quirking a brow at me as my lips tilt up at the corners.

"And yet you're still standing here and not fucking off like I ordered." My words fall flat as I hiccup, but she doesn't laugh like I expect, like I deserve.

She crouches in front of me, elbows braced on her knees as she looks deep into my eyes, ghosting over my soul without even touching me.

"I hate to be the one to break it to you, Axel, but being alone is the worst thing for you in this state. Especially after last time."

*What does she know about last time?*

"Let me stick around and I'll tell you," she replies, magically reading my thoughts again as she drops to her butt and crosses her legs, getting comfortable across from me. "Besides, it's either me sitting my sweet ass here with you or I go tell the guys that you're drunk as fuck and toying with a bag of powder."

My eyes cast down to the bag in my hand and my chest clenches. I don't need them out here seeing me like this, but I don't care all that much for this woman seeing this side of me either. She's right though, she is the lesser of two evils, and one which won't require me to explain my shit.

Clearing my throat, I offer the bottle, but she shakes her head and laces her fingers in her lap. "Excellent, more for me."

# SEVEN

## Scarlett

Wetting my lips, I fold my arms around my legs as I sit across from a completely wasted Axel. I have no idea how he got to this stage, but it's clear he's on the cusp of going further with the bag of drugs in his hands.

He didn't come in with Ryker earlier when the others got back from the run, and with the state of him now, I can only assume he's been in here getting more lost with every passing sip of his drink. This isn't okay, the state he's in... it's not right. Axel needs help, but there's no way in hell he'll hear those words from me, so I'm not even going to attempt them.

"What are you doing out here anyway?" Axel asks, lifting the liquor to his lips.

Shrugging, I keep my gaze fixed on him. "Emily left for the night and the guys were deep into a game of poker, so I thought I would come out here and check on my bike," I explain, nodding toward my Harley.

That's not going to happen now though, not when he's slow blinking and slumped against the tires behind him.

"If your story is true, then how did you come to get the bike? I can't imagine them offering you easy access to an escape," Axel murmurs, his words slurring as his eyes close. I lean in and wave my hand in front of his face.

"Hey, I need you to stay awake," I declare urgently, worried I'm going to have to go and get someone to help him, despite his reluctance, but he thankfully pries his eyes open.

I relax a little when he wipes a hand down his face and purposely widens his eyes. "Well?" he asks. My eyebrows pinch in confusion for a second until I remember his question.

"I took it as a prize."

"A prize?" No one should look this handsome when they're wasted and confused, but it somehow suits him. It also seems to have the ability to get me to open up, even if it's only to keep him awake.

"Yeah, it was my father's." My hands run over the material of my leggings, rubbing my thighs in an attempt to warm me up after a cold chill runs down my spine at the mention of the fucker.

Axel's brows rise as he points a finger at my bike. "You're telling me that was Freddie's bike?"

I nod, my veins thrumming with triumph, just as they did that day.

"No way. How the fuck did you get it as a prize? There's no way in hell he would have given that away, not for anything. But from what I heard about him, he definitely wouldn't have put it on the table for anyone."

Wow. It seems my father's legacy precedes him. I'm not surprised.

"When he's dead, he doesn't really have a choice, does he?" I state, my voice calm despite the fact that my heart rate is increasing.

I didn't think it was possible for his eyes to widen further, but to my surprise, they do. He props himself up a little more. "So, somebody killed him and you took his prized possession when no one was looking?"

I smirk, pride swelling my chest as I steeple my fingers on my thighs. "Almost. It was me doing the killing and taking what I fucking wanted."

A bark of laughter bursts from his mouth as the bourbon in his hand sloshes. "You didn't fucking kill Freddie. No. Fucking. Way." He raises the bottle to his lips, but eyes the rim as it gets close before sighing and placing it down on the floor. The bag of powder is placed next to it moments later and despite his ignorance, relief floods my veins.

"If you say so," I reply with a shrug, pressing my lips together as I look anywhere but at him.

"Fuck that, you're supposed to prove me wrong," Axel retorts, and I glance at him with my eyes wide this time.

"I don't have to do anything. I know what I've done, I know what I regret and what I would do again in a heartbeat. Declaring it to you doesn't prove anything."

A smile stretches across his face. The liquor definitely makes him less of an asshole as he waves his arms to the side. "Amuse me."

Fuck. That.

"My trauma isn't for your amusement," I grumble, tucking my hair behind my ear as I stop myself from jabbing my finger at him.

"We can trade."

I cock a brow at him, shaking my head at the craziness he's proposing.

"You'll regret that when you're sober, Axel." I'm right, I know I am, but as he leans forward, legs crossing as he looks deep into my eyes, I know I'm going to grant his every fucking wish.

"Was he the reason behind your trauma, Scar?" His voice is somber, softer than I expected, and just like the sucker I know I am, I nod.

"Yes."

"Hmm." He leans back. "I killed the reason behind my trauma too."

I gulp hard, aware that it almost sounds like he believes me, but I don't want to make a point out of it. Instead, I rub at my chest, easing the reality that weighs heavy on me. "It doesn't erase everything though, does it?"

"Nope." He pops the p, wiping a hand down his face as I shift, uncomfortable on the hard floor. "Lean against the tires, it makes it more comfortable. Or I think it does, but it could be the bourbon talking," he adds with a smirk, and I grin.

Carefully shuffling around so I'm sitting beside him but not too close, I lean back against the tires and sigh. I feel like he's opened a can of worms between us, each one spilling out after the next. It feels real and raw, and even though he might not remember any of this in the morning, I take advantage of the opportunity to vent, to explain, even if it doesn't make any sense.

"I wasn't meant to exist. I was a runt created when he fucked a whore without protection and shocked him to his core when she pushed me out. Only to die five minutes later from complications." The words flow from my lips freely, surprising even me. "So he kept me that way— nonexistent. Completely off the books so to speak, no government's systems, and nothing in between. I didn't exist anywhere but in the Reapers' basement until I hit double digits." It's still a hard pill to swallow, a reality like no other as I envy every child I've ever seen. "I haven't been down in one since," I add, eyeing the bourbon for myself, but I sit on my hands instead. I'm here to keep him company and busy, not aiding and encouraging the alcohol.

"How the fuck does someone have the balls to train a child to kill?" I'm not sure if the question is for me or more to himself, but I answer either way.

"He taught me where it would hurt the most without causing serious damage and showed me where it was fatal. Along with the information on the best cleaning products to get rid of everything I did."

Silence descends over us for a moment before Axel scratches at his chin. "What finally made you snap?" Fuck. That's deeper than I was expecting, but it only confirms the trauma he has too because someone without any wouldn't even consider that question. I consider my response, but Axel seems to think I don't understand. "What made you fight back, Dove?"

My heart flutters at the nickname again. "I used to fight back all the time at the beginning, with every ounce of strength I had inside of me, but they liked that more than me being pliant," I admit, my blood running cold at the memory as I take a deep breath.

"Fuckers."

Gulping, I push out a whoosh of air. "I was ten the first time I met Kincaid. He was nineteen." He still makes my skin crawl just as much now as he did then. "The Devil's Brutes had some kind of ritual, a test to pass to become a member, a sacrificial lamb or some bullshit," I spit out, pinching the bridge of my nose for a second as I try to gain control of my emotions.

"He touched you?" Axel sounds angrier than I feel, and it forces me to drop my hand and meet his gaze.

"He tried, and he would have succeeded if my father hadn't stormed into the room the second Kincaid pulled a dagger from his sheath." The memory flashes in my mind as fresh as the day it happened. "It seems when Daddy Dearest sold me to him for the night, it was for my body and not my soul along with it. It was okay for him to sacrifice me over and over again, but I couldn't be Kincaid's lamb for his ritual." Axel's mouth sets into a grim line, the harsh reality of my past draining the effects of the alcohol from him. He lifts his hand out to me, but thinks better of it at the last second.

It's probably for the best. This is already getting more complicated than ever before.

"What happened?" Axel's frown deepens, a wince flickering across his face as he braces for my response.

"He stormed into the room like a knight on a white horse, charging at the motherfucker to save my honor. For the first time in my life, I felt... hope. That is until we got home and I overheard him talking with his closest ally about the reality of the situation." I can't bring myself to look at him as I speak. The shame and heartache I feel is indescribable, and no fault of my own, but they're there all the same. "I was worthless to him dead. I was his prized possession, his Grim Reaper. He didn't love me, he didn't care even a tiny bit about me. He just wanted me to slaughter his enemies on demand. Even when I was battered and bruised at the hands of his men, it was okay, because I was not dead. I could *never* wind up dead."

I hate to think how many times I wanted it, considered it, but something kept me going.

Survival.

"*You* were the Grim Reaper?"

I glance at Axel, finally having the strength to meet his eyes again as he gapes at me in surprise. "It suits me, right?" I reply with a dry smirk as he covers his eyes with his hand.

"Thank fuck you killed him, Scar. Otherwise I would be doing it right the fuck now for you."

I scoff at him. "In this state? You're not doing shit like this."

He hangs his head with a chuckle, and my chest

somehow feels lighter from blurting some of my truths out to him. Silence surrounds us once again, and my heart rate finally slows. This man better not be an asshole to me tomorrow after this, but knowing my luck, he'll be ten times worse than he already has been. Fuck it though, this has been soothing.

"Next week is the anniversary of the day I killed my mother."

His words hang between us, heavy and daunting as I sink my teeth into my lip to stop myself from gaping. I'm too scared to talk, too scared to frighten him off. Sharing the darker corners of our lives isn't fucking easy, and it's so far from what I expected today to be filled with, but here we are.

"She was deranged, psychotic, and totally fucked up," he continues, and my heart breaks for him. "I remember how she would stroke my hair as she let *them* touch me. Woman after woman, night after night. She said my daddy was her greatest addiction, but he was never truly hers, so she found another one instead. Unfortunately for me, it involved her watching women…"

My pain turns to fury, my hands clenching in my lap as I fucking long to reach out to him, but I refrain.

"I'll kill them all, every last fucking one," I bite, meaning every single word.

No wonder he fears a woman's touch. Look what pain

she caused him for her own selfish gain. I'm glad she's dead. She fucking deserves worse, a life of never-ending torture or something far more sinister than death. While I've used sex to cover the pain I felt at the hand of others, it's had the opposite effect on him.

"Stereotypically, it should be me revealing the fact that I was trained in brutality and you were the one exploited sexually," he says with a humorless laugh.

"I wish you didn't know the pain of either," I admit, a sad smile tainting my lips as his expression mirrors my own.

"Same." His head leans toward me slightly, his eyes stormy with emotion. "It seems the apple hasn't fallen far from the tree though. I have my own addictions now, just like she did," he murmurs, waving his hand at the bourbon and powder beside him.

"We all deserve the rush of an addiction, Axel. You just need to choose better ones." I shrug, responding honestly, which seems to surprise him. But I'm not going to sit here and pretend that we should all be perfect civilians, because that's not how this works.

Axel stretches his legs out, pursing his lips, as he assesses me before speaking. "What's yours?"

Rubbing my lips together, I consider my response, but I've been honest this far, there's no need to stop now. "I was never handled delicately as a child, and I don't care for it now either. But the rush I get when *I* ask a man to be rough with me, to fuck me into the mattress or choke me on his dick… fuck, it's like nothing else. It's my choice, my body, my rules, and I fucking love it."

He nods slowly in response, mulling my words over. "Maybe a new addiction is what I need."

"I highly recommend it, Axel, because this shit here"—I point at the same two vices he's familiar with—"they're not going to serve you well. Shit, they're going to serve you nothing but an early trip to your grave." I'm sure that's harsh, but it's true.

Axel opens his mouth to speak, when my name is called in the distance and I recognize Gray's voice. He clears his throat beside me, taking longer than usual to rise to his feet as he pats off his jeans. "As fun as this has been, please put some distance between us before he gets fucking excited over nothing," he grumbles, my pulse ringing in my ears as I nod quickly, rushing to my feet along with him.

"It'll be our little secret."

He rolls his eyes before looking at the incriminating evidence on the floor. I don't think twice when I reach down to grab the bag of drugs before shoving them deep into the trash. "As will this." I wink at him, and he smiles, his shoulders relaxing back as he leans on the heels of his feet.

"Th—"

"Hey, Sweet Cheeks, what…" Gray stares from Axel to me and back again, his pupils pinging between us before he places his hands on his hips. "What the fuck is going on in here? Is he giving you trouble?"

# EIGHT

## Scarlett

Gray's brows knit in confusion as he continues to stare between us, and I'm at a loss for words until Axel breaks the silence.

"She's ruining my fucking buzz, man. Get her out of here."

*That motherfucker.*

Shaking my head at him, I snicker. "Please, you were on the edge of passing out. I was doing you a favor."

Gray's eyes widen with worry as he zones in on Axel, taking two steps toward him as he rakes his fingers through his hair. "Fuck, Ax, you didn't touch—"

"No," Axel grunts, interrupting Gray, who turns to glance at me for confirmation. I shake my head, and Gray sags with relief, his chin hitting his chest.

My gaze skims past him for a moment, resting on Axel,

who offers me the faintest hint of a smile before it vanishes again.

"Good," Gray finally murmurs, turning to look at me again. "I came looking for you to see if you wanted to hang out for a bit."

I cut the distance between us and squeeze his arm. "That sounds amazing, but I don't think he should be left alone just yet," I admit, feeling Axel glare daggers into the side of my head, but fuck, it's the truth.

Whatever we just shared, whatever moment that was, it was important, special somehow, but it doesn't override my need to ensure he's safe.

"You're right," Gray replies, his hand moving to my waist as he pulls me in close. "But I don't think you being here is the best idea. Especially not with this unpredictable prickle pants." He points at his friend, and a burst of laughter sprouts from my mouth. "I'll get Ryker."

"Don't get Ryker," Axel replies quickly, which only confirms my suspicions from earlier. The state he's in has to do with his Prez and friend. Something tells me that all links back to the revelations that came out in Church, but hopefully they can get past it.

"But—" Gray starts to push, but I cut him off, lifting my hand to his chest and rubbing gently. "I'll head out. Come find me when you're done."

Gray nods reluctantly, pressing his lips to mine for a

brief moment before I take a step back. As I edge toward the door, a bark of laughter from Axel has me glancing back over my shoulder, and I'm surprised to see a sneer on his face.

"Aren't you scared to leave us alone? I can see the outline of his cock from here. He's hard... and I'm hungry." Yup, there's the Axel I've been waiting for. My gut clenches, my mind overloaded with thoughts and need, but I smother it all down and shrug instead.

"Nothing is exclusive here." Another twist to my stomach. "But I am disappointed that I'll miss your little show."

Gray storms toward me, a mixture of anger and dominance flashing in his eyes as he comes to a stop in front of me. He grips my chin, tilting my head up to force my gaze to his, and I quirk a brow at him.

"He's being a dick, Scar, ignore him. And this is exclu—"

I cut him off with my lips, pushing past the hold he has on me to stop him from saying shit just to calm the tension in the garage. Breathless and needy, I take a step back, and my lips tingle with the need to do it again. "Come find me," I repeat and rush outside.

The chill in the night air cools my skin, but not enough to battle the inferno rising inside of me. I take a deep breath, followed by another, before I shake out my limbs and head toward the main building. As I near the double doors, Euro steps out, lighting a cigarette.

I smile politely when he sees me coming. "Hey, how are you holding up?" So much has happened over the past few days that it's all melting into one and I feel like I haven't slept.

"I've been better," he grumbles, his face scrunching in distaste, and I take him in properly for the first time. His eyes are a mossy shade of green, his nose crooked from one too many hits to the face, and his dirty blond hair is tucked behind his ears, slick with gel.

I don't mention the fact that this asshole hasn't even said thanks or anything, and point toward where his wound is. "Do you need me to check it over or anything?"

"Nah, it's all good. One of the bitches is taking care of me," he replies with a wink, and I cringe so hard I almost shiver. Some men are just assholes and he's one of them.

Before I can piece together a somewhat civilized response, the double doors behind him burst open and Emmett comes racing out. My heart rate instantly spikes, adrenaline courses through my veins as I instantly fall into defensive mode.

"What's happening?"

"Everything's dandy, baby," he sings, winking at me as he sprints past, heading for the garage.

It takes a second for my brain to understand that there

isn't an instant threat, and a further moment for my body to loosen. These men are going to be the death of me, I'm sure of it. They give tornados a run for their money with the craziness that surrounds them.

Offering a tight smile to Euro, I head inside. The bass of the music isn't as harsh as it usually is in here. It still manages to make my body thrum with each beat, but it doesn't feel like it's ricocheting in my chest for a change.

My gaze slides to the Prez's booth where I find Ryker slouched back against the leather seat with a beer bottle pressed to his lips. His eyes are hooded, his brows knitted as he stares off into the distance. Something tells me this links right back to the other intoxicated man I just left in the garage. They're both acting the exact same, so hopefully they'll get over it and move on.

There can't be cracks within the club when you've got the Devil's Brutes knocking at your door.

Considering whether to keep him company or go to my room for some peace after the heavy heart-to-heart with Axel, I pause in the middle of the room. Before I can take a step in either direction, hands grab at my waist, hoisting me in the air before placing me over their shoulder.

Panic bubbles to the surface, remnants still remaining from when Emmett came charging outside, but it quickly subsides once more when the sound of Gray's laugh meets my ears. It's a split second later that his hand spanks my ass, and I squirm in his grasp.

Fuck.

"Ryker," he hollers at the top of his lungs, spinning around to look in the Prez's direction, but I can't be sure since all I can see is his denim-clad ass. Not that I'm complaining about that, it's a damn good ass. "I need you in Church. Now."

My eyebrows pinch, intrigue and confusion flitting through my mind as Gray starts walking with me still over his shoulder. I know the second we're in Church when the noise dies down, the soundproofing in here well worth the money, but when I pat at Gray's thigh to put me down, he ignores me.

"What the hell is going on, Gray?" Ryker grumbles. The door clicks shut behind him as it suddenly becomes the three of us.

Gray's hands on my thighs pull me down his body, inch by inch, until my feet finally touch the floor. I feel his stiff cock against my stomach, see the desire in his eyes, and taste the hunger in the air between us.

As he nudges me backward, my ass presses into the table,and I sit on the edge. He spreads my thighs and stands between them like it's a damn throne or something, before turning his attention to Ryker.

"She thinks this isn't exclusive and then I realized that the conversation we had the other day without her was exactly that; without her. We need to get her up to speed real quick, man."

I glance at Ryker who moves to my right, hovering over his seat as the head of the table, and watch his eyes darken. "Oh, it's exclusive alright," he murmurs, staring intently at me.

"What is?"

"Us," Gray answers, and I finally register that a moment ago he said they discussed something without me. Fuckers.

"Who is 'us' specifically?"

Gray rolls his eyes like it should be obvious, and as much as I like to assume it is, my life hasn't been peachy and assumptions get me nowhere.

He places his palms flat against the wood on either side of me, leaning in until his face is an inch from mine. "Me, Ryker, Emmett, and... Axel."

My head rears back, a huff tainting my lips as I gape at him. "Axel?" He can't be serious, can he?

"One day," Ryker adds, and I glance at him out of the corner of my eye. His hands are fisting the top of his seat, intent clear in his eyes as he looks between Gray and I.

"Okay," I reply with a dramatic eye roll. It should be just as obvious to them as it is to me that it's never going to happen. Would I want it, though? The flutter in my stomach is answer enough as I sink my teeth into my bottom lip.

"I'd say we have a point to prove, wouldn't you, Ryker?" Gray's voice is darker, huskier, and I gulp, desperate to clench my thighs together, but with him perfectly between them, it's impossible.

"She's already fucking panting, so it won't be too hard." I turn and glare at Ryker, but the smirk on his face calls my bullshit. He's not wrong. "Strip her, Gray," he commands, and I lift a palm, plastering it against Gray's chest to stop him before he can even consider starting.

"I'm not a club whore, remember? You can't just tell me what to do and expect me to fall in line, asshole." I keep my eyes fixed on Ryker, who only grins wider at me.

"Good. If you did, then I wouldn't be as drawn to you as I am. You're too rebellious to fall in line." Each word is aimed at my pussy, and it throbs in response.

Gray must see my resolve dissipate as my hand drops from his chest, and in the next moment, my black t-shirt is being torn down the middle.

"You fucking didn't," I gasp, turning back to my favorite fucking blondie who loves to drive me insane. "With the amount of clothes you guys are literally tearing through, you better be prepared to take me shopping," I grumble, hating how much I enjoy watching the smirk spread across Gray's lips in response.

Tearing the remainder of the top, it hangs loose at my sides as he nods. Of course this fucker had to prove a point.

"I'll make the arrangements, Sweet Cheeks."

I hook my finger in the belt loop on his jeans, drawing him in as close as possible. It brings our lips a breath apart, before I cut the remaining distance and crash my lips against his. They're still warm from our moment earlier and the fire inside of me reignites, drenched in gasoline that gathers between my thighs.

"Are you ready, Scarlett?" Gray asks, eyes hooded as he grips my thighs. "I'm going to fuck you on the Church table, cementing the fact that you're ours and ours alone, while Ryker chokes any protests out of you with his cock. Any objections?"

My mouth and pussy moisten at the thought, desperate for exactly that, and the fucker knows it.

"Make my day, Blondie," I breathe. My tongue flicks along his bottom lip before he claims me once more.

I shake the torn t-shirt from my body, before feeling hands immediately at my back, unclasping my bra and releasing my breasts. His calloused fingers run down my spine, making me shiver, before lips press against the column of my throat.

Ryker.

Holy shit.

Goosebumps prickle over my skin at the mingling touches from them both as one of my hands reaches up into Gray's hair, while the other blindly searches for

Ryker. "Pants, Scar," the latter murmurs just before hands grab my waist and lift me off the table, while another set discards the remaining clothes on my body.

My boots hit the floor with a thump, moments before the light chill in the air coats over my skin, licking against every sensitive spot that's needy for attention.

As my ass touches the cool table top, Gray steps back, making me groan, before I feel the touch of leather draping over my shoulders. Looking up into Gray's eyes, all I see is awe and desire, and it makes my heart lodge in my chest.

Too scared to blink, I keep my eyes locked on his as I slowly place my arms through the sleeves, watching as satisfaction morphs his features.

"Hot. As. Fuck." Those three words come from behind me, which tells me Ryker approves too. Releasing a shaky breath, I glance at the length of myself.

Rubbing my lips together, I try to place exactly what I'm feeling, but it's useless. I can't describe something I've never felt before, it's impossible.

"Fucking stunning," Gray declares, tipping my chin back up to meet his gaze as I smile softly at him.

"As a little girl, I vowed to never, *ever* wear one of these," I admit, completely caught up in the moment as I see the worry darken Gray's gaze. "But maybe it wasn't that. Maybe I was just waiting for the right one." His teeth sink into his lip as his eyes gleam with need. "Maybe I was waiting to feel the cool, worn leather of a Ruthless Brother's cut." I should probably slow down to think about this, considering that this is all moving way faster than I can even process, but nothing has ever felt more right in my life. If everything is taken from me tomorrow, then at least I had this moment first.

"Fuck yeah, you were."

Gray unzips his jeans in the next moment, and his cock juts in my direction.

"Please," I beg, before he can utter a word, and Ryker chuckles as he rounds the table and steps up onto it once at my side. My jaw goes slack instantly, excitement getting the better of me as he, too, drops his zipper to reveal his thick length.

"It looks like someone is ready," Gray murmurs, capturing my nipple between his teeth and making me groan as he sinks his teeth into the needy flesh. A cry rips from my mouth.

Thank fuck for the soundproofing.

"Open that hot mouth for me, Scar," Ryker mutters, looking down at me with half-mast eyes, and I swipe my tongue over my lips before doing just that.

Gray's fingers reach for my core, stroking through my folds, as Ryker's cock weighs down on my tongue. *If this is what being claimed looks like, then stamp my ass and call me Ruthless.*

"Fuck, you're beyond wet, Sweet Cheeks," Gray groans, moving across to my other nipple as I continue to whimper at his expert teasing.

"Stretch me with your cock, Gray. Please," I groan, my head falling back as my eyes close, inviting Ryker to push his cock further into my mouth.

He grunts in response, his fingers retreating from my body as the telltale sound of a condom echoes around us before I feel the nudge of his cock at my entrance. That's exactly what I need right now. With Ryker's cock filling my mouth, I can't respond, so I place my feet on the table and tilt my hips for better access.

Swallowing his length, I hum with approval as Gray inches into my core, stretching my pussy to perfectly mold around his cock. I look at Ryker, tilting my head so he has the perfect angle to thrust to the back of my throat, and I practically sob when they both slam into me in sync.

No taking turns, no easing me in, no delicacy; just raw, urgent ecstasy. Exactly how I like it.

With my palms flat against the wood, my body melts between them, Ryker's hand curling into my hair as he cups the back of my head, holding me up, while Gray grips my waist and takes me over and over again.

My mind swirls from the pleasure running through my body. Today has been… crazy as fuck, but it's like it's put me on the brink of a climax, my foreplay coming in the form of a moment with Axel, waking up in Emmett's bed, and both Ryker and Gray claiming me.

Nothing makes sense but this. The way I feel, how in tune my body is with theirs. All of it.

The fall is close, the swirling inside of me rising with every breath I take as the leather on my shoulders reminds me who I belong to now. Prying one hand from the table, I sweep my fingertip over my tight clit, my body shuddering with the move before I repeat it, again and again, until I can barely fucking breathe.

Ryker hits the back of my throat, making my eyes brim with unshed tears as Gray hits my G-spot three times in quick succession, and I fall apart. My moan is captured by Ryker's cock as I hollow my cheeks and suck for dear life, while my climax is drained for all it's worth by Gray's cock slamming into me.

Euphoria sweeps over me, making the hairs on my arms stand on end as my muscles go weak.

"Swallow me, Scar," Ryker bites, his hips moving faster and shallower before his taste bursts over my tongue. I manage to blink my eyes open in time to see his own roll to the back of his head with pleasure, and I suck a little harder with delight.

He slips from my mouth, his hand untangling from my hair. Gray takes a handful instead, steering my attention back to him as his hips slam unrelenting into me. "Mine," he growls, before crushing his lips to mine, finding his own release as his movements become stilted, drawing out every inch of pleasure.

I feel like I'm floating, drifting between reality and make-believe as heaven casts its angelic glow over me. I could get used to this.

"Fuck, Scarlett. You're right," Ryker murmurs, kissing the lobe of my ear. "You were always meant to be with the Ruthless Brothers and never as a Ruthless Bitch," he adds, eyes full of wonder as he waits for my gaze to lock on his before he speaks again, but Gray beats him to it, releasing my mouth.

"Nah, she's our Ruthless fucking Rebel."

# NINE

*Ryker*

"Any further questions?" I glance around the table. Church is filled to the brim with members, each shaking their head. I pound the gavel, and everyone disperses, leaving me to slump back in my seat with a sigh.

This is beyond fucking ridiculous. We have no more information, no details to give us the upper hand with the Brutes, nothing to go on. At this stage, it's a lost cause, but they haven't retaliated since we cleared out Kincaid's men, so something is on the horizon. I know it. I can fucking feel it.

Getting information on these fuckers is harder than I thought it would be. No one wants any involvement, no other clubs willing to make a stand, which just leaves us. Ruthless to the very end.

I turn my attention to Shift as he reaches the door.

"Don't leave any stones unturned. We need something, anything, you hear me?" My tone is more scathing than necessary, but I can't help it, and if he thinks so too, he doesn't utter a word as he nods.

"You got it, Prez."

He leaves the room with everyone else until only Gray, Emmett, Axel, and I remain. Laughter filters in from the bar, making me pause for a beat.

Scarlett.

*Fuck.*

It's crazy to me that a month ago, I wouldn't even recognize her in the street and now I know it's her by her laugh alone. Is it a distraction or a God-send? Fuck if I know.

Axel slams the door shut behind everyone, the frame rattling as I quirk a brow at him but I keep my mouth shut. We're all pent up and frustrated about the situation. Lives have been lost, everything has gone to shit, and we need to exert that anger somewhere. Door frames be damned.

"I was listening to that," Gray grumbles, frowning at Axel who looks confused as fuck.

"To what?"

"Her laughter, it's like a fucking symphony," he says with a swoony sigh, and I shake my head at him. At least I'm not as bad as him… right?

"She's something alright," Emmett chimes in, adjusting

himself in his pants. Axel grunts, but the grizzly fucker leaves the door ajar for us.

"You guys have never been ruffled like this before," he comments, slouching back in his seat as he assesses the three of us.

"That's because we hadn't met *her* yet," Gray explains, like that's all there is to it.

"But there's still so much we don't know about her and we're just letting her in willingly," I add, still unable to wrap my head around it all.

Silence covers the room for a moment before Axel clears his throat, his gaze fixed on his fingers as they tap along the table top. "She's broken just like the rest of us, but by some fucking miracle, she's used her pain to mend herself. I've never witnessed someone with so much darkness have such an air of lightness around them, the type that says I pieced myself together without anyone's help."

I wet my parched lips, my heart lodging in my throat at his deep words. My eyebrows raise when I process them again and again and realize it's Axel we're talking about here. Glancing to the others to see if they've noticed too, I find Gray with a smirk on his lips and I know there's something I'm unaware of.

"What am I missing?"

Gray sits taller like he was hoping I would ask.

"You're missing the fact that this asshole was wasted in the garage last night, and I walked in to find him being almost civilized with Scarlett." He wiggles his eyebrows at Axel suggestively as I turn to glance at him too.

My gut twists with worry. Was he drinking because of me? Fuck. I shouldn't put the weight of this on myself, but it's hard to deny it. I can tell by the glint in his eyes, but I should be able to say how I feel and act accordingly without worrying about this kind of stuff. I can't walk on eggshells forever, but he also deserves a friend who is going to be there for him.

Through thick and thin.

His eyes finally shift from Gray's to mine, and I can see the storm in them. He knows exactly what I'm thinking without me saying anything. I might be mad at him, but I need him to see I'm still here to help. "Do you need anything from me?"

Axel assesses me for a brief moment before shaking his head and sitting taller in his seat. "I'm good, but I think it's us that need to do something for you," he replies, catching me by surprise. Before I can ask what the hell he means, he continues, "Get out of here. Take a minute, regroup, and you'll be better focused when you get back. Then we can hopefully come up with something to put an end to this bullshit with the Brutes."

Laughter from the bar area trickles in ever so slightly,

stirring my cock at the thought of her again as Emmett pats my arm. "Take her with you. Have some fun just being Ryker for a minute."

I should disagree, I should explain why none of that will help, but they're right. Without a word, I push my chair back and head for the door. I step into the bar to find a few people in here, but my attention goes straight to the girl at the bar that's laughing with Maggie.

Scarlett fucking Reeves.

Her hair is piled in a messy bun, a few tendrils loose and framing her face, making me want to cup her cheek and bring her closer. She's wearing a pair of jeans and a fitted black ribbed top. A flash of ink on her arm is a reminder of what she let Emmett do.

Shit.

My dick hardens by just looking at her. If I expect to get out of here, I need to move now before I choose to just take the twenty steps to my room with her over my shoulder instead.

"Rebel," I holler, and her head whips to me instantly, a ghost of a smile touching the corner of her lips. "You coming?" I add, taking a backward step toward the exit.

"Where?"

"Does it matter?"

"No." Her reply is instant and I have to bite back a groan.

"I didn't think so." Turning, I head for the doors, swinging them both open at the same time and spotting my bike parked to the left. Her hurried footsteps are hot on my heels, and by the time she's at my side, I'm already seated on my bike with a helmet extended in her direction.

She takes it, places her dainty hand on my shoulder, and swings her leg over the back of the bike. Her arms settle around my waist as she gets comfortable, and I grin from ear to ear.

*And she said she doesn't take orders. Would you look at that?*

---

My jeans ripple around my legs as we speed over the highway. Dotted trees turned into shrubs and cement barriers as we headed further and further away from Jasperville earlier, but now we're making our way back.

Seconds turned into minutes, and minutes drifted into hours. Each one passing with Scarlett pressed against my back like a second skin. It's clear she knows how to ride, she leans into the corners naturally with me, enjoying the speed just as much as I do.

Turning off the highway, we travel a block or two as we take each right turn, before we're back on the highway again, heading in the opposite direction. We haven't spoken. Not a single word, but none have been necessary. Her presence has been enough, although the semi in my pants hasn't faltered the entire time. Having her pressed against me is too fucking good apparently.

Her hands flex around my waist, luring me deeper into her web as I spot the sign for Jasperville in the distance. Not wanting to head home just yet, I pull off a few junctions early, eyeing a classic diner I'm familiar with. It's in no man's land, completely open to every crew and club. Neutral ground run by Delia, once the old lady of Bryn Michaels, an original Ruthless Brother. Shot dead by a rival club, he was taken too soon at twenty-two, widowing Delia with a baby. She stepped away from the life, but made a difference all the same when she set up this place.

Rolling the bike to a stop, I knock the kickstand down and take off my helmet. "You hungry?"

I glance back over my shoulder to find Scarlett removing her helmet too. "I could eat."

I stretch out my arms above my head as I stare in awe at her shaking her hair out, before securing it in a hair tie on top of her head.

Such a fucking vision, even when it's the most mundane shit.

I offer her my hand, and the corner of her mouth tips up as she places her hand in mine. She swings her leg over the seat, and I grasp her palm properly, lacing our fingers together. It's foreign, a move I've never made before, yet it feels as natural as my next breath.

Pulling her toward the diner, our steps fall into sync. There aren't too many cars in the small parking lot, and inside isn't overly busy, so I push against the red-framed door and head for my favorite spot.

Soft jazz plays over the old sound system, the worn leather booths having seen better days, but the homey atmosphere has people coming back time and time again. "Ryker, honey, we'll be with you in a minute. Take a seat."

I smile at Delia, who stands behind the counter working the coffee machine. She's in her late sixties now, but still one hell of a woman. If anyone steps inside here and attempts to cause trouble, she'll be the one to handle it.

"Take your time, we're in no rush," I reply with a wave, before taking the booth furthest to the left. Scarlett slides into the spot across from me, eyes casting over the room as she takes it all in, while I confirm that the fire exit door beside me isn't locked shut.

"This is cute," she murmurs, reaching for the menu and running her finger over the items.

"You haven't been here before?" This place is well known in Jasperville. I don't think I know anyone that doesn't know Delia and the pecan pie that she's famous for.

Scarlett shakes her head gently, nibbling on her bottom

lip nervously as she looks up at me. Her finger is paused on the menu, while I don't even bother to get one. I know exactly what I'm having. What I *always* have.

"No, I uh…"

"What?"

"Well, I wasn't allowed free rein like this. I couldn't just go to a cafe, not even after a job, and I only learned this place existed on my last job." Her words grow quiet, like she's considering whether to proceed or not. "I watched Banner for a few weeks before I made my move. He would come here every Friday with Billy."

My eyebrows raise in understanding. She didn't know this place existed until she was paid to kill our president and sergeant at arms. Now, her pause makes sense.

"Every Friday? I wasn't aware of that." Scarlett gulps hard, releasing a breath I wasn't expecting. It dawns on me that she was likely expecting anger from me at the mention of their deaths. "You know, I believe Banner had something to do with my father's death."

Whatever she's about to say is interrupted as Mary-Ann stops at the table with her pad in hand. "What can I get you guys?" She's in her mid-thirties, but still pops gum really big and loud like it's attractive. The bags under her eyes tell everyone she needs a good night's sleep and the thinness to her frame says she prioritizes other things over herself. But despite all of the invisible weight she's silently carrying on her shoulders, her smile is wide and her attitude is always too peppy.

I make a mental note to tip her big today. Scarlett glances at the menu with panic in her gaze. "Hey, Mary-Ann. I'll take a bowl of chili with some cornbread and a slice of pecan pie."

"Like always, Ryker. I shouldn't even bother asking you anymore. You want a large orange soda to go with that?" I nod, smirking at her comment, and then her attention turns to Scarlett. "And what will it be for you, hun?"

Scarlett rubs her lips together, brows pinched in discomfort as she looks from Mary-Ann, to the menu, and to me, before dropping her gaze back to the menu. Her finger is still pressed where she paused it earlier and I notice she's only three items down on the list, but before I can think anymore on it, she clears her throat, distracting me.

"Can I get the same as Ryker, please?" Her smile doesn't quite reach her eyes as she looks up at Mary-Ann, but she doesn't seem to notice as she nods in response. "Just a coffee instead of the soda, if you don't mind."

"Of course, hun. It'll be right out." Mary-Ann leaves without another word and Scarlett slumps back in her seat, avoiding my gaze.

Stretching my arms out on the table, I try to find a way to ask what I want to without being a dick, until I realize there's no way around it. "Scarlett…" I wait for her to look at me, and when she does, there's resolution in her eyes like she knows what's coming. "Can you read?"

Her lips purse instantly, fingers flexing as she regards me. "Barely," she admits. "Any kind of pressure and it all just becomes a jumbled fucking mess."

"Is it because you've never been taught or because of dyslexia maybe…" I don't know what I'm fucking saying, but the need to be supportive and understanding is overwhelming. I'm neither of those things, the fact that none of her old club remains is an example of that.

"I've never been to a doctor in my life, never mind someone who can diagnose me with anything, but I think it's a lack of knowledge. I've tried to teach myself, learn from videos and shit on the internet, but it's harder than it looks." She sits taller in her seat, almost defensively like she has something to prove, but her statement only makes me admire her more.

"I think you were a little preoccupied surviving to waste your time on shit like reading, writing, and math." Her eyes widen at my words, tongue flicking out over her bottom lip. "We'll help you," I add. It's as simple as that, we can make whatever she needs work. Despite all of the craziness around us, she slayed Kincaid's men for us, and ultimately… we owe her.

Big time.

"Okay," she murmurs. Soon, the drinks are placed down on the table. We both offer our thanks to Mary-Ann, who barely hangs around to hear it.

"So, you're a boss bitch killer, huh?" I change the subject, leaning toward her strength instead of what she may deem a weakness.

Her eyes blow wide as she sinks down in her seat. "What the fuck, Ryker? You can't say shit like that out loud."

"I can say whatever I want," I reply with a chuckle, and she rolls her eyes at me, but she's still nervous, I can sense it. Apparently conversation is no longer a strong suit of mine. Tapping my finger on the table, my head tilts slightly as I look deep into her eyes.

"I'm sorry your father died. I agree with your thoughts on Banner though. When I heard the gossip about it all, I knew it was an inside job."

I freeze for a second, my Adam's apple bobbing for a moment before I nod. "If I had gone into the warehouse with him, he would still be here," I admit, refusing to consider the alternative. I'm a champion, a winner, I wouldn't have fallen at Banner's hands. Ever. Not that I need to dive into all of that. "I'm sorry your father was murdered too," I offer, remembering learning of Freddie's death.

Scarlett chuckles, swiping a hand down her face as she leans forward and braces her elbows on the table. "So you guys didn't gossip this morning, then." It's not a question, it's an assessment.

"What am I missing?"

"I'm not sad that he's dead, Ryker. I was simply inconvenienced with the clean up I left for myself." Understanding washes over me.

"You're the Grim Reaper."

Scarlett laughs, shaking her head as she wags a finger at me. "Axel's response was the exact same, tone and all."

"You told Axel that?" I clarify, and she shrugs.

"That's irrelevant. I—"

"Ryker, long time, no see." My blood runs cold before exploding into an inferno of rage as I turn to glance at Porter fucking Hallman. After what he set up with the Brutes at the sheriff's office, putting Emmett at risk like that, I want to rip his damn throat out here and now. As if sensing the war inside of me, I find Delia looking over at us and I bite back my anger.

"Fuck off, Porter," I grunt, looking straight at Scarlett, who instantly shrinks in her seat. He's not in his officer uniform, but he fucking smells like a pig and walks like a cop so she likely knows what he is.

"That's no way to speak to the deputy of this town, Ryker. I could take you in for that disobedience alone." I hear Scarlett's sharp intake of breath, and I stretch my legs out under the table so mine brush against hers, offering her as much silent support as I can without drawing attention to her.

"What do you want, Porter?" I finally glance at him and his face instantly irritates me.

"I was just checking in. It's important for the sheriff's office to have a good relationship with the clubs in these parts," he states, and I snicker.

"Do you want me in your pocket to balance out the fact that you're in the Brute's pocket?" I ask, quirking a brow at him.

"You just keep talking and you're going to put a bigger target on your head," he grunts, slamming his palms down on the table. Scarlett remains rigid in her seat.

"Deputy Hallman, you're going to have to leave." Delia's voice carries across the room as the music is halted and everyone turns to look in our direction.

"Delia, you're not above the law. I don't know how many times I have to tell you—"

"In here, your law doesn't mean shit. If you want to question that, I'll get the sheriff on the line right now." Her voice is like steel, unwilling to back down.

Annoyed, Porter's hands ball into fists. Whatever he's desperate to say remains locked down deep inside him as he plasters a fake as fuck smile on his face. "I'll be seeing you, Ryker." He doesn't even look in Scarlett's direction as he turns and tilts his head at Delia. "Ma'am."

I watch his every step until he leaves, and the second the door closes behind him, our food is placed in front of us. I don't offer any thanks this time as I continue to track Porter's every move, right down to the cell he pulls from his pocket while glancing over his shoulder at me.

"Eat up, Rebel, our fun just got fucked in the face with a floppy dick."

# TEN

## *Scarlett*

What the fuck is going on right now?

I knew leaving the compound would cause issues, but I didn't expect a run-in with the cops. My spine burns with tension, my thigh pressed into Ryker's leg under the table as I try to keep myself grounded instead of spiraling like last time… and every single time before.

That guy barely paid me any mind. His issues fell more with Ryker, but it still has me on edge. "Who was that?" I ask, still not reaching for my fork as Ryker dives into his food across from me. Anger knits his brows together as he keeps flitting his gaze outside and back.

"That's Porter Hallman, we went to high school with the fucker, but more recently, he's the bastard that set up the hit on Emmett and Euro when they were arrested at the compound."

Distress claws at my insides once more, but I take a few deep breaths to try and bite through it. I would love nothing more than to rush out there and end him for that bullshit, but in my mind, since he's an officer, it puts an invisible force field around him.

"Eat, Scarlett," Ryker adds, waving his fork at my plate.

It smells incredible. My stomach grumbles at the reminder that I've not eaten yet. Grabbing the cornbread, I dip it into the chili and take a bite, groaning in delight as the flavor bursts over my tongue.

"Holy shit, that's good." I don't look up at him until I'm done with the bread and halfway down the bowl with my spoon poised at my lips. His chili bowl is empty, a pecan pie placed in front of him, but his eyes are fixed on me. "What?"

Shaking his head as if I've pulled him from a trance, he glances down at the pie. "Nothing."

"What the fuck is that?" I balk, lowering my spoon as he glances up at me, a soft smile ghosting his lips.

"What the fuck is what?"

My eyes narrow. "What's with you glancing down and holding back what was going through your head?"

Bracing his elbows on the table, he meets my gaze straight on. "You know you're hot as fuck, right? Like hot hot, doesn't even know how hot, especially when you're in your own little world eating some food. It should be illegal and it's distracting because I'm supposed to be sitting here devising a plan of action against fucking Hallman. Instead, I'm thinking about the fact that Emmett announced he was refusing to buy any more condoms because he wanted to feel you for real next time and I'm sitting here thinking about how tempting that sounds." My thighs clench at the rawness in his tone, need and anticipation threatening to tear me apart.

All I can do is gape at him, whiplash from the chain of events that have just unfolded leaving me speechless. When I can finally remember how to work my tongue, I clear my throat and lean back in my seat. "That's not going to happen because I can't get birth control and there's no way in hell I'm considering the alternative."

Ryker's attention drifts to his pie for a moment as he takes a huge bite, making me discard the remainder of my chili to join him. "Why can't you get birth control?"

I roll my eyes and lift a forkful of pie to my lips. "Because I don't exist, remember? That means I can't just stroll into a doctor's office for it."

Realization dawns over him as he purses his lips while I try the pecan pie, groaning with delight when it melts in my mouth. That's criminally good.

"Could we maybe rope Emily or one of the girls into helping? Like get the meds set up in their name or something?" He's really fucking considering this. It's not a bad idea; it's probably the most realistic idea, but it's still crazy as hell.

It's a classic Ruthless Brother's move, their own level of madness, but despite the chaos it may involve, I find myself leaning toward it. "We can speak to her."

A smile spreads across his face, his eyes darkening with a glint of need, and I feel my cheeks heat. Neither of us says another word as we finish off our food. Ryker leaves a pile of cash on the table before taking my hand and drawing me toward the door, making sure to wave at Delia as we go.

The second we're outside and the sun is on my face, I smile.

"I'm really fucking impressed with how well you're handling the run-in with Hallman," Ryker murmurs, pulling me into his side as he whispers against my ear. I shiver at the move, pride in myself making me preen too.

"Inside I'm panicking, but since it wasn't a raid where they charge in with their guns raised, I don't think it's registering the same." I don't even know if that makes sense, but he nods and pulls me toward the bike.

As I reach for my helmet, Ryker pauses my hand and places something in it. A key? Looking up at him, excitement starts to ripple through my veins as he nods at his bike. "You driving us home, Rebel?"

"Fuck yeah." I squeal at the top of my lungs, cringing the second it happens, but he just laughs at me. I don't know whether I'm more excited to be in control of the bike or have Ryker hold on to *me*. Either way, my fingers are itching to feel the vibration of the handlebars.

Placing my helmet on my head, I reach for the clasp when screeching tires distract me. My heart sinks when the telltale MC cut flashes before us as a bike rolls to a stop. I know who it is by their stance, their cock-sure attitude even when they're simply breathing, but as they remove their helmet, his jet-black eyes reveal him.

Kincaid.

Clearly we didn't eat quick enough because my gut tells me that Porter guy called up his friend here. Fucker.

Ryker doesn't even stiffen beside me as he moves ever so slightly to put himself between Kincaid and I. A protector to the very end, even when he knows what I'm capable of. It's a bizarre feeling, having someone stand between you and danger. I'm so used to being the human shield that this catches me off guard.

Rising from his bike, Kincaid folds his arms over his chest as he eyes Ryker like a disgruntled piece of shit on his boot. "You made quite a dent in my men, Ryker. I should kill you on the spot in retaliation."

I have to hold back a laugh at his audacity, but I leave the speaking to Ryker. "You shouldn't have sent them to our compound to begin with. It's not my fault they didn't realize what they were walking into, especially without their leader." The dig twists Kincaid's lip into a snarl as he takes a step closer, but Ryker doesn't move an inch.

"You should have paid your dues by now." Kincaid's change in subject irritates the fuck out of me, my hands balling at my sides as I glare at him, but it goes unnoticed.

"I ain't got any dues to be paying, Kincaid. I keep telling you this and you keep ignoring it." Ryker sounds bored, like the man before us hasn't been wreaking havoc on his club, but it brings me too much joy to watch Kincaid's irritation grow. He lives for being feared, it's what fuels him, but he's definitely not getting that response from the Ruthless Brothers. Maybe he's finally met his match.

Kincaid shakes his head, swinging his arms out wide as a wolf's grin touches his lips. "I'm going to be a good guy here and offer you seven days to get your head out of your ass or I'm coming for you and there'll be no mercy *this* time," he bites, teeth practically snapping as his eyes finally drift to mine. "I'll be seeing you too, Scarlett. It's long overdue." He moves to his bike.

"Fuck you, Kincaid."

"That's the plan, princess," he retorts, before revving his engine and leaving smoke in his wake as he hightails it out of the parking lot.

Ryker and I stand in silence for what feels like an

eternity, processing what the fuck just happened, when he finally turns to look at me. "I don't know what the fuck that was, but he's delusional," he grunts, his words relaxing my body despite there not being any soothing tone to it.

"He's up to something. He would never give you an extension like that. He's either rallying more men or there's something bigger at play here." He nods in agreement. "What's his angle?" I add.

He squeezes my shoulder in comfort. "I don't know, but we need to find out if we want to protect the club."

# ELEVEN

*Scarlett*

Pressing my palms into my eye sockets, I try to rid the fog from my sleep-deprived brain. When Ryker and I returned to the compound yesterday, he instantly went into 'prez mode' and the guys were all holed up in church for hours. Emily wasn't here and even though Maggie offered for me to relax at the bar with her, my social limit had been maxed out.

I may not have spiraled in the diner over Porter Hallman's surprise arrival, but it's played on my mind ever since, or more so the fact that he knows Kincaid.

He. Fucking. Knows. Kincaid.

Someone who despises me and knows my biggest secret. He knows I don't exist. Is this going to be held over my head for the rest of my life? Either way, it leaves me riddled with anxiety. The tightness in my chest kept me awake most of the night as I caught up on the crime podcasts I'd missed, but they offered no comfort.

My stomach churns, a reminder that I haven't eaten since the diner, which was almost twenty-four hours ago at this point. Lifting my face from my hands, I exhale with a whoosh, before rising to my feet and heading for the door.

It's quiet in the hallway as I make my way to the kitchen, where I find Maggie at the fridge.

"Morning," I call out, wanting to make my presence known, but she still jumps a little in surprise as she turns to look at me.

"Sugar, you scared the crap out of me," she gasps as she pulls a carton of eggs out of the fridge and closes it behind her. "You okay? You look like a zombie." Her words are humorless as concern creeps into her eyes.

"I'm good, just a rough night's sleep," I admit, making my way over to the coffee machine as she hums in acknowledgment.

"Well, I'm going to have the grill going tonight. We deserve a little get together after everything that's happened this past week, and I feel it's only right that we celebrate the lives we lost."

I pause, coffee mug in hand as I gape at her. How the fuck did I forget about Eric's death? Emmett and Emily have lost their father and the world keeps on turning. How does that happen?

Shaking my head and focusing on Maggie again, I pour two mugs as I nod. "You're right, Maggie. Count me in, whatever you need help with, I'm there."

"This is why you're good for our club, Scarlett." My eyebrows furrow, uncertain as to what she means by that. I'm no good for anything, I've been told so enough times in my life. I keep my mouth shut though, not wanting to bring my insecurities to life when there are bigger things to handle. "Do you want some eggs?" she offers, swiftly moving on from such a statement, but before I can say anything, Emily waltzes into the room, her finger instantly pointing in my direction.

"There you are," she sings, before glancing at Maggie. "Don't be feeding our girl, Mags, we're going out for food today." Her smile widens as I carry two coffee mugs to the table.

"We are?"

Emily nods eagerly in response. "Yup, you coming too, Mags? It's going to be fun." She wiggles her eyebrows and I definitely know I'm missing something.

"I'm good, I've got my hands full with the food prep for tonight, but it will be good for you girls to get out of here for a bit," Maggie replies, before mouthing her thanks for the coffee and taking a big gulp.

Taking a seat at the table, I eye Emily. "Why are we eating out?"

Not that I mind, but after yesterday, I feel a little more hesitant than I usually would. Especially with Emily present, I'll be on high alert for her safety more than my own.

My new friend takes the seat across from me, her gaze serious as she locks eyes with me. "Do you want the pill?"

"The what?"

My nose scrunches as I lean back in my seat, and Emily giggles.

"The pill, ya know, for stopping procreation," she explains, before creating a hole with her left hand and stabbing her pointer finger from the other hand vigorously into it. *Give me fucking strength with this woman.*

I take a deep breath as Maggie chuckles behind me, clearly enjoying this. "Uh, I mean, I don't want to be procreating, but I also really don't want to be having this conversation right now. So…" I trail off as they laugh unabashed from the top of their lungs. It takes a moment, but I let the tension release from my body and grin at them.

This is only going to be as awkward as I fucking make it.

"So, where are we eating before we figure this out?" I ask, just as Emmett appears in the doorway. A smile touches the corner of his mouth when his eyes land on mine, and I return it with a shit-eating grin of my own.

Everything has been utter madness since the showdown

that revealed my skills to the Ruthless Brothers and I feel like I haven't seen him properly since he found me out by the waterfall. "Hey," I murmur, tucking a loose lock of hair behind my ear.

"Hey, beautiful," he replies softly, making my cheeks redden. Emily fake gags.

"You two could procreate with just the tension in the air," she chimes in, her nose scrunching.

Emmett rolls his eyes. "Will you stop with the procreating talk," he groans, rubbing the back of his neck. "Let's get this over with, shall we?" He points over his shoulder for us to follow, and Emily is out of her seat and bouncing after him in the next breath. I can still hear her teasing continuing from here as I drink the last drop of my coffee. I really should have made it stronger to survive this damn conversation that's coming.

Emmett's coming too? I don't think my brain can take any of this.

I'm in a pair of black joggers and a long sleeved black t-shirt, with my combat boots. I'm not really sure how I'm supposed to dress for this kind of thing, but this will have to do.

"Wish me luck with these fuckers," I murmur to Maggie, who laughs in response before I follow their voices through the bar to the front of the compound.

My shoulders roll back and my body relaxes the second

the sun's rays touch my skin. I could sleep right now with that beating down on me, wrapping me in a cocoon and making me feel safe.

"Let's go, snowflake. I'm already stressed out about all of this, don't drag it out and send me over the edge," Emmett grumbles as he tucks his loose blond hair behind his ear.

*Sexy. As. Fuck.*

I almost explain how he's the distraction in all of this, but I can feel Emily's beady eyes on me so I slam my mouth shut and simply nod in response. I climb into the back of the SUV with Emily, Duffer takes shotgun beside Emmett, and before anyone can speak a word, he's tearing out of the compound.

"So, how is this even going to work?" I lace my fingers together in my lap as I look at Emmett in the rearview mirror, but it's Emily who replies.

"I spoke with Ryker." His jaw tightens at her words. "We're going to get them prescribed under my name for you."

I gulp harshly, nodding in understanding. "Thank you for doing this. I hate that I make things complicated and can't just do it myself, I—"

"Hush, it's nothing honestly, and you don't do any of that bullshit. In fact, you make us happy and you're amazing, so in comparison, we still owe you." My jaw is slack as I stare at her, utterly speechless and caught off guard with whatever this is... Kindness? Appreciation? Friendship? "Besides, this is all for me because it makes Emmett flustered and I love nothing more than having fun at his expense."

Emmett's hands tighten on the steering wheel as Emily giggles again, and I smirk.

"Let's have some fun then."

---

The SUV door slams shut behind Emmett and Emily as she practically drags him toward the doctor's office. There's a skip to her step, while Emmett looks more than reluctant, his knuckles almost dragging across the floor like an ape in defiance. A hot as fuck viking ape if we're being specific. The gleam in his eyes when he glances back at the vehicle sends a shiver running down my spine.

This is all happening because he wants to feel me bare, without the consequences of 'procreating'. I didn't expect my day to be looking like this, but here we are.

A brown paper wrapper is thrust into my line of sight and I relax back into my seat as I take it from Duffer. Emmett insisted I move to the front, just in case there was an emergency, and placed Duffer in the driver's seat as a getaway driver. It would have been amusing to call him a drama queen, but there's been a lot of deaths over the past month, and he's right to have a fall back plan in place. It's the exact reason Ryker chose him as his VP—he plans, he considers, and he protects. Another three factors that add to his hotness along with his blond viking looks that melt me, even just from a fleeting glance.

"Thanks," I murmur to Duffer, pulling the jalapeño cheddar bagel with cream cheese from the wrapper and taking a big bite. Emily insisted we stop by the cute little deli near campus that she loves and I can instantly see the appeal. I groan as I sink my teeth into it again, and Duffer chuckles.

"Emily definitely has you onboard with the deli then. The first few times she went, I just waited outside. Then the fourth time she came out with a bagel for me, even though I'd declined, and I've been hooked ever since." He grins, taking another bite.

"Food is heaven," I declare, not really knowing what else to say, when his face falls a little solemn and he looks at me out of the corner of his eye.

"Food, when you've never been able to indulge in more than a piece of buttered bread and the odd piece of meat, is a raw mixture of heaven and hell. Addicting, devilish, and orgasmic all at once."

"Those are the truest fucking words I've ever heard."

An understanding smile passes between us, before we

continue devouring the bagel-y goodness in our hands. Reaching for the bottle of water in the center console, I unscrew the cap as Duffer clears his throat. "I have a confession to make."

My stomach instantly drops, uncertainty clawing up my spine as I side-eye him. I try to remain calm, fighting the instinctive need to beat the fuck out of him or run for my life. I need to hear his confession before I make any decisions, but nothing good ever comes from a sentence like that.

"Emmett knows, that's why he insisted I come with you guys, despite the circumstances." He waves his hand in the air as my body relaxes ever so slightly. If Emmett trusts him on the matter, then it can't be that bad... I hope.

"You're going to have to spit it out because you're making me nervous," I admit as he rubs his hand over his chin.

"I know who you are."

*Nope, I take it back. Kill and flee, I repeat, kill and flee.*

"I don't know what you mean." My voice is barely more than a whisper as I replace the water bottle in the holder, hand slowly drifting to the door handle.

"I didn't realize it until you came out guns blazing at the compound when the Brutes showed up. I was young, real fucking young, so I don't remember very well, but we've met before."

My heart is lodged in my throat, my breath ragged as the cords in my neck strain. "Met. Where?" I don't mean to grind the words out through gritted teeth, but fuck if my defenses aren't up.

Duffer nervously rubs at his lips, his face downcast as he looks up at me from the corner of his eye. "My mom's name is Rita, Rita Borland, or it was bef—"

"Rita? As in the Reaper's whore, Rita?" My mind swirls with the memory of the woman who loved me fiercely and lost her life. The woman I cared for when the drugs consumed her. The woman that gave me strength when I had none left. The woman... who had a son, a little boy, a year or two younger than me, called—"Dylan?"

A smile spreads across his cheeks, but the pain still remains in his eyes. "The one and only."

My hand clasps his shoulder, the leather cool against my palm as I gape at him. "Dylan Borland." His name hangs in the air between us for a moment as I try to wrap my head around it. "I haven't seen you since..." The memory of that night burns the back of my eyelids, the haunting look I see on Duffer's face reflecting in my own.

"Since you pinned me to the floor and sobbed until the sun came up."

Guilt trickles down my spine as my jaw falls slack. "I didn't... I... you..."

"You didn't want me to see her like that, I know. I

know and I'll be forever grateful to you for that."

My eyes squeeze shut as I take a deep breath. When I pry them open, there's a smile touching his lips. "When I left, I was placed into the system, never that far away from here. It seems like they like to keep the crazies all together." I snicker at his light joke. "I did come to visit you one time though, when I was having a rough time, but the second I showed my face at the gate, I had a gun in my face and a threat on the Reaper's tongue."

Darkness clouds his eyes, and I feel it too, anger building at those motherfuckers. "I'll kill him."

"He's already dead," he replies, patting my hand on his shoulder as I pout, annoyed that someone beat me to it. "But the warning was clear. I knew about you, about their Grim Reaper, and that made me a liability, a threat. I might think I'm cool now, Scarlett, but shit, I was scared as fuck. I was too frightened to ever show my face after that."

"I'm glad. You did the right thing."

There's so much more I want to say, so much I want to catch up on, but I can't find the words. The last time I saw him, I was maybe nine? I literally pinned him to the ground, the pair of us screaming in pain at the loss of his mother. The next day, he was gone and I was back to being the Grim Reaper. Gone was my flicker of hope, and all that remained was pain and anger.

That was the day I knew I would kill Freddie, I just had

to be calculated and careful.

"Oh, fuck." Duffer laughs, pointing out the front window toward the doctor's office where Emily and Emmett are. They're completely flustered. A grin spreads across my face, and I fail to cover it with my hand as they climb into the back of the SUV.

"Get us the fuck out of here, Duffer. Now," Emmett grunts, folding his arms over his chest as Emily tries to suppress a laugh, but fails miserably.

"How did it go?" I ask as the vehicle starts to move. Emmett chucks a white paper bag at me, making Emily laugh even louder.

"Next time, you take my fucking cum instead and name our firstborn Emmett, okay?" My eyes almost bulge as Emily fake barfs and Duffer laughs.

This fucking man.

"It was that bad, huh?" I smirk at Duffer's casualness as Emily claps her hands.

"It was worse."

"How could it be worse?" I frown, twisting further in my seat to look at him.

"She thought Emmett was my…" Her words trail off as she gets the giggles again. I spy him out of the corner of my eye as he glares at her, face red, but doesn't offer to finish her sentence. "She thought Emmett was my boyfriend luring me to the dark side."

My head falls back as a bark of laughter escapes. "That's too funny."

"Don't make me have Duffer pull this vehicle over so I can spank your ass," Emmett grunts, a challenge in his eyes.

"In front of your sister? I don't think so," I retort, knowing full well I'm playing with fire, but he makes it too enticing.

"Try me."

Two words, just two damn words and I'm squirming in my seat. "Save my punishment for another time, Viking."

Laughter echoes around the SUV, and as I turn to face forward, a hand wraps in my hair, pulling my head back, and I squeak with surprise before Emmett's lips crush into mine upside down.

The angle is awkward, the pain warring with the pleasure as I'm pulled over the center console, but only enhancing it as he claims me with his mouth.

"Your punishment is coming, Snowflake. When you least expect it."

# TWELVE

## Scarlett

"Why can't we just show up to the get together tonight in exactly what we're wearing now?" I ask Emily with a pout, and she rolls her eyes like I'm the one being ridiculous.

"That's cute, but hell no, we're looking fire. It's the only option." She stands in front of the floor-length mirror she dragged in here, ruffling her hand through her hair for it to fall flat again straight away.

The second the SUV rolled to a stop at the compound doors, she jumped from the vehicle, swung my door open and pulled me along with her. I didn't stop her, and Emmett didn't call me back, so her speed slowed as we entered the club and we've been tucked away in my room ever since.

"I need to do something with my hair, give it some more life than this," she grumbles as she continues to assess her reflection. "Curls maybe, I don't know."

"Girl, we both know you're asking the wrong person for this. I've perfected the art of a messy bun and a slick ponytail, and that's all I have to offer."

"Yeah, but your hair is the perfect texture. Mine is just meh."

Rolling my eyes, I push up from the bed and move to stand beside her in the mirror. I've never had a friend, not like this, but my gut clenches with the need to cheer up my ball of sunshine. "Em, your hair is stunning exactly as it is, but we both know there is some tool or technique that will give you the vibe you want. I'm all hands on deck to make it work." The corner of her mouth turns up, encouraging me to continue. "Your wide eyes reflect like fucking orbs of magic in the sun, or some shit like that, your skin is like fucking glass, and those cheekbones are perfectly angled." Her smile turns into a laugh as she nudges me with her shoulder.

"Thank you."

"You're welcome."

"It doesn't get you out of getting all dressed up for tonight though," she says with her eyebrow raised, and I crinkle my nose.

"I don't think a damn earthquake would stop you from doing your thing right now." She preens at my statement, whatever weight that was pressing down on her slowly dissipating as she searches out her overnight bag that she brought.

"Have your way with me," I declare, taking a seat at the foot of the bed and she starts unpacking hair products and make-up.

Something tells me there's something more at play than her just wanting to be cute tonight, or more specifically *someone*, but I don't push the subject. She'll spill it to me when she's ready.

She goes from combing my hair and working magic with her curling wand, to tinting my lips after completing a full face of make-up, before throwing a bag at me. "Go get dressed, we don't have long and Maggie will be waiting for us." Without another word, she turns back to the mirror and starts working on her own skincare routine before she glances back at the make-up. She quirks a brow at me when I still haven't moved, and I sigh as I peer inside the bag.

Reaching in, I feel the silky material before I see it. Crimson red, deep and tempting, with long sleeves, a low neckline, and a short hem. I don't bother leaving the room, changing where I am, and a shiver runs down my spine when I catch a glimpse of myself in the mirror. Mixed with the curly updo and smokey-eyed make-up, I look hot as hell. This is a confidence boost if ever I needed one.

"Blue or black?"

I look at Emily at the sound of her question, her hair now full of volume and bouncy with curls. Her make-up is lighter than mine, enhancing her natural beauty as she holds two dresses in front of her. "Blue, it brings out your eyes," I murmur, wagging my eyebrows, and she shakes her head at me.

"Perfect, I'll be good to go in two minutes. You look hot," she adds, and I fake pose dramatically, making her giggle.

"Thank you for this. You have to let me repay you."

She waves her hand dismissively at me, and I let it drop for now, but lock that information away for later. Emily shimmies the dress over her hips, slipping her arms through the spaghetti straps before spinning on the spot.

"Emmett is going to be beating up every man out there when they catch sight of you."

"Please, I could stay home and still get in trouble somehow," she replies, making me frown.

"Where is home now? What with your dad and…" I slam my lips shut, hating the taste of the words on my tongue, but she smiles softly at me.

"I was already staying in the dorms on campus. It was the only snippet of freedom I've been allowed, hence Duffer being my full-time shadow." She doesn't sound all that sad about it, and I bet Emmett preferred that over her staying here. Even if she is here all the time, it's separation from a life she doesn't deserve, want, or need.

"If he gets extra growly tonight, I'll karate chop him in the throat, no problem." I wink, slipping my feet into my sandals before heading for the door.

"Oh, I would pay to see that." She chuckles, leading the way through the clubhouse. The bar is empty, the bass from the music coming from outside, luring us closer.

Dusk casts a glow around the compound as we step out, a warmth still in the air as the entire space is filled with people. Members, old ladies, children, and Ruthless Bitches. Everybody has shown up to celebrate those lost in the attacks from the Devil's Brutes.

When I killed my father, splaying blood everywhere, the Reapers did nothing in his memory. Nothing except keep a hold on me. There was no celebration, no pain, just a new man to fill his boots and the anger still raged inside of me.

Maggie is getting help from Shift over by the grill, while Ryker, Axel, Gray, and Emmett are sitting at the same table as last time. I move to head in their direction, but Emily quickly catches my arm and steers me toward the grill instead. "They can feast on you later, you're mine for now," she says, and I snicker, falling into step with her.

The second we're within arm's reach, Maggie smiles

brightly, wrapping her arm around my shoulders. "You guys are finally here. What do you want to drink?" She sounds like she's already been having a good time and a taste of the liquor that's beside the grill. If anyone deserves to let their hair down though, it's her. She takes care of everyone here and even though she might run this ship like a pro, it must be tiring at times.

"I'm good with water. Do you want me to take over the grill?" I offer as she digs into the cooler and retrieves an icy-cold bottle for me.

"You're good, I've roped Shift into it," she says with a wide smile, wagging a finger at her son who smirks in response.

"She gave me no choice. Something about birthing me and repayment."

It feels strange to see him here like this, connecting him to Kronkz, my only friend before I came here, and the guy that set up all of my hits and lined my bank account. He's now more than a voice at the other end of my headset or a reply to my texts. He's a human being standing before me, and it makes me feel a bit awkward.

As if sensing my thoughts, he places the tongs down and lifts a bottle of beer instead. "Can I steal Scarlett for two minutes?" he asks, and Maggie nods, stepping back as she wraps her arm around Emily instead.

"Of course, you guys stay here while we fetch some

more drinks."

"We can do that," I offer, but they've already left, chuckling among themselves without a backward glance.

*Well then.*

I take a sip of my water as I turn to face Shift, my free arm banding over my stomach as I try to not let the awkwardness lingering between us take effect.

"I feel like you need to punch me in the face or something, cut the tension and put me in my place." I almost spit water everywhere as I bite back a laugh.

"How did you come to that conclusion?"

"You're the fucking Grim Reaper, Scarlett. In front of me, in the flesh. The same woman I've been contracting to complete assassinations. All while being my closest friend outside of the club. Now you're standing here and I'd rather you didn't kill me like you're so well trained for, but a pinch to my flesh just won't suffice in comparison."

It still sounds like a whole lot of craziness to my ears, but before I can think better of it, I rear my arm back and punch him in the chest. It's not quite the face, but it will do.

"Fuck, Scar," he grunts, taking two steps back as he presses his palm to the injured area. A bubble of laughter rings in my ears from a distance, and I glance to my right to find Ryker, Axel, Gray, and Emmett watching our every move with smirks on their faces.

"Now you made us have an audience."

"*Please*, like they weren't watching you already," he replies with a grin, and I roll my eyes at him.

"Feel better?" I ask, changing the subject as he stands up tall, a wince still twisting his face.

"I appreciate you didn't go for the face at least," he remarks. "But in all seriousness, I just wanted to say I'm glad you're okay. When you went silent on me after Banner's death, I was worried. I'll never truly understand what your life was like before here, Scar, and I won't embarrass myself and even try to imagine because I know it'll be ten times worse, but your voice sounds lighter now than it ever has."

His words hang in the air for a few moments as I take them in. One at a time, savoring the truth as my chest bursts with emotion.

"I'm still fucking lost, Kro, that's going to take a long time, but I can't deny that you're right. I feel different. I can't quite describe what it is about this place, but it warms my soul," I admit, tucking my hair behind my ear. It's hard not to use his nickname, adjusting to Shift may take me a minute.

He opens his mouth to respond, but lips press against my right cheek, cutting into the moment.

"Sweet Cheeks, you look hot as fuck and you're wasting it all on my brother," Gray murmurs against my ear, making me shiver.

"I was just catching up with my friend, Gray, calm down." Shift offers his brother a bottle of beer, and Gray takes it with a clink.

"In what fucking world is your only friend my brother, Scar? That only shows that you were meant to be mine," he states, before sinking his teeth into my earlobe, and I groan.

"Fuck. If this is a pissing contest, I want no involvement," I bite, struggling to keep my eyes open as need claws at my insides. One touch from this man and I'm putty in his hands.

Shift chuckles and winks at me before glancing at his brother. "Keep her safe, brother. She's my bestie."

"You know it," Gray replies without missing a beat.

"We good?" Shift asks, and I nod.

"Always." Slipping out from under Gray's arm, I take a step forward and wrap my arms around Shift's neck in the next breath. "You kept me going on days I didn't think it was possible to go on and that's always going to mean something to me." My voice is low, the words just for the two of us. He doesn't utter a single one in response and I'm relieved.

Turning, I link my arm through Gray's, resting my head on his shoulder as we join the gathering, but we barely make it two steps before anger ripples through my veins.

"What the fuck is that?"

Gray frowns in my direction before following my line of sight. "I don't fucking know."

"I thought you said we were exclusive." I hate the whine to my tone, but turning around to see Molly hovering over Ryker as she cups his face enrages me.

"We are."

"I don't fucking like that." I want to puke at the sound of myself in my own ears, the twisting in my gut not relenting as I watch her with him.

Ryker glances at me out of the corner of his eye, irritation flitting across his face, but not at her, no, it's aimed at me.

What. The. Fuck?

"She wasn't there when I came over. I'm sure there's an explanation, Scar, but we're not going to get it standing here." I hate Gray's words of reasoning, and when he encourages me to take a step forward, I reluctantly move.

"Did you just say that to get in my pants or something, because I don't know if you know or not, but you were in there without that bullshit," I grind out, and Gray glares at me.

"No, I didn't. *We* didn't. That's ridiculous."

"More ridiculous than that?" I ask, pointing at the bitch that's now sitting in Ryker's lap.

"Maybe you need to lay claim on him, Sweet Cheeks, mark him as yours."

I scoff at that. That's the complete opposite of what I would do. "Am I pissed off? Yes. Am I unexplainably hurt? Yup. Am I going to make a scene about it? No. Nope. Nada."

My stomach twists more and more as we get closer and Molly's voice gets louder as she smirks at me.

"Ryker, baby, you dancing with me?" she asks, dragging her fingertip down his cheek. He shakes his head. "But you promised to show me a good time."

I want to rip her throat out. She's pushing my buttons on purpose and I can't stand it. Where's Emily right now? I could really benefit from getting the fuck out of here.

"Ryker," Axel grunts, catching me by surprise as he folds his arms and leans back in his seat. The table goes quiet, like it catches everybody off guard, but he doesn't say another word as the two of them stare off with one another. Jaws tense, eyes squinting, and nostrils flaring. "Enough, Ryker," Axel repeats, making Molly laugh loudly for no reason.

"Ryker, why don't we…"

I turn my back to them, refusing to let her continue to get under my skin. Placing my hand on Gray's shoulder, I smile tightly. "I'm going to go and find Emily. Alone." I step away to leave when Molly calls out my name.

My body stiffens and it takes me a hot minute to calm myself enough to turn toward her. When my eyes lock on hers, a sneer taints her lips. "Leaving us so soon, Scarlett? We were just getting to the fun part." She snuggles further into Ryker's side, her hand falling to his denim-clad thigh as she squeezes, and my heart rattles with anger.

I take one involuntary step toward her, finger aimed in her direction as my emotions get the better of me. "This is your free pass because I don't want to spoil the evening for everyone else, but the next time you push me, I will make good on the threat I laid out the other day," I say, practically trembling with anger.

"I don't recall," she replies sweetly, and even though the words ricochet in my mind, I don't speak them out loud. She knows what I fucking said, she doesn't need a reminder.

*"The next time you lay a finger on me, I'll gut you and watch you bleed out for everyone to see until your eyes roll to the back of your head, before I let your body slump to the floor without care. Next time you touch me, I'll make an example out of you."*

With my head held high and my shoulders rolled back, I head for the club doors to search for Emily. I'm two steps away from the double doors when I hear it.

"Rebel."

Fuck.

"Don't call me that," I snap, not bothering to turn. I know exactly who is hot on my tail.

"Don't be stupid, Scar."

Whirling around on the spot, I glare at Ryker, surprised with how close he actually is to me. There's barely a foot between us, but he wastes no time cutting that too. Standing toe to toe, my chest heaves with each breath.

"Don't call me stupid when you act like that. This… all of this," I state, waving my arms out wide. "It's all new to me, it's something I didn't expect or want, but here we are, and this kind of shit isn't going to fly." God, I sound like a needy bitch, but I can't help myself.

"Neither is you throwing your fucking arms around Shift."

What the fuck?

"Are you for real right now? I was saying thank you. Thank you for shit you don't know anything about. That man was my only friend for years, my only lifeline outside of the club, and that's not going to change. It also doesn't mean that I'm going to throw myself at him, but if I want to hug him, I damn well will."

Ryker rubs at the back of his neck, lips pinched as he listens to me. "I can handle—"

I lift my hand, stopping his words as I shake my head. "I don't care. I really don't give a fuck. Pushing me like that because you're jealous is petty and immature, and it's the wrong way to go. Hurdle number one in whatever the fuck this is," I grunt, waving a hand between us. "I've just realized that I have a hard limit with people touching what is supposed to be mine. Bitches or club whores included. Handle that."

# THIRTEEN

## Scarlett

Sleep clings to every part of my body, my brain slowly flickering awake as my limbs protest. My mouth widens as a yawn escapes my lips, before my eyes start to blink open. Running my fingers through my hair, I attempt to brush it back off my face as I sense another body lying beside me.

I see the sleeping form and memories come flashing back to me. After storming off on Ryker, Emily found me as I entered the bar area of the clubhouse. She took one look at me and called it a girls night, men be damned. We spent the rest of the night holed up in my room with snacks and movies.

She looks peaceful beside me, angelic, and it blows my mind once more that she has a connection to an MC. She's too pure for this world, too soft and sweet.

Blindly reaching for the tray of birth control pills on my nightstand, I pop my second one. I haven't really felt any nausea, but if the way I popped off at Ryker has any connection, then I'd say my hormones are definitely in full swing.

Latex-free dick better be worth all of this. My thighs clench at the thought, of course it fucking will be.

Hungry, I slip from the sheets as quietly as I can and throw on a pair of leggings and my boots, opting to leave on the oversized Metallica t-shirt that I wore for bed.

Once upon a time, I would have just left this room in the t-shirt alone, but I'm getting wiser. Things usually go to shit out there and I'm determined to be prepared at all times.

Swiping a hair tie off my nightstand, I fix my hair as I make my way to the door. With my ponytail in place, I tiptoe through the doorway before clicking it shut, only to find Emmett propped up against the wall beside me. He's asleep, a fact I'm sure he would hate to be called out on, but it seems like someone was protecting his little sister for the night.

Nothing makes him hotter than his fierce love for his family, his sister. The long blond hair and thick beard definitely help, but his soul is something else entirely.

Not wanting to wake him either, I tiptoe down the hallway to the kitchen, only to find Molly standing at the fridge.

Fuck.

This is really not what I need to start my day off. Am I being an irrational cow all on my own or can I blame this on the pill? I'd prefer the latter, but does that make me a cop out? Either way, as much as I want to claw her fucking eyeballs out, the need for coffee wins out. I literally have no clue about any of this, and excuses aren't my thing, so I have to accept that the green devil sits on my shoulder too.

I move toward the coffee pot without uttering a word, praying like hell the bitch will give me some reprieve before she starts. I almost laugh at my own embarrassing hope as I turn on the coffee machine. Within five seconds, her voice echoes around the room.

"Well, if it isn't the whore that keeps on giving. Have you managed to sleep yet or have your legs just been a revolving door for every Ruthless Brother in sight?"

Tapping my fingers on the countertop, I take a deep breath before turning to look at her. There's no use pretending I can't hear her, I'm sure she'll only get louder. I give her a pointed stare as the corner of my mouth tilts up. "Are you jealous? Isn't that what you want? The Ruthless Brothers between your thighs, claiming you over and over again."

Her scowl deepens, arms folding over her chest as she knocks the fridge door shut with her hip. "The difference is they're going to worship me when it happens, not use me like they do you."

A snicker parts my lips. "Do you want me to fake cry for you now, will that make you feel better?" I mock, and she sneers in response, taking a step toward me.

"You don't know who the fuck I am, and maybe it's about time you learned." One hand falls to her hips as the other jabs at her chest. "I run this fucking house. The Bitches are mine, the Brothers are mine, even the Prospects are mine, and there's nothing you can do about it." I stare at her, tilting my head to the side to assess her better. "What?" she finally grunts when she doesn't get an angry response from me like she hoped.

I shrug. "I'm just trying to figure out what your problem is. Daddy issues? Hmm, nah, I've got a shit ton of those and we're not syncing." I shake my head as I deepen my stare. "Mommy issues? I didn't have a biological one to ever figure out what those look like, but we'll say no for now, but it could be." Anger starts to ignite in my gut, the restraint I was trying to uphold melting at the sight of her scrunched up face. Taking a step toward her, I don't stop until my finger presses against her chest. "Or maybe it could just be that you're a massive. Fucking. Cunt."

She bares her teeth at me, before saliva hits me square in the face.

Did this motherfucker just spit at me?

Shock leaves me gaping at her for a split second as I

try to calm the rage inside of me, but she's crossed the line in a sprint and there's no turning back. With my finger still pinned between us, I use my weaker arm to fling back and punch her in the nose.

"Oh my god," she gasps, cupping her face as blood splatters around us, but I'm not done yet. Grabbing her throat, I squeeze tight as I lift her clean off her feet and turn, slamming her down onto the dining table beside us. Her grunt turns to a sob as pain vibrates through her into my arm, before I'm leaning over her, snarling with a kitchen knife pressed to her neck.

When the fuck did I reach for it? I don't even recall the action. My face feels like it's ready to explode as anger controls my every move.

"It's going to make my fucking day having your blood on my hands," I bite, seething with fury. "Make. My. Fucking. Day."

"You're a crazy bitch," Molly grunts, blinking up at me with a wince, and I shake my head.

"No, you're crazy for thinking I'm going to put up with your bullshit. I've already warned you twice, I don't know what you're expecting."

My chest heaves, rising and falling harshly as I try to taste the oxygen barely passing my lips.

"What the fuck is going on in here?"

If those words were spoken by anyone else but him

right now, they'd magically pop the bubble of rage I'm in, but his tone only pisses me off more.

"Of course you're going to sweep in here and save her. Fuck off, Ryker," I grunt, not bothering to look up from the bitch struggling against my hold, putting a show on for the man she's hot for.

"Rebel, put the fucking knife *and* the girl down." His voice is calm, like he's trying to placate me, but it doesn't erase the irritation this bitch causes.

"I'm *done* with her bullshit, Ryker. *Done*."

Molly lightly taps at my hand, being dramatic as fuck as I angle the blade better, making her still.

"She's nothing but a fly on shit, Scarlett. Her death isn't the answer."

"It is if I say it is."

"Put her down, Rebel."

My heart twists at the nickname, my decision faltering for a second until she gleams up at me and snarls, "Do as you're told, bitch."

The blade pierces her skin ever so slightly, but the scream that rips from her lungs belongs to that of a massacre.

"Don't fucking encourage her, otherwise I'll assist her in getting rid of your body," Ryker grunts and closes his hand around mine. I melt into his touch, releasing my hold on the knife as he takes it from my hand, before lifting me clean off the ground, holding me away from the bitch who deserves more than she's gotten today. "Get the fuck out of here, Molly, before I change my fucking mind." There's no question in Ryker's voice, but she still manages to push.

"But I'm bleeding, Ryker, I need you to help me." Her plea falls flat when he growls, and the next sound is of her feet scurrying away.

Slowly, Ryker drags me down the length of him until I'm standing on my own two feet again. I turn on the spot, my hands instantly going to his chest as he stares down at me, then I push with all my strength against him.

He barely moves, but it's enough to clear a path between me and the door. I don't waste my opportunity and rush for the bar area before stumbling outside. I inhale sharply, angry and frustrated with myself more than anything with how she manages to get under my skin like that. A truth I hate to admit.

"Scarlett, wait the fuck up," Ryker hollers, but instead of making me stay, it pushes me to rush toward my bike.

I need a minute to breathe without the confines of this club that doesn't belong to me. A club that shouldn't have me in such a hold, but I can't deny it time and time again. I thank my earlier self for dressing properly and opting for my combat boots as I swing a leg over my Harley Davidson and rev the throttle.

"You're not going anywhere," Ryker declares as I slip

my helmet on and fasten the clip.

"I can't stay here right now. It feels like you're suffocating me, trying to put a lid on my actions and feelings, and fuck, I've lived through enough of that already. She spat in my face, Ryker, and to me, that's worse than stabbing me with a fucking blade. If I want to respond like that, then I should be able to without question."

He stands in the open space, arms folded over his chest as he shakes his head. "You can't be serious, Scarlett. You can't just kill people because you feel like it. Your life doesn't have to be like it once was, it can be different here."

I scoff. "It can be different, but I have to watch you flaunt women in my face when you're mad or jealous? Thanks, but *fuck* that." I roll forward on the bike, but Ryker doesn't move.

"We can talk about this inside."

"The time for talking was last night, but you decided to take action instead. Now, I need a minute."

"I don't want you to ride like this, not when you're angry, Rebel." The concern is clear in his tone, but it doesn't change how I feel.

"I don't want to have to deal with any of this right now, so I'm choosing not to." Placing my feet up on the pegs, I move past him.

"Don't ride, Rebel, not like this, please," he shouts,

loud enough to be heard over the sound of the engine as I head outside. Emmett and Emily are standing at the doors to the clubhouse, confused. I should feel some kind of guilt or need to explain, but I don't.

I speed off, putting some much-needed distance between me and the clusterfuck of thoughts and emotions that invade my mind when I'm on this side of the wired fence.

Maybe some space will offer me clarity. I hope.

Turning the flat pebble in my hand, I run my thumb over the smooth surface before skimming it over the water. The sound of the waterfall is the only backdrop for me as I mull over my thoughts and my embarrassment.

The main conclusion I've made is that I'm a raging bitch. Fuck PMS, this is worse. My hormones are on steroids that have me on the brink of insanity, and as much as I want to point at the pills I've taken over the past two days, I only have myself to blame.

It's all me and the proximity around these men that pull out crazy fucking feelings from inside of me.

I shouldn't have shown my hand like that. I shouldn't have let her see how easy it is to get under my skin.

Wiping a hand down my face, I sigh. I definitely woke

up on the wrong side of the bed this morning. I wish I had just rolled over and gone back to sleep, but realistically, this kind of confrontation with Molly was on the cards, just waiting to happen. It will again, and again, and again.

Is it worth it?

Being with them and having to put up with her? Is it really worth my effort?

My heart clenches, giving me the answer I know is true. I might be out of my comfort zone here, but there's nowhere else I'd rather be. Even if I had to deal with her bullshit and Axel's moody side every day, I would still be here.

I must be a sadist to put myself through it, but I would never throw ultimatums out there. That's not who I am, and I refuse to operate like that.

My stomach grumbles, interrupting my thoughts and forcing me to my feet. Maybe I should stop by the diner Ryker took me to on the way home. At least then I might not be a raging *hangry* bitch. I'm already a handful, there's no need to make it any worse.

Decision made, I breathe in the fresh air and appreciate the waterfall for one more moment, before climbing onto my bike and heading back down the dirt road. It doesn't take long for the town to come into view and I take the quick route to the diner, remembering the turns from the other day.

When I'm near, I spy a motorcycle in my rearview mirror and my back stiffens. Slowing down, I drive more casually as I take the next turn, drawing away from the diner to see if they follow suit.

My breath stutters as they follow after me, remaining a good distance behind so I can't tell what the cut is that they're wearing. Taking random turns, they continue on my tail enough for it to be more than suspicious.

Someone is fucking following me.

With my heart hammering, I consider my next move and decide my best option is to head back toward the compound. As expected, they stay close all the way. Almost fifteen minutes pass when I see the entry to the compound appear ahead.

I don't want to slip into the gates and not know at least what club it is, so as I get closer, I suddenly slam on the breaks. Glancing over my shoulder, I find the emerald green marking that links the driver to one club and one club only.

The Ruthless Brothers MC.

Those assholes sent out a detail on me? Is this a joke? Motherfuckers.

Picking up speed quickly, I barely fit through the small gap in the gate as a prospect opens it for me. I skid to a stop in front of the clubhouse, not bothering to look back as I rush inside and slam the door shut behind me.

"Hey, what are you doing?" Maggie asks me curiously, the only person present thankfully as I move to the side of the door and push my back against the wall.

I lift my finger to my lips, and her eyebrows pinch, but she doesn't utter a word as she wipes the glass in her hand clean. Seconds pass in slow motion, my breath held as my senses are on high alert, but as predicted, the door swings open and a Ruthless Brother steps through the door.

"Mag—"

His words cut off as I grab the gun at his waist, pulling it from the holster with practiced precision before aiming at him.

"Care to explain what the fuck you were doing?" I bite, hearing him curse under his breath as he looks back over his shoulder at me. I'm not familiar with who he is, I don't even know his name, I just recall him shooting at the Brutes with me when they attacked. "Why were you following me?" I push, annoyed he's not responding as his shoulders slump.

"When did you spot me?"

"On the outskirts of town, heading toward the diner."

"Fuck, straight away then." My eyebrows raise in surprise at the fact, but I don't acknowledge it.

"Where are they?" I keep the gun pointed at him as I move to his side slightly, watching as his gaze trails over to the doors leading to Church. "Are they all in there?" I ask, looking at Maggie who nods in response, aiding me even when she doesn't fully understand what's going on.

Nudging the fucker toward the door, I try to take a deep breath to release the tension in me, but it barely scratches the surface. I didn't get to make Molly bleed as much as I wanted this morning, and now I'm right back to being desperate for the crimson color coating my skin.

As we come to a stop by the door, my brows furrow when I hear them murmuring but nothing is audible.

"Open the door," I mutter, and to my surprise, he does just that. I push this asshole inside and knock the back of his leg, forcing him to his knees with a thud.

"It doesn't make any sense. How can they gather shit on us and we're grasping at straws at how to respond. It's impossible for them to be one step ahead all of the time like this. What the fuck?" It's Shift that speaks, but I ignore him, glancing from Ryker to Emmett, and the pinch to the latter's mouth tells me who organized the detail. Fucker.

"Anyone care to explain why this guy was following me?" Silence greets me. "Fuck you guys. I was about to help you with your little situation, but if it's not working both ways, then I'll keep my mouth shut."

"What do you mean?" Axel asks, shocking me that he's the first to speak. Staring at him, he rolls his eyes. "It was obviously Emmett, and you already fucking know it."

I wet my lips, glancing around at each guy, noticing a

few nods that confirm the assessment as the man himself pinches the bridge of his nose.

Sighing, I drop my gun, unlock the mag and disassemble it before letting it clatter to the floor.

"Well, it's also obvious to me. You've got a mole."

# FOURTEEN

*Axel*

We've been going over every single detail we have on the Devil's Brutes for what feels like an eternity, until she steps in, and within seconds declares exactly what I've been silently working out.

A mole.

My eyes turn to slits as I glance around the table. A. Fucking. Mole.

I knew it, I could feel it in my bones barely minutes before Scarlett stepped in. I could see it in her eyes too, that's why I interjected, forcing Emmett to at least acknowledge that his 'secret' detail was futile, and got her to say those words out loud.

"Everybody out. Now," Ryker grunts, slamming the gavel harder than usual into the wood. I expect some kind of pushback, some response or bullshit of an excuse to explain why they're not the mole, but none come.

The last guy to leave is the guy at Scarlett's feet, and he glances up at her for permission to move before he does. I sink my teeth into my fist, knowing that now isn't the best time to laugh, but it's fucking eye opening what control this woman can yield.

Without glancing back, Scarlett kicks her leg back, her foot connecting with the door and slamming it shut. She doesn't utter a word as she rounds the table, taking her usual seat at the other end, flopping down before pointing a finger at Emmett. "Don't ever try to have me followed again."

"Your safety is—"

"My safety is of my concern. Not yours. There're boundaries and you're fucking pushing them. If there's a major threat to my life, then sure, we can have a conversation about it, but don't do it behind my back."

Emmett stares at her hard, his jaw working as he twists his lips. "Heard."

Scarlett takes him at his word and draws her attention to everyone else at the table. Her gaze starts at Gray, working her way around to Emmett, Ryker, and then me. There's a hint of appreciation in her eyes, acknowledging the fact that we communicated like civilized humans. I almost want to tell her not to get used to it, but that would only draw more attention our way.

"What makes you say there's a mole?" Ryker asks, hands steepled together with his elbows on the table.

"What makes you *not* come to that conclusion?" she retorts quickly, cocking a brow at him.

"Our men are loyal. Ruthless Brothers wear our green with pride, they don't betray us."

"Like Banner didn't betray your father?" Her snap is quick. It's not intended to hurt him, but I see the wince on his face. "Sorry," she murmurs, glancing down at the table. "I just mean, you know what Banner was capable of. I know what Billy was—"

"Billy? What the fuck does he have to do with anything?" Gray asks, his brows knitting in confusion.

Scarlett inhales deeply before responding. "You know Billy was my father's right-hand man when he was alive. He's always been a Ruthless Brother and never an Ice Reaper, but he had an important role at Freddie's side. He knew all about me, all about the basement, and… was used as a punishment toward me when I stepped out of line."

Her words go quiet toward the end, like she's admitting something out loud for the first time and is testing the weight of it on her tongue.

"What the fuck are you talking about?" Ryker glances at me out of the corner of his eye before turning his gaze back to Scarlett.

"That's why you killed him when he wasn't on the hit

list, isn't it?" Her eyes find mine the second I say it, and she offers a small nod as confirmation.

"What did he do—"

"Don't finish that fucking question," I bite, pointing my finger at Emmett in warning. My ears ring as he holds his hands up in surrender.

"I'm sorry, Scarlett, I just…"

There's no explanation or excuse he can say that will take the sting out of someone confronting you with that question. It might be meant with care and worry, but it still stings all the same.

I turn to face her once more, only to find her already staring straight at me. I might hate her and what she represents, or I did. Fuck. I still do, I'm sure of it, but that doesn't take away the pain I see in her.

It's the same as mine.

Worse maybe.

"What do we do now?" she asks, changing the subject. I can sense the others around the table desperate to cling to the information about Billy, but despite the facts she may have, he's dead now. She did that.

"I don't know," I reply, breaking the bubble and helping her change the topic. "But I think we need to keep everything on a need-to-know basis for the time being."

Sighing, Gray leans back in his seat. "Are there any suggestions?"

I shrug. "We could run everyone through the mill, no one's behavior has stood out, but now they know we're watching too."

Ryker nods in agreement, but before he can speak, Scarlett interjects, "Is it one of you?" Her arms are folded over her chest, the question soft from her mouth as she looks over each of us. I glare at her in response, more than sure that the others are likely doing the same as well, when she reluctantly waves a hand dismissively at us. "What? I was just checking."

"Could Shift have any involvement?" Emmett asks, scratching at his beard as he glances at Gray. "He came home, and apart from the attack slightly after, everything has gone quiet."

"But he wasn't here when the information was being leaked so that's impossible," Scarlett replies, beating Gray to the punch, and he turns to smile proudly at her for defending his brother. "Besides, that man *is* loyal as fuck."

"Okay, what about Euro?" Ryker asks, and Emmett's face scrunches.

"Man, that guy's been shot at and was summoned to the sheriff's office with me to meet our maker."

"True," I grumble, irritated that it's not as simple narrowing down who the fucking mole is in comparison to realizing there is one.

"Could they have been injured in the crossfire when

the compound was attacked?" Scarlett asks.

"No, everyone was clear and good," Gray replies, lips twisting with annoyance.

"What about the guy you sent to spy on me? I've never really seen him before." Scarlett points to the spot like he's still there, and a smile touches my lips at the dominance she invoked over him.

"You mean Cash?" Gray clarifies, and Scarlett shrugs. "He's only recently been initiated as a fully fledged Brother. He generally stays under the radar and runs details, errands and that shit."

"So it's not out of the realm of possibility," Scarlett clarifies.

Fuck.

"I need a fresh head. Someone investigate more into this while I take care of another matter," I state, rising from my chair and fixing my hair into a bun.

"Where are you going?" Ryker asks, knowing full well where I'm headed.

"No, where are *we* going," I reword, waving a hand between Scarlett and I.

"We?"

I smirk at the squeak to her voice and nod. "Someone deserves a visit, it'll be good for you to be there too. Let's go."

I don't glance back, the telltale sound of her boots

catching up to me is the only confirmation I need.

---

I double-check that she's still behind me on her bike. Usually I would hold up the end of the pack, but since she has no idea where we're going, I need to lead the way. She's stayed right behind me the entire time, effortlessly cutting across town with me.

As the houses get bigger, the quantities drop, indicating we're in the suburbs. They're not going to like the sound of our bikes, but fuck them. We won't be here long.

I spot the number I'm looking for up ahead and slow, noting the car in the driveway as I cut my engine. Scarlett does the same as I take my helmet off, rolling my shoulders back before standing.

"Where are we?" she asks, running her fingers through her hair as she moves toward me, leaving her helmet dangling from the handlebar of her Harley.

"You'll see," I murmur in response, earning myself a trademark eye roll that she's so good at. I smirk in response, making her scoff.

"You're an asshole, you know that?" She falls into step with me as I head up the driveway.

"So I've been told."

She doesn't respond for a second, but I feel her eyes on

me, before she snickers. "Well, I'm a raging bitch, so this works."

I pause mid-step, my brows furrowing as I glance her way. "Who the fuck said you were a raging bitch?" The anger in my tone is undeniable and fuck knows where it comes from.

"Me."

I assess her slowly, waiting for the joke, but she stands before me unapologetic and as determined as ever.

"Fair enough then." Digging into my cut pocket, I pull out the balaclava I grabbed as we left the club and thrust it in her direction. She takes it from my hand without touching me, like she's highly aware of my pain, but I don't call her on it. As much as I would like to know the how behind her knowledge, we have stuff to do here.

"Why aren't you wearing one?" she asks, just as I test the door handle to find it unlocked, and I smirk.

"Because I want this fucker to see my face."

She swoops the balaclava down over her face and tucks her hair away. All I can see are her deep blue eyes, and my hands clench.

Fuck, that's hot. Hotter than it should be.

Wiping a hand down my face, I turn away from her, worried she'll be able to read my expression. Kicking the door open further, I stomp over the wood flooring and head for the kitchen.

"Hello? Who… Fuck."

A delirious smirk spreads across my face as I throw my arms out wide. "Porter Hallman, it's been a long fucking time."

His Adam's apple bobs as he looks at me, lips twisting, as he flexes his fingers at his side. He doesn't have a weapon on him, and if he did, he would have reached for it by now. Perfect, that just makes this even better. Although, a bit of blood loss would still be worth it.

"What are you doing here, Axel?" He takes a step back, and I move forward, not giving him the space he desires.

"What do you mean, Hallman? You dropped in unexpectedly, and uninvited I might add, on Ryker. I felt the same was due in return." I snicker mockingly as his eyes narrow and his tongue runs over his teeth.

"We just happened to be in the same place at the same time. It was coincidental," he replies, sniffing like this conversation is beneath him.

I take in his huge open plan kitchen/dining area. I take two steps toward the kitchen island before swiping every fucking item off it like a petulant child.

"I'm so sorry, wrong spot at the wrong time. I didn't mean that, it was… just coincidental," I say, the mocking and humorous tone dropping as I turn to glare at him.

"Listen, man, I don't know what your issue is, but—"

"My issue is you, motherfucker. My issue is you luring

two of my brothers out to the sheriff's office with a target on their back. My issue is you showing up at the diner and not too long after, Kincaid makes an appearance. Don't tell me that's a coincidence too?"

His mouth opens and snaps shut a few times as he tries to throw an excuse at me, but fails miserably.

Stupid fool.

"What is it you're here for, Axel?" he finally asks, eyes narrowing in my direction as I turn to face him head-on.

"I'm here to teach you a lesson."

"A lesson?"

"Every move you make now comes with consequences. Cop or not, you're dirty as fuck and my hacker friend has created a spectacular file on you, ready to hand over to the FBI at my say so."

"Impossible," he grunts, his face scrunching in annoyance as I smile at him.

"Try me." I move closer, impressed that he doesn't take a step back as I stop when we're toe to toe with one another. "I'll hand you over to the law and burn you at the stake, then take your fucking remains and *literally* burn them in my backyard." Excitement buzzes through me as I sneer at him.

"Do you have any idea who I fucking am? What I'm capable of?"

I've heard enough.

Grabbing the collar of his polo, I yank him toward me, while plowing my fist into his face, watching with glee as his head rolls back on his shoulders and he flops in my hold.

What the fuck?

Rattling him a little, I pout, glancing over at Scarlett who has remained in the doorway. Her eyes are wide, but… heated? Not possible.

"He wasn't supposed to pass out so easily. This feels like a huge letdown, I have a lot of energy still swirling inside of me," I admit, and her eyes light up.

"We can wait until he comes around and go again," she offers, practically giddy.

When I drop the fucker, he lands in a heap of his own limbs on the floor before I step over him. "Help me set these up and we'll see what state he's in." I wink, offering her two small cameras. "This is what we're *actually* here for. Surveillance."

She nods, not uttering another word as she rushes off to place them. I set my two up in his entryway and the other in the kitchen. They're barely bigger than a dime, perfectly hidden away where he can't see. A few moments later and she comes running back into the room.

"Done."

I don't ask her where she's hidden them, I'm happy with the two I have and I know she's no fool when it comes to watching someone. I trust her in that at least.

"Is there any way we can shake him awake?" she asks, coming to stand over his unconscious body.

"Unfortunately not, but you can kick him while he's down if you want," I offer, and before I can even take a step toward the door to leave, she does just that, kicking him straight in the gut.

"Let's go, Reaper," I grumble, feeling her glare at me the second the nickname passes my lips. I expect her to argue back, but she doesn't take the bait.

I wave my hand for her to exit the house first, then slam the door shut behind me. The movement is so hard and fast that the glass in the window pane shatters. It offers me a hint of satisfaction, but nowhere near enough.

Scarlett keeps the balaclava over her face as she mounts the bike and secures her helmet in place. Before I take my own seat, I move toward her, gripping her handlebars tight as I look her dead in the eyes.

"People only have as much control over you as you're willing to give them. From now on, you give them none. Cops and Ruthless fucking Brothers included."

# FIFTEEN

## Scarlett

I spot Maggie's SUV pulling into the driveway as I polish the steel on my Harley. Dropping the rag and leaving the rest of the work for later, I hurry over to the main compound to help her inside with the shopping bags.

"Hey, you don't need to do this," she says as I open her trunk, and I give her a pointed stare before reaching for as much as I can. "Thank you," she breathes, accepting my help without any further complaint.

Her SUV is filled with bags to feed everybody here, and I notice that no one rushes to their feet to help as I step inside the bar area. There are a few tables filled with Brothers and Bitches mingled between. No one bats an eyelid.

Fuckers.

"If anyone actually wants to be fed this week, then

get your ass up and help Maggie with the food," I holler, not caring if it's my place to interject or not. The chatter stops as everyone eyes me. I look at the Bitches' faces, the sneers on their lips, but they quickly disappear when the men stand, nodding at me in acknowledgment before heading outside.

"What the fuck? She's not the boss," Molly hisses, a bandage over her nose from our last altercation. I want to give her a piece of my mind, but someone beats me to it.

"She's fucking right though. At least half of us are still breathing because she stuck her neck on the line for us with the Brutes." I glance at the guy coming to my defense and I have to hide my surprise to see it's the one I had a gun aimed at yesterday.

I manage to keep my emotions in check as he juts his chin at me, before holding the door open and swinging his arm in front. With muted curses and disgruntled steps, the Bitches follow him outside.

Maggie steps inside without a bag in her hand, eyes wide and finger pointing in my direction. "I don't know what you just did, but I'm officially claiming you for myself. You're a damn queen," she announces, making me roll my eyes at her as I carry on into the kitchen.

"Who is?" Gray's voice catches me off guard for a split second as I find him working the coffee machine. Noticing the bags in my hand, he takes them from my hold and places them down on the dining table.

"Scarlett is," Maggie explains, and a smirk lines Gray's lips at the statement.

"She's my queen."

"Nope, she's ours now. I'm willing to share, but she is mine," Maggie says, nudging her son playfully as he chuckles.

"Fine, I can make this work. Let me go bring the rest of your bags in and we can work out the semantics." He winks at his mom, who pats his chest with a chuckle.

"No need, our *queen* over there must have said something to everyone in the bar because they're carrying it all in now."

One by one, everyone filters in, dropping a bag or two down on the table, before murmuring their thanks and swooping back out again. Gray's eyebrows are practically in his hairline until the last person leaves.

"You're right, Ma, definitely a queen."

"I'm a caffeine queen if you're offering." I point to the coffee pot as it fills and he wordlessly pours me a mug. "Thank you." I take it, loving the feel of the heat coming from the mug.

"You two get the hell out of here, I can put it all away," Maggie says, and before I can protest, she shakes her head at me. "Honestly, I have a system, you helping will only delay me because I'll redo it as soon as you leave."

"She's not joking either," Gray adds, pressing a kiss to his mom's cheek before throwing his arm around my shoulder. "Besides, I want you to myself for a bit. I've just set our video game up in the lounge. I was making coffee, hoping to lure you in from the garage."

I smile, leaning into his hold as we fall into step. "That sounds perfect to me." I wave over my shoulder at Maggie as we leave, before stepping across the hallway to the lounge. The loading screen for Apex fills the television, and two controllers are perched on the coffee table.

Placing my mug down, I reach for a controller, but the second my hand wraps around it, I'm lifted into the air with a squeal before Gray unceremoniously drops us down onto the sofa. "You're a menace." I chuckle, trying to catch my breath as his arms tighten around me, and I nestle into his lap.

I could definitely play like this. Surrounded by his touch, his scent, and hopefully have a chance to indulge in his taste too.

"The things I want to do to you, Sweet Cheeks," he murmurs against the shell of my ear, raising goosebumps down my neck and over my arms.

"The things I *want* you to do to me," I reply with a sigh, feeling the press of his cock beneath me as I bask in his hold.

"Gray?" Shift's voice travels down the hallway, making

him groan beneath me before he hollers back.

"What?"

"Do you know where Scar... Oh, she's there, hey." Shift stands in the doorway with a folder in his grasp as he rubs at the back of his neck, his gaze flicking between the two of us before he clears his throat. "Can I steal your girl for a minute or two?"

Gray's face falls to the crook of my neck as he groans in frustration at the interruption. His lips graze my skin, before he sighs. "Fine, but don't be hooking her up with any fucking jobs and putting her in danger."

Lifting from his lap, I try to gauge what Shift wants to talk about, but he gives nothing away as I move toward him. "I would never, but you probably have to consider whether she wants to take jobs on or not because that's for her to decide, not you."

Fuck, I wasn't expecting that at all. Deciding not to get into any of that right now, I shake my head and point for him to lead the way. I follow after him as he comes to a stop outside my room.

"Are we okay to talk in here?"

I shrug, reaching around him to unlock the door before stepping inside. He knocks the door shut behind him before glancing down at the folder in his hands. When he doesn't get into it straight away, I fold my arms over my chest. "So, what's up?"

His lips thin as he tries to figure out what he wants to say, before he takes a step toward me. "I, uh, I'm probably overstepping, like *way* overstepping, but I…"

"Spit it out. It's not like you to be all stuttery and shit." My nerves start to spike a little, worry making its presence known as he waves the folder at me instead of responding.

Taking the manila file from his hands, I open it up to see a variety of documentation. I stumble back a step to fall onto my bed.

"What is all this?" I ask, knowing full fucking well what it is, but I need to hear it from his lips.

"It's a chance, Scarlett. However you want it to be."

I don't look up as I run my fingers through everything, before settling on the small card at the front.

A driver's license, photo and all.

Bringing it closer to my face, I focus on the letters at the top and slowly take my time despite the adrenaline coursing through my veins.

"Charlotte Winters."

I open up the passport in the pile and glance at the top line of the other documents to find the same two words on all of them.

"I know it's not your real name, or the name the Reapers bestowed upon you, but I didn't think—"

"Thank you," I breathe with a gasp, my throat catching as it clogs with emotion.

"You can be whoever you want, wherever you want, without worry. I've even had your fingerprints altered in the system so they still don't link with yours."

How is any of this even possible? How was it as simple as this? I'm sure there was more to it on his end, but it's just in my hands so casually and naturally that I'm at a loss for words.

"Why? Why would you do this for me?"

Shift doesn't move an inch, waiting for me to draw my eyes to his once more, and only then does he offer me an insight. "Because you deserve it. Even if we didn't owe you as a club, I would have done it for free. Knowing your past is a painful privilege, Scarlett, and I won't ever let that be a liability for you again."

"The club doesn't owe me anything." I say with a frown, refusing to latch onto his words and focusing on the semantics instead.

"Please, we owe you for the exact same reason you just had every motherfucker out there following your orders." He quirks a brow at me, like it's really that simple, and I cast my eyes away.

As I run my thumb over the driver's license, hope and excitement blossoms in my chest. It's a feeling like I've never felt before, like the chains and claws of my past hooking me down are slowly releasing me from their grasp.

"Thank you," I mumble again, unable to find any

alternate words to express my gratitude. With the papers clenched tightly in my hand, I rise from the bed, arms wide as I go to hug him, when he steps back, wagging a finger at me.

"No way, I've heard the bullshit that caused last time, I'm not doing it again. I want my prez to like me, you know." There's a smile on his face, but that doesn't calm the irritation that itches at my skin.

"You either hug me or I get you in a headlock, either way my arms are going around your throat. Whether it's a nice gesture or not is up to you." My eyes widen as I tilt my head and stare him down, the grin on his lips finally meeting his ears as he steps into my waiting arms.

"You're going to be the death of them all, Scarlett. In the best way possible. Me too at this rate, but at least it will be worth it," he murmurs, hugging me. He offers me a quick wink before spinning dramatically and disappearing from my room.

What a fucking whirlwind.

Glancing down at the papers in my hands that contain my first ever official documents, I shake my head in disbelief.

Literally, that man is a goddamn whirlwind. My actual savior.

Tucking everything away safely in my duffel bag, my eyes fall closed as I fasten the zipper, and I take a deep breath. I can't stop the smile spreading across my face as the reality of what he's offered me sets in.

With my head half in the clouds, I practically float back to the lounge in search of the other *White* brother. I snicker at the memory of Gray's full name being Gray White, before slamming into a hard chest blocking my access.

Startled by the fact I didn't even realize someone was standing there, I blink up into deep green eyes.

"Can we talk?" His words register in my ears but don't process in my brain for what feels like an eternity as I just stare up at him dumbly. He takes my silence as defiance, and his hands fall to my waist. "Please, Rebel."

"Fuck off, Ryker, I'm trying to spend time with my fucking girl and everybody is getting in the way," Gray complains as he comes up behind us. I can practically hear the pout on his lips.

"It won't take long. Besides, wasn't it you who told me to pull my head out of my ass?" Ryker retorts, and I shake my head at him.

"If you need someone to hold your hand and guide you into this, then you're clearly not ready for an actual mature conversation." I press my lips together, taking a step back, but he doesn't let me get far. His hands tighten on my hips, before my feet are swept from under me and I'm tossed over his shoulder with a grunt.

I can still hear Gray's protests in the distance as Ryker

trudges away from the lounge, my head bobbing with every step he takes until we're turning to the right. His scent wraps around me like a noose as he kicks his door shut.

"Are you going to listen and talk with me if I put you down or are we going to stand like this for a little longer?"

I huff at his fucking attitude, before hooking my fingers through the belt buckles on his jeans for leverage as I bend my legs and thrust my knees into his chest. The move startles him, his feet back tracking a few steps, and the feel of his arms loosening around my thighs makes me grin. Not wanting to waste a single second, I push off his ass cheeks, redistributing my weight to catch him off guard as we both fall onto his bed.

"What the fuck?" he grunts, but I don't respond as I push up to my feet, smirking while I fold my arms over my chest.

"I was only up there because I allowed it to be that way, although, it's cute that you thought otherwise."

Ryker gapes up at me with a mixture of annoyance and awe in his eyes as he slowly rises to sit at the foot of his bed. "And you somehow seem delusional over the fact that I'm obsessed with you," he grumbles, giving me a pointed stare as he rearranges his dick beneath his jeans.

Fuck.

"What is it you wanted to talk about?"

Ryker braces his elbows on his thighs, lacing his fingers together as he shakes his head. "I want to apologize."

*Oh.*

"For what?" I ask, shifting from one foot to another as my nerves creep through my veins. They've barely simmered down since my conversation with Shift, but now it's for an entirely different reason.

I care.

"Where do I start?" He swipes a hand down his face. "For the shit I pulled with Molly in response to you doing nothing wrong. To stopping you from doing whatever you fucking wanted yesterday, and most of all, for making you feel like you didn't have a choice. That's the one thing I want you to have more than anything in the world." My heart hammers at my ribcage with abandon, echoing in my ears as I struggle to breathe. "I know I don't know every piece of your past, but I know enough to believe that you should never live anything even remotely close to that again. Especially not on my watch." Anger shimmers in his eyes, not at me but for me.

I gulp a few times as I try to piece together a response. How do I keep finding myself so damn speechless? I hate it.

"So, were all those words supplied by Gray too? Or did you rope the others into it as well?" His anger quickly morphs into irritation as he purses his lips.

"They're my own fucking words, Scar. Gray just gave me a reality check over my bullshit. All he did was confirm what my subconscious already knew, but it took me a minute to get over the embarrassment of admitting I'm wrong." He reaches a hand out toward me, but I'm a little out of reach, so he drops it into his lap with a sigh.

My head and heart war with one another, until my heart soars and ushers me to take a step forward, in between his spread thighs. His hand instantly moves to the back of my thigh, stroking over the bare skin beneath the frayed leg of my shorts. When I place a hand on his shoulder, his tension ebbs away.

It's seems we're all just as crazy as each other here, lost to these newfound emotions and confused as fuck by what it all means. Silence descends over us as we bask in each other's presence. I hid away from him yesterday after I got back from Porter's home with Axel, but apparently that separation may have worked in our favor. I can't keep doing that though, hiding away, like I don't live here. That's no different than how it once was.

"Maybe it would be a good idea for me to find somewhere else to stay. This isn't my club or my family, and when things turn to shit, I cower away and hide, which is just history repeating itself and I can't keep letting myself do that."

Ryker's head rears back, his jaw tightening as he

shakes his head. "There has to be an alternative to that, Scarlett. One where you're still close but you don't feel like that because the distance between us all but fucking killed me. Which is the most bizarre shit I've ever said, but you have me hooked, Rebel." He shrugs, like it's just as simple as that, while I continue to blink down at him in bewilderment.

All I've ever known are brutal men in motorcycle clubs, and now, I'm watching one be brutal with everyone but me.

"The shit with the Bitches, Molly especially, needs attention. All I've ever known is showing strength in actions and death, she makes my fucking blood boil so it's an easy go-to for me to want to snap her fucking neck. She spat in my face, Ryker, that's fucking vile. I'd rather be stabbed."

He stands abruptly, laces his fingers with mine, and tugs me toward the door. I barely manage to keep up as he rushes down the hallway toward the bar. I almost consider asking if he can just make it easier and toss me over his shoulder again, but he stops just inside the bar area, eyeing the space filled with members and whores before pulling me toward the Prez's booth.

His hand tightens in mine as he pounds his other fist into the wooden table a few times. The room goes silent. "Scarlett isn't a Ruthless Bitch and she never will be.

We've never had a woman become a Ruthless Brother, but the way she saved our asses against the Devil's Brutes ranks her fucking higher than most." I stare at him, mouth wide as he goes on a tangent I wasn't expecting. "With that being said, she's a part of this club, our own Ruthless fucking Rebel. If she says shit, you do it. If she needs anything, you damn well get it, but most of all..." His eyes turn to mine, fire burning beneath the surface as he drinks me in before turning back to the mass of people hanging on his every word. "If you so much as consider touching what's ours, then I'll slice your fucking fingers off."

"So, she's what? Your old lady now?" Molly hollers, appearing from the far corner of the room, her face red with anger and her fists clenched at her sides.

"Not yet, but that's because Gray would kill me if I claimed her as my old lady right now," Ryker says with a laugh, like he's delirious or something. Is he high right now?

"Damn fucking straight I would. All I want is to spend some time with her and everyone keeps cockblocking me," Gray grumbles from the door leading into the back. His arms are folded over his chest, there's tension in his tone, but the smile on his face and the glimmer in his eyes tell me he's enjoying this little speech.

"So who does she belong to?"

I glare at the prospect who scrubs his head as he glances

from Ryker, to me, and then to Gray. "My fucking self, you idiot. I belong to myself."

I want to leap over the table between us and kick him in the dick, but the gentle squeeze of Ryker's hand stops me. "She belongs to herself," he reiterates, looking down at me with a softness in his eyes I've never seen before. "If you have to ask that question, then you're definitely not one of the members laying claim."

"Anything else?" Gray asks, eyebrow quirked as he smirks at Ryker, who shakes his head in response. "Excellent, now can I please have her fucking back?" he grunts, before turning and heading for the lounge.

Ryker turns his attention back to me, before claiming my mouth in front of everyone. A round of cheers ignite around us, but I can't pull away from him. His hold is possessive, it's over the top, and it's hot as fuck.

We part with a gasp, before I push up on my tiptoes and murmur in his ear, "Carry on like that, and I'll share with you the idea I have about the mole."

# SIXTEEN

## Scarlett

I feel blissful from my fingertips all the way down to my toes. Apparently making up with Ryker is a lot more fun than being mad at him. Since I woke up, I've been contemplating whether the agitation between us from before is worth recreating, just so we can work it out of our systems again, but I decided against it. I'm holding out my next anger fuck for Emmett once we finally have the conversation about him putting a detail on me.

I'm not actually mad, but I'm definitely onboard with the aftermath if it looks anything at all like last night. My thighs are bruised and my calves ache, but that doesn't stop my sex drive from careening forward, desperate for their touch one more time.

Ryker declared me to the fucking club like it was nothing, and even though I'm not an old lady or a Ruthless

Bitch, it makes my chest blossom with pride. I mean something here, despite my preference to fly under the radar, and I can't deny that I like it.

The morning I came back with Emmett, I chose to be here and now I have to act like it too. No more excuses, no more bullshit, nothing. Just me. What will be will be, the rest can burn to the ground at the flick of my matchstick.

"Are you even trying?"

I glance up to look at Emily, guilt heating my cheeks as I shake my head. "Nope."

"At least you're honest," she grumbles with a shake of her head, but there's no annoyance or anger in her tone.

"Sorry, the words are all jumbled and I got lost in my head," I admit, and her hand quickly launches in my direction as she plants her hand on my shoulder.

"Hey, it's no biggie. We've been at this for a while now, we should call it a day. Besides, I have classes again in twenty minutes so I should probably find Duffer and head out."

Leaning back in my seat, her hand drops from my shoulder but I squeeze it before it can fall too far. "Thank you," I breathe, repeating a word I've said more times in the past few days than I have my entire life.

Ryker must have told the guys, or at least Emmett, who roped Emily into helping me learn to read. It's hard, but as embarrassing as it is, I'm obsessed with learning. I want to be more than I was made to be, and doing this feels like a step in the right direction.

"No problem. I'll leave this stuff with you for now so if you have a clear head again, you can take a look." She rises from her seat, clenching my hand before grabbing her backpack. "Speak to you later," she calls over her shoulder, heading to the door when Shift appears in the open space. "Oh, uh, hi."

The pair of them smile tightly, the awkwardness affecting even me before Shift steps to the side. "Hi, are you heading out already?"

"Yeah, classes," Emily stiltedly responds when Duffer appears at Shift's side.

"You ready to go, Em?" Her gaze flicks between the two of them, and I lift my hand to cover my grin. It all adds up. Her nervousness, her cute outfit the other night, it's all for Shift.

Tucking a loose tendril of hair behind her ear, she offers Shift a tight smile, before waving at me over her shoulder and rushing for the door. Duffer has to bolt after her, leaving just Shift and I. He doesn't meet my gaze for a second as he wipes his eyes, but when he does meet my stare, I see it.

These two are cute on each other. I can practically feel it in the air around me. I can list at least five reasons why they both wouldn't agree it's a good idea, but if I've learned anything in this life, it's that nothing should get in your way. Not even yourself.

I don't say a word though, I just smile at him instead.

"Do you want a coffee?"

Do I want a coffee? What kind of question is that? "Please," I answer instead, keeping my sass to myself as someone else responds too.

"Coffee or cock, Sweet Cheeks?"

I grin at the sound of Gray's voice as I glance back toward the door to find him leaning against the frame. "That's a silly question."

"How come?" He raises a brow at me, still waiting for an answer as a hot mug of coffee is placed in front of me.

"Because coffee is the liquid of Gods," Shift says, and I chuckle.

"Nope, that comes from cock, Shift. You've got it all wrong," I reply, making them chuckle as I settle my gaze on Gray. "Is that offer real or are you teasing?" I don't want to take a sip of my coffee if he's being real, not with how my body is reacting to him right now.

"It can definitely be on the menu, but I just booked out the gun range in town for us if you want in?"

My eyes practically roll to the back of my head as I swoon in my seat. "Cock and a glock, that's the perfect day."

"Then what's your sweet ass still doing sitting there?"

I blink my eyes open and rise from my seat, smiling. I dismiss the coffee and cut the distance between us. "Lead the way, Blondie."

Gray wraps his arm around my shoulder, leaning in to press his lips to the shell of my ear. "You want me to stop at the coffee shop on the way too, don't you?"

"If the offer is on the table I won't say no."

---

The windows are down, soft rock plays on the radio, and there's a takeaway coffee cup in my hand as we cross town. Most girls probably want some cutesy shit like a picnic in the park, a candlelit dinner for two, or something extravagant. Not this girl; a trip to the gun range is an easy way to my heart. "What made you come up with this?" I ask as he drives the SUV.

"It was actually Axel's idea."

"Axel's," I repeat in surprise, blinking at him as he nods.

"Yeah, he fucking owed me after he got your bike from the Reapers." My lips clamp shut, not wanting to draw attention to the fact that he's clearly still not over that. "I'd say someone who cared about you would recommend it, wouldn't you?" He's prying, but his friend is as troubled as I am, and I'm not commenting on it at all. That will only lead to hurt and heartache on my end.

The SUV rolls to a stop, and I look out the windshield to see the gun range, so instead of offering him a response, I quickly jump down, coffee still in hand, and rush for the door.

I can hear Gray's footsteps right behind me, but I don't wait for him as I step inside. The familiar smell of gunpowder and lead fills my nose as I scan my eyes over the rows of guns lined up behind the glass cases on the wall. The shelves have all the ammunition you could dream of, but since these fuckers in town are always after a free weapon, the good stuff is out of reach.

"Scar, is that you?"

My head whips around to the counter, and I grin. "Colin, it's been too long."

He beckons me closer with a crook of his finger, just like he used to, and I hurry toward him. "What brings my favorite girl out here?" he asks, glancing over my shoulder and I follow his line of sight.

"I'm being treated to some time at the range." I wag my eyebrows at him, and he chuckles.

"Do you want me to clear everybody out?" Colin asks as Gray comes to a stop beside me. The men shake hands, and Gray frowns at me.

"You two know each other?"

"She's the best gal to ever walk through those doors,"

Colin declares, pointing at me, then he heads toward the side door that leads to the shooting gallery. "Potentially the greatest ever," he adds with a wink before disappearing.

It seems I didn't need to answer for him to clear the space out. He's so used to this being the case that it's second nature at this point.

"I feel like I'm missing something." Gray places his hand on the small of my back, making me shiver as I turn to face him properly.

"Colin's place was about the only spot I was allowed to go. When I was a child, I would be put in the trunk of a car and driven out here, but when I got a bit older, I was eventually able to come down here on my bike."

Gray opens his mouth to respond but pauses as he glances past me. "What the…" A trail of men step into the shop area, eyes casting our way as they trudge toward the door. "What's happening here?"

"I practice alone. It's always been that way. Colin shuttles everybody out to accommodate me. I pay him kindly for it." I shrug, keeping my head held high but my gaze slightly off from the other members being escorted out. Nobody utters a word, throws a slur in my direction, or complains. The bullet hole on the wall behind them likely has something to do with it. That was the result last time someone tried.

Colin locks the door after the last guy leaves, and Gray

steps to the side. "Is everyone afraid of my girl, Colin?" His grin spreads wider than imaginable in response. "Holy fuck. That's hot as shit," Gray says with a whistle, making me roll my eyes as I sip my coffee.

I hear the jingle of keys as they sail through the air and I quickly reach out to catch them. "You've got ninety minutes, Scar." He heads for his office on the other side of the room, closing the door without a backward glance. Gray takes that as his hint to lead us to the good stuff.

With our hands laced together, Gray pushes the door to the shooting range open and I instantly relax in the familiar surroundings. "Who knew you could wield all of this power without breathing a single word?" I preen at the compliment as I place my coffee down and move to the wall of guns.

Excitement gets the better of me as I eye each weapon up, before settling on my favorite handgun. Gray's arm rubs against mine as he leans in for a similar model.

"Are you ready to show me what you've got when we're not actually under attack?" he asks with a smile, and I meet it with one of my own.

"Are you?"

"Game on, Sweet Cheeks. Let's go." He leads the way back to the small table, where I check over my gun while he grabs some bullets from the other wall. Looking out over the range that's set up, it's clear why Colin's place is a favorite in town.

Instead of being a standard blacked out room with individual zones, it's much more open and enticing, bringing the outside in as you take your shots. The ground turns to turf a few steps in front, with barrels and targets hanging up to a hundred yards away. There's a fan blowing further away toward the right, upping your difficulty level, with some of the mannequins changing in size too.

"Your smile is so big your jaw will be aching later," Gray muses as he comes to stand beside me, and I shrug.

"It's worth it." We load our weapons, anticipation running through my veins as I bounce on the balls of my feet. "Where do you want to start?" I ask when I'm all set, but Gray waves his hand for me to proceed. Considering a pair of ear defenders, I boycott the stand and move toward the left of the room where the shots are easier.

Placing my feet shoulder-width apart, I relax my shoulders back and exhale slowly as I stretch my arms out in front of me. I pull the trigger twice, moving slightly between the two closest targets and putting a perfect hole in the middle of the red circle.

"Did I mention you're hot as fuck?"

"Show me how delicious you are too," I murmur, ringing out shots until my chamber is empty, before I turn to face him.

He winks before settling his eyes straight ahead. "Did

anyone tell you that you're hot as fuck today?" I ask as he lines up his shot, a smirk teasing his lips as he keeps his eyes fixed forward.

"Not yet, but I'm definitely open to hearing it," he replies, before aiming down the sight on the next set of targets behind the ones I aimed for. Bullet holes ripple in the center of the red circles just like mine. It looks like this is quickly going to become a challenge and that only makes me more excited.

Reloading my gun, I repeat the same process as I eye the third row of targets, popping each of them off in succession with ease. My veins are thrumming with a buzz, the sound of the bullet piercing through the air still audible to my ears as it makes me shiver. As I move to take a step back, I hit a solid wall behind me in the shape of Gray, whose hands quickly fall to my hips as he locks me in place against his chest.

"Want to make this more fun?"

"I thought you'd never ask," I reply, not actually knowing where he's going with this but eager to find out.

"Good girl," he whispers against my ear.

My thighs clench as I bite back a moan. "Let's aim for the trees at the very back, and whoever hits the closest gets head from the other."

I rub my lips together as I stop myself from yelling yes at the top of my lungs, instead I take a deep breath and agree. "You're on, but I don't see how I'd be considered a loser when I love *giving* and *receiving*." I wink at him playfully before I take two steps to the side, watching as he cups his dick, before I aim down the sight.

The bullet sails through the air, marking the red circle just as I have all the others, and Gray whistles before following suit. He doesn't waste any time raising his gun and sending a bullet through the air, managing to hit the same spot as I do. From this distance, we can't see who has the most central spot, but when I turn to glance at Gray, he waves his hand.

"It'll be more fun to hold out to the end," he states, before stepping to the right.

"To the end?" I ask, needing clarification as he smirks at me.

"Yeah. Next challenge, whoever gets the most central spot on the rolling barrel targets gets to choose who goes on top." His eyebrows dance as excitement pools in my stomach.

"You're on." Moving to stand beside him, I nudge him to go first.

In a flash, he's hit the target, the red circle pierced with his shot once again as I roll my shoulders back and line myself up. I take a deep breath or two, and on the final exhale, I pull the trigger, matching his mark as the barrel continues to slowly spin in place.

"Nice. Ready for the final challenge?"

I nod eagerly as he moves us to the far right. I can see the slight flutter to the targets from the fan running at the back, but I quickly turn to Gray to see what the challenge is. "Whoever makes this shot gets to choose where the fucking actually happens."

At this point, none of it fucking matters, my body is alive with excitement from the weapon in my hands, the bullets darting through the air, and the sexual tension naturally floating between us. I couldn't give a shit who chooses any of this, it's a close call that's for sure, but either way, I'm going to be enjoying myself.

Aiming my gun at the full body mannequins at the furthest distance, I glance over my shoulder at Gray. "Straight for the head?" I ask, and he nods, a wicked glint in his eyes. I tilt my head back, consider the blow of the breeze and then pull the trigger.

When the bullet embeds itself in the center of the red circle on the target's head, I spin excitedly, dropping the weapon on the nearest table and throwing myself at Gray. He's definitely not expecting it, but he manages to catch me while still holding his gun.

"If I lose this shot now, it's because of this," he grunts, pressing his lips to mine before sliding me down the length of his body. Heat sizzles between us, the air thick with tension as he moves to take his shot. It's on the tip of my tongue to call out 'fuck it, I'll let you win', but I let it play out instead.

"Are you ready to go and see who the winner is?" Gray takes his ear defenders off, unloads the remainder of his gun and sets it on the table.

I rush in front of him, heading back to the first target with excitement. Stopping in front of the target, I can see the slight difference between the two bullet holes based on the size of the bullet, and a grin spreads across my face. "I hope you like eating pussy, Gray," I sing, turning back to glance at him as he comes to a stop.

He leans down to get a better look."How do you know whose is whose, Sweet Cheeks?" He already knows the answer; I can see it in his eyes, but he wants to hear it from my lips.

"Different bullets leave different marks, Blondie, that's why your holes are slightly bigger than mine."

"So fucking hot that you know that," he groans, and I smirk. I would much rather know my fucking ABCs, but at least I'm good for something. "You can have this one, Scar, but you might not be so lucky on the next." He grabs my hand, pulling me along as we move to the barrels. Holding it still with my hand, I roll it back slightly to get a better look. This time, it's a little more difficult since the bullet holes are touching.

Running my tongue over my bottom lip, I decide to let

Gray call this one, and when he turns to me with a wide grin on his lips, I know it's going in his favor. It's exactly why I kept my mouth shut. "I do rather like it when you're above me, your tits bouncing in my face." He smacks his lips, making me laugh as he pulls me in close.

"That sounds like a damn good time to me," I breathe, our lips so fucking close yet not close enough. "But the question really is, where?"

With our hands still intertwined, we run to the final marker, playfulness laced with desire as we stumble to a stop in front of the mannequin. Shoulder to shoulder, we stand pressed together, scrutinizing the bullet holes, and with every breath I take, the feeling of victory ripples through my bones.

"Admit it, Gray. Let me hear it." Turning to face him head-on, I lean on the mannequin with wide excited eyes and a huge grin. He purses his lips for a moment, but he knows the smaller hole is more central.

"You just tell me where, Sweet Cheeks, and I'll be there."

My heart thunders in my chest, need clawing at my insides as I glance at myself. I'm standing here in a gun range, in a simple Pink Floyd tee, a pair of leggings, and combat boots, and this man looks at me like I'm a million bucks.

Releasing a needy breath, I grab the hem of my tee

and pull it over my head, revealing my needy breasts and pebbled nipples. "Here. Now."

Heat rises in his gaze, his tongue sweeping across his lower lip as he shakes off his cut. "Keep going," he grunts, kicking his boots off, and I follow suit. I'm not sure how much time we have left, but I need this more than my next breath.

Slipping my hands beneath the waistband of my leggings, I pull my panties down with them, leaving myself bare.

"Fuck, Sweet Cheeks," he groans, fisting his cock, with his jeans and boxers mid-thigh. I watch in awe as he strips the remainder of his clothes from his body, before dropping to the grass. I tilt my head at him in confusion, but he instantly explains. "I'm eating your pussy, Scar, but I want you riding my face until you come."

*I think I just fucking died.*

He reaches for my hand when I'm close, pulling me down to my knees as they land with a thud on either side of his head. He's placed me in the perfect position, his cock glints in my direction as I look down the length of him, leaning toward it subconsciously.

I run my tongue down the prominent vein in his cock, groaning at the stiffness under my tongue as his fingers dig into my thighs. Wiggling my ass slightly in his face, I moan again as he takes the hint and glides his tongue between my folds, circling my clit briefly before repeating the process.

Fuck.

"God, Gray." The words are like a prayer on my lips as I arch my hips to grind against his face. The slight hint of stubble on his cheeks makes me weep with ecstasy as it grazes my swollen nub.

Needing more, I drag my tongue over his cock once more, before taking the head into my mouth. Closing my eyes, I keep my movements soft and in time with the strokes of his tongue on my pussy, falling in sync, as my body prickles with hunger.

I take him deeper as he places two fingers at my core, sinking them inside me excruciatingly slowly as I desperately try to take more of him. When his cock hits the back of my throat, his fingers are plunged deep into my center, pushing perfectly against my G-spot.

"M-more," I garble, humming around is cock. He retrieves his fingers and slips his tongue into me instead.

"Always so fucking needy, Scar," he murmurs, lips rolling over my folds as he speaks, and I suck him down harder, hollowing out my cheeks.

His thumb presses against my clit as he works his tongue at my entrance, leaving me gasping and grinding with abandonment as I lose myself to my senses. "That's it, Sweet Cheeks, come on my face."

He's panting just as hard as I am, my mouth going slack around his cock as I try to breathe, but I'm too amped up. I need to find my release. With one hand clenched around my thigh, the other is used to thrust three fingers inside me, stretching me further as his teeth sink into my ass cheeks.

I'm tumbling over the edge before I can catch myself, my release tangling me up into tight knots before I come undone. My hips don't stop moving as I drag out every ounce of pleasure, humming around Gray's cock in delight until he tears me from him.

"You're going to make me come before I'm inside you, and we can't have that."

Sweat clings to me, the loose hairs around my face sticking to me as I try to find the strength to move. Lifting my leg over Gray, I rise, spinning around and throwing my leg over him again, facing him just as he described.

He stretches out to grab a condom from his jeans. Then, he sweeps his tongue over my taut nipple, making me shiver. Between these men, I'm going to be a ticking time bomb, constantly set to explode at any given moment.

He rolls the condom down his cock. Positioning myself above him, I look deep into his eyes as he lines his dick with my entrance. In the next breath, I'm sinking down onto him, my body tightening around him as I gasp with ecstasy.

Once he's all the way in, I give myself a second before

he wraps his mouth around my nipple, teeth grazing the pebbled flesh. "I want you bouncing as high as you can go while I keep this little bundle of sweetness between my lips."

My back arches, desire coursing through me as I respond with actions instead of words. Rising just enough for the head of his cock to remain, I circle my hips slightly before slamming back down with a groan as his teeth bite into my skin.

Gaping, I gasp for breath, clinging to his shoulders as I repeat the motion again and again and again. A kaleidoscope of colors bursts around us as the pain quickly morphs into pleasure. Every fiber of my body trembles, the need to come once more taking over me as my movements become urgent and jagged.

Gray's hands grab my waist, forcing my hips higher and lower as his mouth moves to my other nipple, sinking his teeth into me once more as I cry out. I can't stop taking him, the need to make him come desperately taking over as I clench my core, making him groan.

"Fuck, Scar. Fuck." He releases one hand from my waist, but I don't stop bouncing, my clit catching the smallest bit of friction between us. "Come for me, Sweet Cheeks. Fucking come for me," he grunts around my nipple, his free hand landing a harsh blow to my ass cheeks and sending me free falling over the edge.

"Ah, Gray, fuck…" Each word is elongated from the remnants of my orgasm as it rushes through me. On my next downward stroke, he holds me in place, his cock pulsing inside of me as he finds his release too.

My forehead falls to his shoulder, and I cling to him, gasping for breath.

"I've never wanted anyone more than I want you." I smile against his skin at his words. "This is it for me, Scar. I can't explain it, and I really don't fucking care to. All I know is my world revolves around you."

With my heart soaring in my chest, I lift my head and meet his gaze. "I don't think any of us will ever be able to explain it, but that's what tells me it's worth it. The club, the trouble with the Brutes, the mess with the Bitches, all of it is worth it if we have you."

# SEVENTEEN

## Scarlett

My finger taps the table top as I find myself in the kitchen for the second day in a row, the words on the paper before me swirling in my mind as I fucking try to make sense of it all. The sun set hours ago, and here we remain, trying to learn some damn words.

It's frustrating as hell, giving me a headache and putting me in a bad mood, but I refuse to give up.

"Just take a deep breath and try again, Scar. Stop getting mad at yourself." Emily's voice remains as soothing as it was when we first sat down. I don't know where she gets her patience from, but I'm definitely not gaining any from her.

Stuttering, I try to sound out the word, so I take another deep breath and try again. "Flower." The word sounds wonky on my tongue, but Emily whoops anyway. I can manage standard words, like cat and dog, and I can manage foods and drinks if I'm given some time, but other words are just… stupid as fuck.

Don't even get me started on the silent letters and sounds some of this bullshit makes. Emily swears she's not making any of it up, but that seems impossible.

"I'm going to get you some cute pens and a notebook tomorrow, so we can give writing a try."

I glare at her, but she doesn't falter. *Stubborn, just like her brother.*

"She's this bossy with me too if it makes you feel any better." I startle at the interruption from Emmett, glancing toward the door where he stands with his hands tucked into his pockets. His blond hair is swept up in a hair tie and his beard looks extra long and thick. Fucker. I'm mad at him, which means I'm not supposed to find him hot.

"It doesn't," I pout, making Emily chuckle behind her hand as Emmett grins. It's the first time we've spoken since I called him out in Church for sending someone to follow me, and we haven't really hashed it out since.

The glimmer of hope in his eyes tells me that's exactly what he's here for, and I can't help but feel overwhelmed with all of the talks I'm having lately. It's just one after another and it's exhausting. Productive and positive at the end, but draining all the same.

"What do you want, Emmett? We're busy," Emily

says, leaning back in her seat and squinting at her brother.

"I wanted to talk with Scarlett, but I didn't realize she had a bodyguard now," he grumbles, matching her stare.

Before the pair of them can continue at each other's throats, I wave my hand between them. "It's fine, Emily, honestly. I really could use a break anyway, it's all melting together." The smile on her face is almost one of relief, surprising me even further as she puts her things away in her bag, before turning to face Emmett.

"You've got five minutes, asshole. Make him weep, Scar," she declares with a wink before sauntering past her brother.

"Is she going to be okay on—"

"Duffer's waiting for her on the other side of the door," he interrupts, calming my worry, but I still quirk a brow.

"Are you sure?"

"On my life." He shrugs, stepping further into the room, but he doesn't take a seat. Silence blankets us, and even though nothing is being said, there's no awkwardness. It's almost fucking comfortable, but the elephant in the room is just present enough to cause a wedge. "I'm sorry."

I blink up at him, lips pressed together as I just stare, surprised that those two words fell so casually from his mouth. "I wasn't looking for an apology, Emmett. I'm looking for it to not happen again."

"I can't promise you that." He folds his arms over his

chest, resting against the chair.

"And why is that?" *The audacity of this fucking man.*

"Because I want you safe. I'm not saying without your permission, and I'm not saying permanently, but if something or someone comes looking for trouble, the first thing they'll use against us is you." My lips twist, hating the fact that he's right, but it doesn't stop the ache in my chest.

"I can't promise to go along with that, Emmett, and you have to see that it's hard for me to consider other people's feelings when it comes to my own safety. But I'm also willing to not rule it out." It's the best offer I've got.

"Deal." He reaches for my hand and pulls me to my feet. Cradled in his arms, I bask in his scent as he rests his chin on my head. "I've fucking missed you, Snowflake."

"I've been right here," I mumble into his t-shirt.

"I know, but there's been so much going on, from running shit for the club and you being occupied with the other assholes, it's been hard. I knew sharing you would be hard, and it's completely fucking worth it, but it's going to take more juggling and compromise than I expected. Maybe even a schedule."

Tilting my chin up so I can look at him, I sigh in content. "It might be easier when you're not pissing me off." I stick my tongue out, and he snaps his teeth at me, making me grin as I wrap my arms around his waist.

"I'll work on that," he murmurs, tucking a wayward piece of hair behind my ear as he inches closer.

His lips press against mine delicately at first, setting my soul on fire and melting my bones in his hold. It's soft, gentle, and a complete contradiction to what I know he's capable of, what I've felt at his touch, but that only makes it even sweeter.

"What are your plans for the rest of the evening?" I ask against his lips, and he kisses me again before responding.

"I'm either sitting in here with you as support while you work through all of this, or I'm taking you into the bar for a bit to let your hair down." My eyes widen, and he smirks. "Don't give me that look. You can have my dick later, but for now, I actually just want to be around you."

A tremor runs through my veins at his words, and I swoon even harder. Making up is definitely my new favorite thing, unless I could just feel like this all the time without the fuckups that get us here, that would be even better.

"I'm done with all these stupid words for the day. Take me out for a drink," I breathe, stepping up onto my tiptoes as I kiss him back.

"I'm sorry I told Emily about this. When Ryker mentioned it, I—"

I cut him off with another sweep of my lips against his, before pressing my finger against his soft, plump mouth.

"It's okay, I appreciate it. Thank you."

Taking my hand, he kisses my knuckles before pressing his lips to my forehead. "Am I in the dog house for anything else before we leave this room?" he asks, cocking a brow at me, and I tap my finger on my chin thoughtfully.

"No, I think you're good."

"Thank God for that." As he leads me toward the bar, I wince a little when the door swings open and all the noise hits me. The chatter quickly melts into the background as I smile at the song playing. I love a good country song or two from time to time when I need to relax, and this is one of them.

I spy Ryker, Gray, Duffer, and Emily in the Prez's booth, and I head over to join them with Emmett's hand still laced with mine.

"What do you want to drink, Snowflake?" Emmett asks against my ear as I take a seat.

"A beer would be good." I almost ask why he doesn't ask someone to get it for him like I've seen the four of them do before, but something tells me his chivalrous side is on full display tonight. If it's for my benefit, I'm definitely not complaining.

"Hey, did you make him work for it?" Emily asks, shuffling into my side as soon as he leaves, and I roll my eyes at her.

"Don't tell anyone, but he's not really that much of an

ass, and as mad as I want to be, I get it too. Doesn't mean I like it, but it also makes it harder to be mad at him."

She smiles from ear to ear, turning to face Duffer with her hand out. "Twenty bucks."

"No fucking way. Scarlett definitely put him through the wringer, I don't believe you," he retorts, batting her hand away as Gray and Ryker laugh at them.

"You bet on me?" I gasp, pointing between them but they just chuckle.

"I said that you were soft on him, just like you're soft on Ryker, Gray, and Axel, but Duffer was adamant you would be a tough nut to crack. If anything, I took your side and earned twenty bucks so don't give me that look," Emily says with a laugh, and I shake my head at her.

"You're crazy. Slightly richer, but definitely crazy," I grumble, but she just preens when Duffer slaps a twenty into her hand.

"She is most definitely a tough nut to crack," Gray says from across the table, his words directed at Duffer but his gaze fixed on me. "But when you get to her center, she's just—"

Ryker cups his hand over Gray's mouth before he can finish, making everyone at the table laugh at his expense. "Whatever you're about to say, shut the fuck up because we both know you'll spoil it." He winks at me, and I bask in the playfulness.

God, this is exactly what I needed.

The press of a cold drink touches my arm, and I turn, expecting to see Emmett there with the bottle of beer he went to get. Instead, my mood sours when I come face-to-face with Molly.

*When will this bitch take a hint?*

There's no bandage on her nose now, a surprise to me because God fucking knows this woman will milk anything she possibly can. Especially if it means painting me as the bad guy. "What the fuck do you want, Molly?" I ask through clenched teeth, watching as her gaze shifts to Ryker's the second I speak, but he doesn't say anything.

"I was just wondering why little Emily was sitting at the big boy's table. I never imagined Emmett would let her whore herself out, but then again, I never thought he'd let her be friends with one either. Especially since he worked so hard to keep her away from the Ruthless Bitches." My hands clench in my lap, irritation getting the better of me, but she's not done speaking yet. "Is it your turn for the rite of passage, honey, or are you too fucking chicken?"

Emily tenses up. Now I understand why she's being targeted. Just as I play a weakness to the guys, Emily plays the exact same role for me.

"How about you do us all a favor, Molly, and fuck off," I say, casting her a scathing look.

"I'm fucking done when I say I'm done, bitch. Don't

make Ryker put you in your place again." She jabs at my chest, a glint of excitement in her eyes, and I scoff.

That's exactly what she wants. She wants to push my buttons and cause a scene in front of everyone so Ryker will interject and save her ass again. This is probably because of the declaration he gave the other day and now she wants to make it look like trash in comparison.

Even though I don't want to react and give her exactly what she wants, I also refuse to let her get away with it. That fact wins out over everything else.

Grabbing the neckline of her low slung tank top, I pull her toward me with a growl, making the smile on her face falter and widen again in a split second. "Face, arm, or leg, Molly? Ryker said no killing, but that was for my conscience more than your well-being, and he didn't mention shit about mangling your body parts."

Her mouth gapes open, her eyes blinking at me as she wildly searches my gaze, before tilting her head toward Ryker. She doesn't get a chance to say a single word before he adds on to my statement.

"She's right, Mol. Mangling is definitely on the table. If not by Scarlett, then I'm sure Emmett will do it when he finds out what you're saying about his sister."

Fear flashes in her eyes, before anger darkens them. "Let go of me," she bites, her hand wrapping around my wrist as she presses her long fucking talons into my skin. It only makes my grip tighten as I yank her closer.

I'm ready to take this bitch outside and let off some steam, not giving her the audience she so desperately craves, but a large bang halts my thoughts and gathers everyone's attention as all eyes turn to the double doors. They're still vibrating from hitting the wall so hard when they were pushed open, but that's not what has my attention.

It's Axel who has my attention. The panicked look in his eyes as he manically searches the crowd, the tension in his shoulders that leave me on edge, and the bounce in his legs even though he's standing still, tells me something has got him worked up.

"Axel?" Ryker calls out, concern etched in every syllable as his friend whips his head around to look at him, but he stops short when his eyes crash into mine.

The bouncing stops, the erratic and panicked vibe calming as he blinks. Once, twice. And then his mouth opens for all to hear over the country music in the background.

"Scarlett, I need you."

# EIGHTEEN

## Scarlett

Axel wipes a hand down his face, looking just as surprised as I am that he uttered those words. His eyes are pleading, his scattered thoughts reflecting in his gaze as he ignores everyone else staring at him and focuses only on me.

"Where?" I ask, rising from my seat and shoving Molly out of the way.

His shoulders sag in relief as he cuts through the crowd slowly. No one stands in his way, everyone highly aware of the tension rippling off him.

"You can't just go around shoving people. I want an apology."

I turn to glare at Molly. Her mouth is wide as she folds her arms over her chest. If looks could kill, I would drop down on the spot.

"Fuck off, Molly," I bite, turning my attention back to Axel.

"Look at you, even the used and abused take pity on you. You should just leave now, it's never going to get better for you."

"What did you just say to him?" My anger rises in my veins as my pulse rings in my ears.

"You heard me," she retorts with a wicked grin on her lips.

Balling my hands at my sides, I exhale sharply. "Say. It. Again."

There are eyes on us, I can feel them burning into my skin. "Used. And. Abus—"

I grab her hair, tangling my fingers among the mass for extra grip, before smashing her face into the table. The bang vibrates around the room as gasps ring out, followed quickly by low, gravelly laughs from the men.

None of that matters though, it's all about shutting this bitch up. Emily's mouth is wide open in shock, but the glimmer of amusement in her eyes tells me she's okay and not freaking out. The screams and sobs from Molly as she sinks to the floor fill me with a sick satisfaction as my attention turns to her again.

Crouching beside her, I grip her chin, trying to avoid the blood trickling down her face, forcing her to look at me. I really hope she didn't toss out the nose brace. "Don't ever, and I mean *never*, say shit about him again. As a matter of fact, don't even address him at all. Don't look at him, don't speak to him. Don't even fucking speak *of* him. You're done if you do. Nothing will stop me from killing you. Not even Ryker," I bite, every fiber of my body ready to rip her apart.

A hand touches my shoulder gently, and I find Axel standing beside me. "Please." One word, and I nod, forgetting the bitch at my feet as I stand to full height and point for him to lead the way.

He doesn't even look down or acknowledge Molly as he heads for the door leading to the back, her words not touching him like they destroyed me. I glance around the table, noting the concern on both Ryker and Gray's faces. This is either the first time he's publicly asked for help or the first time he hasn't asked for one of the guys because the surprise is vivid in both of their eyes.

"Tell Emmett I'm sorry, I—"

"It's okay, Snowflake. Go."

I whirl around, a soft smile touching my lips as I squeeze his arm in thanks. "I just…" My words trail off as I glance at Axel who is waiting by the door with desperation in his eyes.

"He needs you right now, I get it." He places the two bottles of beer down on the table before cupping my chin. "And I appreciate it." Emmett presses a kiss to my lips, sealing those words to me for the briefest moment. He steps back far too soon, leaving me longing, but I can't waste any more time getting to Axel.

The crowd parts without a word, the only noise coming from Molly's hysterics on the floor, but that's no concern of mine.

I hold the door open as Axel walks through it, trying to give him the distance I know he always needs, while desperately wanting to wrap my arms around him. He stops outside of his room, chest heaving with each breath as a tremble runs through him repeatedly. The door swings open and I'm overwhelmed by his presence all at once.

I don't know what I expected in here, probably something as plain as the others, but it's the complete opposite. The white walls are filled with guitars of different shapes and sizes, a vintage record player sits in the near right corner with shelves upon shelves of records lined up. His double bed is placed against the far wall, tucked away to make room for the drum kit in here. I know he likes to jam out to heavy rock as soon as he slams the door shut behind him, but this is something else entirely.

"You can come in," Axel murmurs, pacing at the foot of his bed.

Rubbing my lips together, I take a tentative step, not wanting to touch anything or get too close to him and trigger whatever is going on in his head. "Where are you comfortable with me being?" I ask, still glancing around the room at the random knicknacks and memorabilia that fills every surface.

"How do you know to say that?"

I pause, glancing at him out of the corner of my eye to read his energy before turning to face him. I don't lie, and I warned them that if he ever directly asked me, I would be honest.

"When you last overdosed, I helped you."

"How?"

"I didn't touch you, not once, the guys made sure of it. Well, I technically checked your pulse, but it was like briefest fucking second to make sure you weren't dead I swear. I have experience with similar circumstances, so I was able to offer them some guidance."

Axel swipes a hand down his face, his lips pursing as he takes in my truth, and I worry that this is quickly going to turn sour. That's not what I want, not at all, but if I want him to trust me, all I can do is be honest. Whether he likes it or not.

"And you never took any credit for it."

"Sorry?" I'm confused, but he finally relaxes his shoulders back, like he's reached an understanding about me in his mind.

"Not once have you used it against me. Not the fact that I was in that state, or the fact that you had to help. You let me continue to be a dick."

"I mean, dick is not the word I'd use, but it was never about that." My chest tightens with another truth. "I could see the same torment in you as you saw in me."

His head tips down, a pained snicker touching his lips before he looks back up. Taking a seat at the foot of his bed, he braces his elbows on his thighs, releasing a heavy sigh. "It's the anniversary tonight." My heart lurches, the anguish evident in his face. He's struggling. Hard. I'll be who or whatever he needs me to be at this moment. Whatever keeps his head in the game. I wouldn't wish that sinking feeling on anyone, especially him.

"Tell me what you need, and I'll make it happen." I'm itching to get closer to him, but I force myself to remain in place, the door still slightly ajar behind me.

Big pleading eyes look up at me helplessly. "I don't want these addictions anymore, but I crave them."

Fuck.

"Have you—"

"No, I came looking for you when it got too much."

Relief washes through me, a hint of pride too as I see the strength in him that he doesn't see in himself. "That's good, Axel. Real fucking good."

"You say that, but I need something to distract me." His head falls into his hands with a sigh.

I lift my foot to take a step toward him but pull back

at the last moment. This isn't about me and my need to comfort him, it's about what works for him.

"We talked about healthy addictions, or healthier at least. We could find something for you."

A sigh leaves his lips as he shakes his head. "That's all I've been thinking about since you mentioned it. What else could consume my veins and offer the same comfort?"

"I don't know, Axel, we're all different, we could—"

"Oh, I already fucking figured it out, Scar, but I'm not so sure it's any healthier." The conflict in his eyes runs deep, making my eyebrows pinch.

"Whatever it is, if it works, it's surely healthier than drowning in alcohol and drugs." I try to keep my tone light so he doesn't take offense to my statement, but it seems to go right over his head anyway. "I can help you, Axel, whatever you need." I lower myself to the floor, feet tucked under me.

"I don't think you'll want to." He doesn't look up from his hands, watching them clench and unclench repeatedly.

"Try me."

He grunts, pushing from the bed before trudging across the room to step into the closet. He's barely in there five seconds when he reappears with a long, thin piece of rope coiled up in the perfect knot.

I look from him to the rope and back again, not able to piece it together on my own. "What is it you need, Axel?"

"I need you."

The rope flies through the air, and I catch it, the material softer than I expect as I run my thumb over it. Confused, I settle my gaze on his. "What does this mean?"

"I can't claim you. I can't make you happy. I can't give you shit, Scarlett." He scrubs a hand down his face, a swirl of emotions in his eyes. "But I can give you this."

"You're going to have to spell it out for me, Axel," I breathe, my body thrumming with anticipation—a dark twisted flick of desire and a drop of uncertainty at the unknown. "What is it exactly that you want to give me?"

He paces again, avoiding my gaze. "You can't touch me, and I can't even consider touching you… *yet*," he whispers, pinching the bridge of his nose. Then he turns to face me with determination in his eyes before exhaling. "I want to tie you up in my pretty knots and watch someone fuck you."

My breath catches in my throat, my world stopping for a split second, before my heart gallops in my chest. I feel dizzy with excitement and desire, both emotions overwhelming my senses as I just stare at him.

The silence surrounding us sends Axel spiraling, but I quickly lift my hand to stop him from pacing once again. "What kind of pretty knots are we talking about?" My voice is huskier than I expect.

Axel huffs, eyes narrowing at me. "I just said I want

to tie you up and watch someone fuck you and your first question is what kind of knots?" I nod. "It can't be as simple as that."

"Says who?"

"Me."

"Well, I'm sorry to be the one to break it to you, Axel, but that's not really how life works. It's not just your say so that makes the world keep spinning. If I accept it as simply as that, then it really is as simple as that."

*Simple. Simple. Simple.*

The word bounces around in my mind, his doubt seeping into my own, but I squash it instantly.

"You have to want this too, Scarlett. Not just because I ask for it." He braces his hands on his hips, giving me a pointed look. "This isn't me demanding; it's a choice for both of us. It goes completely against what you told me the other night in the garage. You like to be the one to ask for it, and I really wouldn't be bringing this to the fucking table if I could get it out of my mind. But since the first moment I thought about it, it's all I can think about."

"Giving you the freedom of this takes strength from me, the strength I crave when I offer myself up on my terms. I'm beyond intrigued and interested to try it," I admit. "So please, tell me what you want from me."

He stares at me for what feels like an eternity before nodding, almost to himself before his whole demeanor changes. "I haven't spoken to any of the guys about this."

Smiling, I stand. "I can do that." His lips purse, like he's waiting for the other shoe to drop, but he's no longer jittery, his body calm as he nods again. Moving toward him, I offer him the rope back. "I won't be a minute. Then you can tell me about this rope and what your vision is," I murmur, watching the fire flicker in his eyes.

I freeze when he grips my chin, tilting my head back to look deep into my eyes. "Hurry."

I don't know how fast he thinks I can go when he has me this fucking dizzy with need, but I rush for the door all the same. I get halfway down the hall when the door to the bar opens and Emmett steps through, concern etched into his eyes as he takes me in.

"Is everything okay?"

I cut the remaining distance between us as I release a breath. "Are you free? We need you."

"Of course." He takes my hand without hesitation, completely clueless of what's about to unravel at his approval. Hurrying back toward Axel's room, I rap my knuckles on the door before stepping inside. The last thing I want to do is catch him by surprise.

Axel waves me in, but doesn't really acknowledge Emmett as I click the door shut behind us.

"What's going on?" My Viking asks, glancing between Axel and I.

Axel clears his throat. "I want Scarlett to be my model," he states, tossing the rope in Emmett's direction. "Then…" His words trail off, whether it's from fear of embarrassment or rejection, I don't know. All I know is he shouldn't feel either.

"You want me to enjoy her," Emmett finishes, surprising me, and when I glance at Axel, his eyes are wide too. "What? Your Shibari skills aren't a secret, and I'm intrigued as hell to experience it. If that's what you need from me tonight, count me in." His gaze fixes on me. "I want Scarlett more than anything, so if I get to enjoy her and help you through this shit, then it's not even a question worthy of an answer."

Axel practically turns to a puddle before me, all of his tension floating away as he toys with the rope in his hand. "I'm just going to try and keep it simple for her first time."

"Then tell me where you want me." I'm bursting at the seams, ready to explore this with him, with both of them.

"On the bed, naked."

My teeth nip my bottom lip as I glance down at the shorts and t-shirt I'm wearing. Kicking my sandals off, I unbutton the denim shorts, letting them fall down my legs without another glance, before reaching for the hem of my cropped t-shirt. It's not a show, but I want to take my time, his eyes on me right now are intoxicating.

His lips part the smallest bit when he realizes I'm not

wearing a bra, and I have to bite back a groan. Slipping my fingers into the waistband of my panties, I glance to Emmett, who nods, his eyes hooded as he appreciates every inch of me. With that final nod of encouragement, I drag the lace material down my thighs.

It should be overwhelming to stand in a room completely bare, with two men still dressed from head to toe, cuts and all, but it's enthralling. I fucking live for this feeling.

"On the bed, Scar." My thighs clench at Axel's raspy voice as I move to do as he says. "Kneel at the foot of the bed, facing the pillows," he orders. I shiver with anticipation. "Do you mind if I braid your hair so it doesn't get caught in the rope?"

I shake my head, unable to find my tongue, but that seems to suffice. He pulls the hair tie from my bun, letting the waves fall down my back before running his fingers through the length. His calloused finger teases my spine ever so slightly, but I feel it everywhere.

He's quiet and precise as he braids my hair, and I remain in place, too scared to move. Not even when I hear what sounds like Emmett undressing. As needy as I am, I need to remain calm.

"I'll be using a jute rope, it's the safest option. I swear I'm fully aware of what I'm doing, and that includes being aware of your nerves and circulation. Communication is key."

"You communicate? Who knew we had to get the rope out for you to be able to do that," I sass, a smirk on my face, and I feel him pause for a moment before a light chuckle fills the air.

"Reaper, I'm going easy on you today. I need to show restraint and you need to try it first, but your sass is going to be fun to punish in the future."

My back arches, his breath right at my ear, and I almost sob with pleasure. It's embarrassing how I react to them, but it's worth it.

"You're teasing her, Ax. Want me to shut her sass up with my cock on her tongue?" Emmett asks, walking around the bed with nothing on, and I groan.

"She doesn't get your cock anywhere near her until I'm done. *That's* teasing," Axel grunts, releasing my hair in the braid, placing it over my shoulder. "Are you ready?"

"Please."

"That's not a yes or no, Scar." I can envision the smirk on his face without even looking at him.

"Yes." Apparently I *can* be quiet and pliant, but only under extreme circumstances.

"If anything hurts or feels too uncomfortable, you have to tell me. Otherwise, enjoy. Arms behind your back, Reaper."

I wet my parched lips, letting my eyelids flutter closed as I hum in response. The rope glides over my skin, banding around my upper arms behind my back as he gets to work. Silence descends over the room, my head lulling forward as I concentrate on every touch, every breath, every fucking ripple along my skin.

There's no guessing how long I sit in position, but when I pry my eyes open, Emmett is stroking his cock as he watches intently. "Fucking beautiful, Snowflake," he mutters, the words going straight to my pussy along with every touch from Axel. He knows exactly what he's doing, he must hear the hitches in my breath as he works. I notice the moment he stops, a loss swarming inside of me as he steps back and a whoosh of air dusts over my skin.

"How does that feel, Scarlett?"

"Which part, the restraint or the goosebumps pebbled all over my skin?" I finally tilt my head to look at him. His pupils are blown, his eyes wide as he assesses me.

"Both."

"Like a fucking dream. Please don't make me beg." I'm pent up, full of need and raging with desire as my blood boils with ecstasy. I'm oversensitized. One brush of my clit and I'm bound to explode.

My stomach clenches as he takes a step toward me, his finger running over the rope holding my arms behind me. His breath flutters over my neck before I feel him press his lips to the top of my spine, it's so faint, so soft that I'm sure I make it up. Until he whispers against my skin, "Thank you."

Another shiver down my spine, another goosebump on my skin, another moan from my lips. Looking through my lashes at Emmett, I pant. "Please, Emmett."

I'm strung too tight. I need him now. Right fucking now.

"Take her, Emmett," Axel says from behind me.

Emmett doesn't waste a second inching toward me, rounding the bed so he fills the spot Axel was in moments ago. He sweeps my braid to the other shoulder as he trails kisses over my skin, making me hiss with need.

"You definitely wound her tight, Axel. She's fucking vibrating," Emmett groans, his hand between my shoulder blades as he lowers me to the bed. Face in the sheets, ass in the air, I'm as exposed as it gets, and I love it. "How wet do you think she is already, man?"

"Dripping," Axel responds gruffly, and I spy him out of the corner of my eye. His cock is in his hand, his jaw slack as he pumps his length, watching me.

Emmett glosses his hands over my ass cheeks, making me stutter before he lines his cock up with my entrance. "Remember what I said the next time I fucked you, Snowflake?"

Fuck.

No condom.

"Please."

His cock is at my core, brushing against my folds before he grabs my hips and slams deep inside of me. "Ahhh." I cry out, my slick pussy allowing him to push in deep, spreading me wide around his huge cock.

"Shit, Scarlett. You feel so fucking good."

My pussy clenches around him in response, words betraying me as he retreats and slams straight back inside of me. He repeats the motion again, this time searching out my clit with one hand as the other grips my hip. With the next pass of his length against my walls, I shatter, screaming with ecstasy as my lungs burn.

His pace doesn't shift, dragging out every drop of my climax, and just when I think the world will stop spinning, his hand slaps down on my ass cheek. One orgasm launches straight into another, leaving me sobbing into the sheets with ragged breaths. My eyes are glued to Axel, his eyes searing my soul as I fall apart.

"Feel me, Scarlett. Feel me come inside of you and make you mine like a good girl," Emmett chants, before slamming into me hard and fast. I feel him explode, painting me with him cum as he juts into me in short, sharp bursts.

When he pulls out of my pussy, my hips collapse to the bed. Emmett kisses my heated ass cheek, before stroking his fingers around my core and slipping them inside, feeling his cum inside of me. I shiver at the sensitive touch. "So fucking beautiful, Snowflake."

I whimper, completely lost to my body as he presses another kiss to my ass before stepping away.

"I'm going to untie you now, Scar. Okay?" Axel's voice is as ragged as I feel. I manage a nod but nothing more. As each binding loosens against my skin, my body comes down from the biggest high, one loop at a time.

My arms drop to my sides on the bed, exhaustion calling me, just as he whispers in my ear.

"It's official, little Reaper. I've found my new addiction, and it's you."

RUTHLESS BROTHERS MC

# NINETEEN

*Axel*

For the first time in a long time, I actually slept last night. On the anniversary of my mother's death of all nights, and it's all because of her. She's unintentionally helping to rewire my brain, but the scarier part is that it's fucking working.

There was a woman in my room, in my safe haven, last night. A woman I intentionally let in here. Scarlett let me bind her arms behind her back in the sweetest fucking knots, and I've never seen a more beautiful sight.

Rising from my bed, the spot that she took gains my attention, making my cock come to life. I need coffee and a reprieve from the scent of her orgasm that still clings to my sheets. No wonder they're all addicted to her. She's a slice of heaven and a sliver of the devil all rolled into one.

A fallen angel. A delectably sweet sinner. The perfect

fit for a Ruthless Brother.

Deciding to leave the sheets as they are for the time being, I quickly dress in my usual denim jeans, a fitted black tee, and my cut over the top. Forgoing a brush, I run my fingers through the ends of my hair, before scooping it up into a bun.

I slink out into the hallway, clicking my door shut behind me as I take the side exit instead of trudging through the club. The mid-morning sun casts over me, and I take a deep breath, letting another layer of my worries drift away with ease.

Lighting a cigarette, I take my time heading to the garage, relishing in the peacefulness that envelops me. The sounds of the birds chirping in the trees, a soft rumble of a vehicle in the distance, and the rustling of the leaves in the bushes lulls me.

It's been a minute since my head felt this clear, since I could focus on anything other than my pain, trauma, and overwhelming thoughts. It could all be back to shit by tomorrow, or the end of the day if it's extra fucked, but I just have to take one day at a time.

There might be hope for me yet.

Stubbing out my smoke, I open the garage door and turn on the overhead light, finding my baby instantly. Hattie the Harley, the only woman I've ever been able to truly rely on. I've neglected her this past week with my mental health taking over everything, and she could use a good clean.

I gather the cleaning products from the storage unit in the corner and open up the large garage door so the water can drain out. Starting with the wheels, I get lost in the motion of making my baby shine, allowing it to distract me in the best possible way.

As I reach for the leather cleaner, I hear a throat clearing behind me and turn to see who it is.

Ryker.

Fuck.

My chest clenches slightly with tension. I'm worried the awkwardness between us is going to take over me and force me right back down the rabbit hole of head-fuck central. It's my own doing, but that doesn't mean I can handle it.

I search his eyes for a moment, but he doesn't offer any words as a follow up so I focus back on the task at hand. Despite my best efforts, ignoring his presence is easier said than done, and I soon find myself turning back to him with my eyebrows raised in question. He's still standing in the open doorway.

"Are we going to get past this shit or not?" Tension ripples through my limbs. Confrontation is never a problem for me, but it's not usually aimed at him.

"I didn't make this happen, Ax," he grumbles in

response, tucking his hands into his pockets with a sigh.

"I never said that you did. I'm fully aware this is my doing, but you clearly came out here for a reason. Get to it." I should be apologizing for pissing off my best friend, but it seems it's impossible for me to be civilized. Not just that though, it feels too raw and vulnerable to offer him that.

"There's a reason you kept it a secret, Axel. You knew, you *fucking* knew." He takes a step inside the garage.

There's a helplessness in his eyes along with a brewing storm.

We're both as fucked as each other, it seems.

Sighing, I discard the rag in my hands as I turn to face him. "You're right. I knew you would be mad and refuse. I'm quite sure you did numerous times after we offered up assassination as an option." Three times that I can remember off the top of my head, but there's probably more.

"That should have been your hint not to do it then." The pointed stare he offers would make anyone else shrink on the spot, but not me.

"Your own rage was holding you back from seeing the bigger picture, Ryker. We couldn't continue under his bullshit any longer and you know it. We were digging for details, slowly piecing the puzzle together, but in the meantime the club was drowning. Fast." Ryker swipes a hand down his face, likely trying to hide the glint in his eyes that shows he knows exactly what I mean. But when he looks up again, there's nothing there at all. "You can be mad at me for it, but watching you slowly drift back to your old self over the past few weeks has made it worth every single fucking second of being pissed."

I need another smoke before I transform into a matador, continuing to anger the big bad bull in the ring before me. Moving toward him, I pause when his hand grabs my shoulder, stopping me from slipping past him.

Our gazes lock, a moment passing between us. One of brothers always at each other's side, of friends that have always shown up, shovel in hand, whenever needed. Drop by drop, the tension radiating between us slowly evaporates without words.

Clearing his throat once more, Ryker squeezes my shoulder. "Last night was the first time you've reached out to someone other than me on the anniversary. Are you okay?" The concern in his voice is real, making me realize his worry for my wellbeing last night outweighed any anger that was still between us. It tells me everything is going to be okay.

My shoulders roll back, relief blanketing me as I nod. "Yeah, I'm good."

We stare off for a few more breaths before he juts his chin at me in acknowledgment. "Good. I'm glad. You seem… lighter this morning." His observation is correct, especially now that this shit between us doesn't pose a threat to our friendship.

"Yeah, she's slightly magical," I murmur with a grin, and he smirks back at me.

"Did you…"

"No. Fuck no," I splutter, almost choking on my tongue as he nods, but he doesn't ask for further details thankfully.

"Okay, go eat. We've got a busy day ahead of us, and I need my best friend and sergeant at arms to be on point."

"Roger that, Prez." I salute him mockingly, and his brows furrow.

"Don't call me that." His mutter is barely more than a whisper as I cock a brow at him.

"You love it, don't fucking lie." I smirk, placing a cigarette between my lips as I continue to stare him down.

He rolls his eyes, mirth in his orbs as he sticks his middle finger up at me. "I do, but not from you, asshole. You're my best friend first. Always."

---

With the weight of the world no longer on my shoulders, I feel like I float toward the clubhouse. I ignore everyone as I step inside, taking purposeful steps toward the kitchen. Coffee is calling my name.

I'm not surprised to find Maggie at the dining table when I enter. She never seems to stop, likely giving me a run for my money with my insomnia most nights if she even actually sleeps at all.

"Morning, honey, how are you feeling today?" The hint of concern in her eyes tells me straight away that she caught my manic state last night, but I don't shy away from it. Not from Maggie at least.

"Surprisingly okay," I murmur, filling a mug up with the coffee already waiting in the pot. Taking a seat across from her, I have a swig before meeting her gaze. "I was lost as fuck last night. My chest felt tight, my vision blurred. It was rough."

She looks intently into my eyes for a moment, a sparkle of hope flashing in her gaze. "And she made it go away?"

I know who she's referring to, and it makes my heart stutter to admit anything out loud. Shaking my head, I reply, "Not entirely, but she made it better."

The smile on her lips spreads. "Progress is progress, Axel. We'll take whatever we can get." She edges forward a little as her expression grows more stern. "Did you…"

"Not a single line, or a drop of liquor either," I admit, pride blossoming in my chest. It feels like a victory, a win against the war within myself.

Maggie extends her hand toward mine, remembering at the last second my aversion to it, and quickly retreats.

I don't know why or how, but in the next breath, I'm reaching for her, clutching just the tips of her fingers. The gasp from her lips rings in my ears, my heart thundering in my chest. I can't breathe, the contact catching even me off guard, but the swell of unshed tears in her eyes is undeniable.

She doesn't do anything in response, even though I can see the urge in the slight tremble of her hand, which I'm grateful for. Squeezing a little tighter, I release her and slump back in my seat. The silence that descends over us is comforting, yet there are words unsaid.

"Why do you gotta make me emotional right now, Axel?" Maggie grumbles with a laugh. She's wiping at her eyes and avoiding my gaze.

"I'm sorry."

I can't explain why I'm apologizing. Whether it's because she's emotional over a simple touch or the surprise of it, I don't know, but I feel bad either way.

"Don't ever apologize, Axel. I'm just glad there's a small glimmer of hope in the air for you. You deserve it more than anyone else I know."

Reaching for my mug, I decide to down the remains instead of responding. I rise, and the look in her eyes tells me she knows the moment has passed. "I'm going to start cooking in a minute. Any preferences on breakfast?" she asks, changing the conversation.

"Surprise me." With a wink, I turn for the door.

I don't know where I'm heading until I come to a stop in front of a door, hesitation flickering through me as I look at the handle.

Scarlett.

I fucking know with raw certainty that everything in the kitchen just happened because of her. I don't know how and I'm not ready to delve into why, but it's true. I needed her in my darkest time and she showed up without a moment's hesitation.

No questions, no irritation. Nothing.

Then I admitted my thoughts out loud, leaving myself vulnerable for the first time in a very long time, and she accepted me fully. She didn't bat an eyelid, if anything they widened with excitement.

Last night was intense, but euphoric, there's no doubting that. I owe her a thank you, a gift, something. She deserves more than I can offer her, I just don't actually know what.

Before I can think better of it, I grab the handle and twist, surprised when it opens. Scarlett is lying on her bed, her hair fanned around her as she listens to...

"Is that Toby Delmann's murder investigation podcast?" I blurt, stepping into the room.

Peering up at me, she smirks. "Knock, knock. Who's there? Axel. Axel who? Axel the asshole who doesn't know how to actually knock." She grins, pleased with her jibe as I roll my eyes at her.

I clap my hands together, staring straight into her eyes as I do it again and again, watching the smile on her face grow as she leans up onto her elbows to look at me. "Am I getting a slow clap off *the* Axel from the Ruthless Brothers? I might need to film this."

"Fuck off," I grumble, flipping her off for good measure. She pushes up to sit on her bed, legs crossed as she faces me.

"You know Toby Delmann's podcast?" Her hands fly to her chest with a gasp.

"Only fools don't," I grunt, taking another slow step into the room and closing the door a little behind me. I don't know what the fuck I'm doing in her room, it's not as gut-clenching as I worried it would be, but closing the door completely could quickly trigger me and change that.

"Right? I'm obsessed with him. I just started today's episode on the Stanton Strangler from 1982. Have you listened to it yet?" Fuck, why am I so drawn to how wide her eyes get when she's excited, and the way she talks more animatedly with her hands flying around.

I shake my head. "Not yet." She pauses the episode as I tuck my hands into my pockets, glancing around the room nervously. "Is it like your resource center for ideas on how to kill people and get away with it?"

Her eyes flash to mine, a smile on her lips as she shrugs. "Possibly. Care to find out?"

"Not today," I reply, happy to continue living and breathing for a little longer.

The room goes quiet as we look at each other. I want to tear away from all of my pain and heartache, cut the distance between us and slip beneath the sheets with her. It's not going to happen, not right now at least, possibly even ever, but it's the first time I've thought about it with anyone.

It's all-consuming and intoxicating.

Addictive.

"Are you busy right now? Or do you want to listen to it with me?"

I consider my options, when a hand slaps my shoulder, pulling me from my thoughts. "Good, you're both here together." Ryker grins, but there's a flash of reckless determination in his eyes. "The guns are being dropped. Are you ready?"

"Fuck yeah," I grunt as Scarlett jumps from her bed. Predator is etched into her every move.

"Count me in."

# TWENTY

*Scarlett*

My excitement for a bike ride with the MC is short-lived when I realize there are no bikes involved today. It makes total fucking sense, but it still leaves me a little deflated. Instead, I'm sandwiched between Euro and the passenger door as Axel drives the truck.

I glance at him out of the corner of my eye, seeing right through Euro as I watch Axel's jaw tighten. My thighs clench. The memory of last night floods my veins, but when he tilts his head slightly and looks my way, I quickly look out of the windshield instead of meeting his eyes.

I'm trying to play it cool, but I'm totally failing. I'm being obvious as fuck, but he's just as mesmerizing as Ryker, Gray, and Emmett. He's also more elusive and has told me numerous times now that we're never going to be anything at all. Yet hope blossoms inside of me.

Flustered, I squash my feelings down and push my thoughts to the back of my mind. Now definitely isn't the time for that. Hopefully, the day is going to smoothly unravel before us, my idea being put into action, or we're going to return home as clueless and irritated as when we left.

Axel takes the turn into the shipment yard and proceeds toward the far left corner. When the truck rolls to a stop, I exhale heavily, releasing the tension building inside of me over what's to come.

I climb out without a word, leaving the door open for Euro to step out as I take in my surroundings. The slam of Axel's door makes me turn toward him with my eyebrow raised. "Real discreet, mountain man." The words slip from my mouth before I can even consider stopping them, and he glares in my direction.

"Let's climb onto the small container over there, it will give us a good view." His grumble is completely zoned into the moment as he points toward that direction, ignoring my sass.

I follow after him as Euro huffs beside us. "Why do we have to take forever on this? The longer we're here, the more chances we're giving the Brutes to hit."

"Maybe," Axel replies, not even looking in his direction as he uses the thick padlock on the container to lift himself up to the top. "But since you were injured last time and we lost lives, it makes sense to be cautious."

Euro doesn't offer a response as he follows after Axel, and I opt to keep my mouth shut and out of the equation. Reaching for the metal pipes on the side of the container, I place my foot on the padlock and hoist myself up in the air. My knee hits the top first before I clamber to my feet, wiping the dirt off my jeans as I cringe.

I've been in far worse situations, covered in more grime than this, but it still makes me shudder every time.

"Where are we looking then?" Euro asks, pushing his hair back off his face.

"Everywhere, dumbass," Axel grunts in response, and I move toward the taller container that's pushed against the one we're on. A wired fence wraps around us, the perimeter of the shipment yard at our back, and the container beside us shields most of our frames while offering us a good view of everything. "Straight ahead, third from the left, that's our container."

I nod and turn, ingraining every inch of the scenery into my mind. There's no stone unturned, no number painted on a container withheld as I commit everything to memory. "Where are the entry points?"

A ghost of a smile touches Axel's lips when I turn to look at him after a moment when he doesn't respond. Giving him a pointed look, he wipes a hand over his mouth as he comes to stand beside me. There's still a good few inches between us, but it feels closer than usual. Closer than when we were sitting side by side in the garage sharing our deepest, darkest bullshit.

"There's only one main gate, but they can either follow our path or come from the opposite angle." He points, and I hum in understanding.

"Where did they come from last time?" He thinks for a moment, turning around and pointing at the far end. "Let's hope they come from that way again then," I murmur, before Axel holds out a handgun for me.

The metal presses against my palm, my fingers wrapping around the handle, testing the weight as I hold it out in front of me. Checking the chamber, I knock the safety off, satisfied with the product he's offering me.

"Where's everyone else?" Euro asks, completely unaware of how serious we're taking this as he lights up a cigarette. I take his calmness as a good sign, like everything isn't as fucked as I think, but it only seems to piss Axel off.

"Watching from other positions around the yard. We need as much distance as possible between us all this time," he grunts, hands flexing at his side.

The telltale sound of motorcycle engines rumble in the distance. My spine stiffens as my gaze crashes with Axel's, who sneers, his head whipping to the only other person with us.

Euro.

He takes one step toward him, and I quickly wave my free hand for him to stop. His nostrils flare as he glances back at me, and I mouth for him to check, pointing toward the sound. It takes a good few seconds for him to relent, turning away from the other member of the Ruthless Brothers with a snarl. While Euro is none-the-fuck wiser.

Tightening my hold on my gun, I close my eyes, listening to the sound of the engines as they get louder and louder, before I blink them open and watch the first bike in the distance. That's definitely the symbol of the Brutes. There's no denying it.

Motherfucker.

"Drop," Axel grunts, crouching to his knees with his back pressed against the container as I do the same. Euro frowns at us for a second before following suit.

I want to rip his eyeballs straight from his damn head, so I have no idea how badly Axel is feeling right now.

"Send it," Axel grunts, and I quickly grab my cell phone and do as we planned.

**Scarlett:**

*Found.*

I've barely hit send when a response comes through.

**Emmett:**

*Fuck.*

**Ryker:**

*Club. Now.*

"Who the fuck is that? Are we being attacked again?" Euro asks, glancing between Axel and I. The audacity of this fucking man. It's not the good kind either, it's the worst. That of a traitor.

"No shit, fucker. We need to leave. Now," Axel bites, his deathly glare moments away from burning a hole in the side of Euro's head.

"You're right." Euro tosses his cigarette, inching toward the side of the container where we came up. It blows my mind how he can act so casually when we know. We fucking know. I'm moving before I realize it, gripping the back of his cut in my fist as I pull him back. "What the fuck?" he grunts in confusion, but I don't respond. Instead, I shove at him, watching as his arms flail at his sides, before he falls from the container with a cry.

"What the fuck, Scar?" Axel grunts, rushing to glance at the man singing out a battle cry in horror. "You could have killed him."

"Please, from this height, that's not possible. Snapping

an ankle or two so he can't run, sure, but death wasn't the plan today." Adrenaline pounds through my veins as I strategically leap from the container, landing with a huff beside Euro. "You're going to be fine, isn't that right, Euro?"

"What the fuck, you stupid bitch. What was that for?" His nose is scrunched, his eyes prickled with unshed tears as he lies on the floor helplessly.

I snicker, tucking a loose tendril of hair behind my ear as I glance down at him. "You're lucky that's all you're getting... for now." I give him a pointed stare, but he doesn't seem to notice as he assesses himself.

Axel's boots hit the ground behind me, and he steps in between Euro and I before I can say another word. "This was a set up, motherfucker, to find the mole within our club, and you just failed with flying colors."

---

Muffled shouts and banging plays a symphony from the bed of the truck all of the way home. I relish in it. Enjoying the pained whimpers as we get closer and closer to his demise.

We managed to leave the shipment yard without the Brutes ever knowing we were there. I'm sure the confusion has them looking for answers, but all they'll get are the remnants of a mole they placed in the Ruthless Brothers' grasp.

"We were supposed to wait for Ryker, Scarlett." Axel's knuckles turn white as he grips the steering wheel, but I just shrug.

"I didn't want him to be able to get away."

"That's still not the point and you know it," he retorts, giving me a questioning glance before turning back toward the road.

He's not wrong, but I'm not admitting he's right or declaring that I regret my moves because I don't. This fucker is as slimy as they come. One hint that we were on to him and he would have been going crazy anyway. I don't know him so I couldn't be certain of his reaction, but in moments like this, defense and attack are standard.

The compound appears up ahead, Axel's foot seeming to press down harder on the accelerator before he skids to a halt in front of the double doors looming ahead.

"You need help getting him out?" I offer, earning another glare from Axel, before he throws his door open and storms to the bed of the truck. He hadn't even glanced in my direction when we were back at the shipping yard. He just hoisted Euro over his shoulder without a backward glance, tossing him in the bed of the truck, tying his arms and legs together before taping his mouth shut.

My eyebrows raise when Axel already has the mole

tossed over his shoulder, marching toward the compound. I catch the doors as Axel swings them open, storming into the bar area without batting an eyelid, but as I follow him inside, I'm surprised to see there's no one present.

I let him lead the way, keeping close behind him until he reaches a door behind the bar, and I freeze when it opens. "I can't go down there."

My teeth clench, my spine locked in place as I shake my head.

Axel pauses as he glances over his shoulder at me with a hint of confusion in his eyes. "What?"

"I can't go down there. If that's where you're handling all of this, then that's cool, but I can't go with you." I gulp, taking a subconscious step back as I try to avoid looking at the stairs that I just fucking know lead down to the basement.

His gaze flicks between my eyes for what feels like an eternity before he nods sharply and turns to go back past me, kicking the door shut. I release a breath I didn't realize I was holding as I watch him drop Euro onto a stool in front of the Prez's booth.

Shaking my hands out, some of the tension that burned up my spine moments ago depletes. I get within two feet of them when the double doors open in a flurry, smashing against the walls on either side as Ruthless Brother after Ruthless Brother filters back into the room.

Ryker, Gray, Emmett, Shift, Cash, and a handful of prospects. Only three of those men look angry, the others look confused. Despite their understanding of the situation, they each look at Euro with a frown.

"Does someone want to explain what on earth is going on?" I glance at Shift, his question lingering in the air, before Ryker takes a step toward Axel and I.

"There was no collection today," he announces, turning his attention to the crowd as he rolls his shoulders back.

"There wasn't?" Cash asks, itching the back of his head as Ryker shakes his head.

"No. We knew there was a mole in the compound somewhere, we just weren't sure where. Until now." He points at Euro who is red-faced and angry in his seat. "There were three drop-off names decided upon, three groups that went out. If the Brutes showed up at one of them, then we would know who the mole is because while I was with Shift at the ferry port, Gray, Emmett, and Cash were at the halfway house. Both places were quiet as a mouse. But not the shipping yard. That had visitors in the shape of the Devil's Brutes, along with Axel, Scarlett, and Euro."

Euro mumbles something behind the tape on his mouth, but it's not audible in the slightest. No one moves to relieve him of the restraint as they let Ryker's words settle over them instead.

"You set me up?" Shift calls out, looking directly at his brother who grimaces. Before Gray can respond, Shift waves his hand dismissively. "It's beside the fucking point, I get it. So the mole is Euro?"

"Yeah, the mole is this fucker right here with two broken ankles and a smashed fucking nose," Axel hisses, hands clenching at his sides as he points down at the traitor before him.

"What? I can't make out his ankles with the swelling, but I don't see a broke—"

Emmett's words are cut off as Axel extends his fist and punches Euro square in the face. Blood bursts everywhere, splattering Axel, the floor, and my arm as I attempt to wipe it off with my t-shirt, a curse slipping from my mouth.

This shit's hard to get out. I'm going to have no clothes left at this rate.

"Never mind," Emmett adds, scrubbing at the back of his neck as the scene unfolds before him. There are no words to describe it, no piecing it back together, it's all here now for everyone to see.

"How are we going to handle this, Prez?" Shift asks, and everyone's attention turns to Ryker once more. It is his place to lead us from here, me included. I'm beyond invested in this.

Ryker spins on the spot, meeting everyone's gaze as he assesses the room, before settling his stare on Euro. A sneer tilts the corner of his mouth as he cocks his head to the side.

"We handle this situation as we always do, Brothers. Ruthlessly."

RUTHLESS BROTHERS MC

# TWENTY ONE

*Ryker*

Anger vibrates through me as I look at the motherfucker who has been tearing us apart from within. Lives have been lost because of him and his actions and he's going to fucking pay for it.

My fingers itch at my sides, desperate to get my hands on him. I feel like a raging bull, my anger consuming me as I breathe in short, sharp bursts. Looking at him now is like I've finally placed Banner where he deserved to be. Banner killed my father, Euro was playing his part in killing this club. In my eyes, that's the same fucking thing.

"Out," I grunt, glancing from Shift to Cash briefly. Nodding, they head for the door without question, the prospects following after them with their lips tightly shut. They can be pissed about being set up later, but for now, they know I have to handle the traitor here.

When the door clicks shut behind them, I turn my attention to Axel. "Breaking his ankles, really? Was that necessary?" I ask, brow cocked.

He waves a hand at me immediately, before pointing at Scarlett. "Don't fucking look at me. That was all Reaper."

The woman in question gapes at Axel for a second, teeth raking over her bottom lip before she turns to look at me. "I don't know what you want me to say, it seemed like a good idea at the time," she states with a shrug.

I almost laugh at the ease within her and the nonchalant shrug as she doesn't deny it.

"No, the correct thing to do was follow Prez's orders, then let him make the next call," Axel states in a tone that tells me they've already had this conversation. All the while Euro grunts from behind the tape sealing his mouth shut.

"He's right," I state, taking a step toward her, but she doesn't falter. Instead, I get another shrug.

"Well, you don't call me Rebel for nothing." She smiles. She fucking smiles.

*Where did we find this woman? And why the hell is my dick stirring to life when I have such a fucking shit show on my hands?*

Swiping a hand down my face, I take my time, hiding the touch of a smile on my own lips as Gray's voice cuts through the air. "Are you guys okay though? Did the Brutes see you?"

*I* should probably be fucking asking that, but my head is all mixed up with this shit. As much as I agreed with the plan and that we needed to figure out if we had a mole, I really hoped we would be wrong.

"It didn't seem like they did. Axel made sure to place us a good distance away where we were covered."

"We would have been out quicker if she hadn't pushed this asshole off the container, snapping his ankles, leaving me to carry him to the truck," Axel grumbles, but there's no real anger in his tone. No. He's fucking impressed despite it all and slightly amused, he's just saying what he's supposed to say as the sergeant at arms of the club.

"I added, what, ten seconds on to the escape, not a moment more, and it was worth every single one," Scarlett retorts, giving Axel a pointed stare that he can't argue with.

Euro's grunts get louder, distracting me from the bickering between the pair of them. "Get this fucker down to the basement. It's time we got to the bottom of this." I roll my shoulders back, so I can focus on what we have to do when we get down there.

"Scarlett can't go down there."

I frown, glancing at Axel as he folds his arms over his chest.

"Why?"

"Because she can't," Axel pushes, as I turn to look at Scarlett.

Her face is void of emotion, giving me absolutely nothing, but there's clearly something there.

Clearing my throat, I nod for Axel to get this dick's body to move. "That's where we conduct business. Always. Scarlett doesn't have to be present for the next bit."

My Rebel scoffs, hands clenching at her sides as she watches Axel follow my orders. "Of course, go with my plan and then drop me at the end of it. I get it, it's fine. Whatever."

Raising my hands in surrender, I take a tentative step toward her. "I'm missing something here. You're going to have to explain it to me."

I really should just be getting on with the job, but my heart refuses to step away when she seems to be in some kind of distress. Her gaze flickers from me to Axel, who walks by with Euro over his shoulder.

A sigh falls from her lips, her chin dipping to her chest for a brief second before she looks back up at me. "It's fine, I'm overreacting. Don't worry about it. Make him pay." The reluctance in her tone is clear.

Any other woman would be running for the hills right now, but if she's the Grim Reaper, then she knows exactly what to do in this moment. She was fucking groomed for it. That fact only escalates the anger inside of me.

While she's here, under our roof, as one of us, it's not her fucking job. It's mine, it's ours. We protect her, not the other way around. She's already placed herself in harm's way more than once for us. That's not what her role is here.

Before I can say anything to her, she turns and heads for the door leading to the rooms. I hear Gray mutter curses under his breath and I feel torn. I want to understand, but it's clear she's not in a position to explain. Although, it's not lost on me that Axel knows.

Pursing my lips, I consider my options as Axel heads downstairs. With my mind made up, I look over at Emmett and Gray, both looking longingly toward the door Scarlett stepped through moments ago.

"Stay with her, we've got this from here," I order, and they move before I've even finished talking.

Thank fuck there's four of us to handle this shit. Bringing this club to victory and satisfying the queen that walks among us needs a fucking community of men to handle. It's worth every moment, and I'll get my time with the girl who has me twisted up in knots.

But for now, I have some pain to cause.

---

Blood drips from my knuckles, each finger aching from the

constant blows, but I'm fairing far better than the traitor in my grasp. His eyes are swollen and bruised, his nose already crooked from Axel's early hit, his clothes drenched in his own blood as Axel aims the sharpened dagger at his throat.

We've been down here for what feels like an eternity that only extends as he continues to offer no information. I'm done already, but I won't back away until we've got what we want.

"I'm going to ask you one more time, and then I'm going to pierce your fucking skin again and again until you bleed out all over the floor," Axel bites. There's specks of blood in his hair and beard, making him look even crazier than usual.

"I-I... I d-don't know w-what you're talking a-a-about," he stammers, irritating me even further.

Without missing a beat, Axel slices Euro's throat. Enough to draw blood, but not deep enough to kill him. Euro cries out, but it's a wasted noise. We all know it.

Frustrated, I yank him forward in the seat, before Axel rips at his cut until he's no longer wearing it. He hisses in pain as I contort his limbs to do as I want to get the leather from him. Once it's in my hands, I feel angry and vindicated all at once.

"You don't deserve to wear this for a second longer." He tilts his head to look at me, a pleading in his eyes that's been there since we brought him down here, but it's useless. Crouching in front of him, I sigh. "How about you do us all a favor and tell us what we want to know. The more you tell me, the less damage Axel is going to do to you and the quicker this will be over."

His gaze travels slowly between my eyes, his tongue peeking out as he calms his sobbing and finally considers my words. I've reworded the same fucking phrase six times at least already, but this one seems to have worked.

"I did it for the club," he murmurs, making my eyebrows rise in surprise. Is he for real? A grunt from Axel tells me how he feels about that statement too, but I keep my focus on Euro.

"Of course you did. Now tell me exactly what you did for the club." My voice is contained, almost sympathetic as my blood boils beneath the surface. I know Axel is going to hate every second of my cajoling tone, but if it gets us what we need, then I'm going to persevere.

"I told them where our drops were and when we would be there."

Fucker.

"Why?" He grimaces as his face crinkles in confusion like he doesn't understand my question. "Why did they want that information?"

"I-I don't know."

"What were they threatening you with?" Surely he has

to know the answer to that question.

He shuffles in his seat with the restraints around his arms and legs making it difficult. "To kill me, to kill my old man."

Axel huffs from beside me. "So how are you protecting the club? Did they even threaten the club?" His fuse is burning faster, irritation getting the better of him.

"O-of course, t-they did," he grunts, running his tongue over his busted lip as he tilts his head in Axel's direction.

"So you aided them to protect yourself and your old man. What about the men's lives you sacrificed in your place? What about the Brothers that are no longer breathing because of your actions?" The fury in my veins matches every note in Axel's questions. Euro, however, blinks up at him lazily as he tries to find a reasonable excuse. "Emmett's old man is dead because of you. Becker is dead because of you. As a matter of fact, why don't you explain to me why you took a shot to the arm as well?"

I stand, pacing behind Axel as he unloads on this motherfucker. Now that we've finally broken past the first layer of his defenses, it doesn't matter who does the talking. Just as long as we get the answers.

"Kincaid said it was to make sure it didn't look like it was me helping, but I know that fucker did it because of the police station," he grunts, a sneer on his lips that matches my own.

I brush past Axel, gripping the fucker's collar as I bring him face to face with me. "You almost got our Brother killed. You helped them target Emmett and you were going to just watch. That's not for the club. Not at all," I bite, unable to hide my anger any longer.

"Someone had to negotiate with the fucking Brutes since you weren't. You're too bothered about your pride, not keeping us safe." His Adam's apple bobs despite the snarl, and I punch him in the stomach, before rearing my stronger arm back and smashing him in the face.

"This isn't about my pride, fuck my pride. Fuck everyone's. The club comes first, and we're never safe in someone else's pocket."

Axel places his hand on my shoulder, and I shake him off as I take a step back. Rubbing at my temples, I take a few deep breaths before I turn to face them. I gather my composure as I understand that this situation isn't going to change.

All he can offer us is bullshit excuses. Nothing more, nothing less. The victory in this moment is knowing the mole is no more, but he's not going to give us any new information that will help piece this all together.

"Can I go now?" he asks, his head rolling to the side as he spits blood on the floor.

I don't bother to answer as it's a stupid fucking question. Instead, I look at Axel. One nod. One simple fucking nod, and my best friend and sergeant at arms knows exactly what he has to do. What's expected.

"Unfortunately for you, Euro, there's nowhere for you to go," Axel murmurs, twirling the dagger in his hand as he steps toward the table lined with tools.

"W-what? No. No, you said—"

"I didn't say shit, that was Ryker," Axel interjects, a burst of laughter in his voice as he spins back around with a hammer in his hands. His eyes are wide, pupils blown and almost jet black as they shine under the dull light. "Ryker wanted to pacify you so you'd open your mouth. Whereas I, on the other hand, want to smash your fucking head in."

Euro's face goes white around the bruises marking his skin, the blood smears doing nothing to brighten his haunted features. "No, please…"

"You should have come to us when they first approached you, Euro. All of this could have been very different, but you chose wrong. Sinners have to pay for their sins, *Brother*, that's always how it's going to be."

Axel is calmer now than he was when we were pushing him. This is control, his comfort zone. Euro attempts and fails to pull at the restraints holding him in place, a sob bursting past his lips as he looks up at Axel hovering over him with the hammer poised.

"That's it, motherfucker. Cry for me, sob, tell me how you'll do better, *be* better. Let those be the last words that part your traitorous lips before I fucking end you," Axel hisses, not wasting another breath as he smashes the hammer into Euro's head.

The sound of his skull shattering echoes around the room first, a shrill cry halted on his lips the following second, before another swing of the hammer is plunged into his chest. Blood sprays the room, coating me as I inhale sharply, looking down at the fucker who screwed us over.

Axel turns to look at me as he drops the hammer to the floor, blood clinging to his face and beard. "Call the crew for a clean-up, I need a cigarette."

# TWENTY TWO

## Scarlett

Anger and irritation courses through my veins as I pace in front of the television hung up in the lounge. I don't know why I'm in here, but I couldn't face my room. It feels suffocating, and this… feels almost similar but not quite as harsh. That may change if I stay in here though.

I want to be involved in the chaos I hope is unraveling downstairs right now, but nothing will have me stepping down there.

Nothing.

Which leaves me filled with pent-up anger and frustration that didn't ease when I shoved that motherfucker off the container. Now, I need to find myself an alternative outlet to channel all of this energy. I just don't know where.

"You're hot when you worry."

I whirl around at the sound of Emmett's voice to find

him leaning against the doorframe with Gray standing beside him. "I'm not worried," I grumble, sweeping my hair back off my face as I continue to pace.

"What's this, then?" Gray asks, waving his hand at my movements as I frown at him.

"This is me being antsy and annoyed. I want to go down there and lay into that piece of shit for putting everyone in danger, but I fucking can't."

They look at me with curiosity, but something stops them from asking why. It takes me a second to realize that the emotional therapy I had with Axel hasn't been shared with them. I can't decide if I'm surprised or impressed.

Right now, I wish he had so I don't have to consider talking about it.

As if sensing my internal stress, Emmett steps further into the room, eyes fixed on mine. "I'm going to assume that's some trauma shit that you don't want to get into right now."

I could fucking kiss him. "That would be correct."

"So you need a distraction *and* to let off steam. Am I right?" He tugs at his beard as he inches closer once more, and I nod.

"Aren't you guys going down there with them?" I ask, trying to deflect away from myself.

"Please, Axel has that shit covered. Ryker's there out of protocol, we're of better use up here," Gray explains, moving further into the room and taking a seat on the arm of the sofa.

"I would love to slice up that asshole in the name of my dad, but I know Axel will get me my justice," Emmett says, a pained flash in his eyes.

"Emmett, I'm so sorry," I murmur, hating that there's been a mole in our midst, and that we aren't downstairs helping take our anger out on him for what he's put this club through these past few weeks.

"I'm good, I just need distracting too. The tension is fucking with me," he grunts, swiping a hand down his face, and I take a step toward him.

The three of us bask in silence for a moment, glancing from one to the other as we try to figure out what the fuck we're doing.

"Can I tempt you with fake killing some fuckers on the big screen?" Gray offers, hinting at a video game.

"I want to, but…"

"I get it, Sweet Cheeks," he says. A soft smile stretches his lips as he helplessly watches me practically bounce on the spot with contained energy.

"The feeling running through your veins has your whole body looking for exertion. Just stimulating your mind wouldn't be enough right now."

I glance at Emmett as he speaks, his words resonating inside of me as I nod.

"That's exactly it." Those three words don't make everything magically disappear, but understanding a little more of what's going on in my head relaxes my shoulders an inch.

"You *know* where my head is going with that, right?" Gray says with a chuckle, making me smirk.

"Is your head ever anywhere else?" Emmett grumbles, cocking a brow at his friend whose smile grows even wider.

"Nope." This asshole pops his p with all the sass within him, and instead of making me keel over laughing at him, it has a different effect.

Reaching for the hem of my sweater, I pull it over my head, shivering at the chill in the air as it tingles over my skin leaving goosebumps in its wake.

"Fuck," Gray mutters, sitting taller as he swipes his tongue over his bottom lip.

"Your chest is heaving with every fucking breath, Snowflake."

One glance at Emmett and his pupils are dilated, his shimmering orbs begging for me as I release a heavy breath. "Make it stop."

He knows what I mean, they both do, but neither of them moves. Kicking my combat boots off, I step out of my pants too, leaving me in my last matching set of underwear that hasn't been damaged by these motherfuckers.

"Please."

Their eyes on my exposed skin makes my breath come harder and faster. I'm on the verge of panting and no one has touched me.

"Who?" Emmett asks as I threaten to melt into a puddle at their feet.

"Both of you."

The hum of sexual tension in the room is palpable, getting thicker and fuller with every breath taken between the three of us.

"Close the door, Gray," Emmett orders, his tone dark and raspy as I gulp.

"Yes, sir," he retorts, jumping up from his spot to do just that as I smirk at the bossy Viking.

"Don't make his ego bigger with your jokes," I breathe, flicking my gaze to Gray for a brief second before settling my gaze on Emmett again.

"Please, we both know you're going to be appreciating his dick getting bigger at the same time," Gray sings, rejoining our little circle as we each look at one another.

A shiver runs down my spine, the tension tightening my muscles burning for their touch. I need to alleviate the pressure inside of me, and that's only going to be possible at their hands.

Gray takes a predatory step toward me, teeth sinking into his bottom lip as his eyes score every inch of me. When he's within reach, his finger trails down my arm, making me bite back a gasp as he continues to walk around me. I can feel his presence behind me, the heat from his body enveloping me as my gaze latches on to Emmett's.

"Where do we begin with you, huh?" Emmett shakes off his cut slowly, his words held in the air as he assesses me. "Maybe we should punish you first for going against the Prez's orders." He cocks a brow at me expectantly.

Shit.

I wasn't expecting that.

I keep my chin high, my shoulders down, and my face impassive. If he's trying to get a reaction out of me with that comment, he's going to be waiting a long time. My silence is seemingly mistaken for submission as he smirks, inching toward me.

He doesn't stop until we're toe-to-toe, forcing me to tilt my head back to maintain his gaze, a power play if I ever saw one. Hands touch my waist from behind, my back arching at the touch as Gray steps in just as close.

"The punishment can be saved for Ryker. Right now, I think we all deserve a taste of ecstasy," Gray murmurs, lips brushing against my neck as he speaks. I have to fight against the need to close my eyes, determined to watch Emmett's every move.

My Viking reaches behind him to pull his tee over his head, discarding the white material without another glance as he looms over me. I didn't want to be the one to reach out to him first, but the scar that tears down his chest lures me close, my finger running delicately over the jagged skin.

The gasp from his lips washes over me, and combined with Gray's touch at my waist, I'm ready to detonate without a push of a button.

"Pain or pleasure, Emmett?" I ask, feeling delicate between them as he grins.

"Both. Always both."

*Yes. Fucking. Please.*

Before I can utter a word, Gray grabs my waist tighter and lifts me into the air. Just like the other day, he takes a seat on the sofa, pulling me down on top of him, but this time, it's different. There are less layers of clothing between us and a level of tension between the three of us that could be cut with a knife.

There's no distracting from this. Nothing that could separate us and we all know it.

Gray parts my legs, hooking his ankles around me to leave me exposed to Emmett, while his arms wrap around mine. I'm helpless, at his mercy, and I love it. My thighs clench at the sound of Emmett's belt escaping the loops, my gaze fixed on the motion until it's being brought toward me.

"Hands."

I don't get a chance to consider his order as Gray offers my wrists up to him. Fuck, that's hot. I keep my gaze locked on Emmett's as he tightens the black leather around my wrists, pulling tight and securing them together. He leaves the strap to fall loose, offering it to Gray who instantly takes it and pulls my arms up above my head.

Fuck.

The irritation that's been bubbling in my veins is angry at the restriction, but the possibility of what they could do to me like this makes it bearable. I want to come, I want to find release from the weight on my shoulders that I can't shift on my own.

Emmett's eyes settle on my chest, my nipples pleading for attention as he kicks off his shoes and drops his jeans and boxers.

My mouth is dry, my need leaving me wordless, my next breath lodged in my throat as he cuts the distance between us, ripping at the lace encasing my breasts before taking my nipple into his mouth. One swipe, two swipes, three... bite.

"Fuck," I grunt, looking at the painful spot, but I can't see a thing as he soothes the mark with his tongue.

I'm so beyond screwed it's embarrassing.

Releasing my nipple with a pop, he looks up at me with a wicked glint in his eyes. He's nowhere near done with me yet, and the way Gray stretches my arms further, peppering kisses along my throat, I know there's more to come.

Emmett's mouth crushes mine in the next breath, claiming me as I desperately want to grab for him but my hands are restricted. I feel a bite at my hips, the material of my panties pinching my flesh, before they tear. The telltale sound in my ears is all too familiar as I sink my teeth into Emmett's bottom lip.

When he leans back, lips red from my mark, I gasp for my next breath before I find my words. "You owe me new panties. Actually, new everything. I can't keep saying this and getting nothing. That was my last pair," I grumble, and he smirks.

"I'll keep you stocked up, Snowflake. Don't worry." I'm about to tell him to put his money where his mouth is, but his lips drop to my core.

"Fuck, Emmett," I moan, my back arching at the touch. I feel like I'm going to snap in two from the way he has my body bending with Gray's assistance.

His tongue swirls around my clit, making my head fall back on Gray's shoulder as I instinctively try to grind against him. Just when I think he's going to thrust inside of me with his fingers, he quickly disappears.

Glaring at the fucker, I tear my wrists from Gray's grip in a quick move as I band my fastened wrists around

Emmett's head. "Don't fucking tease, asshole."

His eyes are wide with surprise, but it's Gray who speaks first. "How the fuck did you get out of my hold?"

It's my turn to grin between them as I pull Emmett's face closer. "This is fun because I want it to be. If I felt like I couldn't escape, I wouldn't be wearing this belt at all right now. So, are we done teasing?"

"Yes, Ma'am," Emmett says, and I lift my arms over his head again. He rises, hands on his hips as he stares down at me. "Gray, I think our lady has ideas of how she wants this to go."

Gray grabs my waist again, lifting me in the air as he rises with me before placing me on my feet between them. "What is it you want, Scar?" he asks, fingers ghosting over my stomach as he stands behind me, body wrapping around mine.

"I want to be filled and exploding as soon as possible," I admit, desperate to get straight to it.

"How does that look to you, Sweet Cheeks?" Gray asks.

Wetting my parched lips, I take a deep breath. "I liked it when Ryker and Emmett took me at the same time. Just like that." My words hang in the air for what feels like an eternity before Gray steps away from me. I'm not sure what's going on until he reaches into the small drawer on the coffee table and turns to face me with a sexy-as-fuck grin.

"You have lube in the lounge?" Emmett asks, sounding as surprised as I am.

"Ever since she came in here and destroyed me at my favorite game. Had to be prepared," he replies with a wiggle to his eyebrows and I grin. The humor lasts seconds at most before the sexual tension creeps to the forefront of everyone's minds again. "You want me to take your ass, Scar?"

I nod, words failing me as he strips. Not one of us has a single thread of clothing on but it feels warmer than ever, the need inside of me heating my bones along with the caresses of their eyes over my skin.

Emmett moves first, taking the lead as he drops to the floor with his back pressed against the sofa. "Take a seat, Snowflake." I'm moving before he even finishes with my nickname.

Placing a knee on either side of his head, he tilts back to look up at me, mouth poised beneath my pussy, just as eager as I am. Using the back of the sofa as leverage, I dip my hips and drag my clit over his beard before his tongue tips out and makes me groan.

I repeat the motion, getting lower each time, before he grips my thighs and pulls me down so I'm firmly sitting on his face as he eats me like a man starved. He pats my ass, gentler than I'm expecting, but I understand why moments later when I feel a fresh set of hands running over the globes of my ass.

Gray.

He spreads my cheeks, teasing my heating skin before he disappears for a second, only to return with the click of the lube bottle. Emmett doesn't let me stop fucking his face as Gray drizzles lube over my ass, focusing on the trail leading to my hole.

Anticipation has me tensing while excitement has my hips tipping to offer him even better access as I ride Emmett's face. Gray draws small circles around my hole, teasing me as Emmett somehow manages to run his tongue in time with him. Neither of them can see the other's moves, but they both know how to play my body perfectly.

I'm a raging inferno in my core, my veins heating with every stroke from both of them. Gray dips his finger inside me, stretching my tight ring as I climax all over Emmett's face. His fingers dig deeper into my thighs, bruising my flesh as he tastes every drop of me.

Tumbling forward, I prop myself up on the sofa as Emmett moves from under me, while Gray continues to tease my limbs. The second finger stretches me further, turning my body to molten lava once more as I fade from my orgasm and instantly reignite, ready to go again.

"She's ready," Emmett states, knowing my body

better than me it seems as Gray retreats, pressing a kiss to the bottom of my spine as I sob with need. "Come on, Snowflake. Let me hold you," Emmett offers out his hand, and I take it, standing on putty legs for a second as he takes a seat on the sofa and pulls me into his lap. "Are you okay?"

"I'm perfect," I reply without even having to consider my response, and he smiles at me.

"You really fucking are," he replies, pressing his lips to mine and I taste my own juices on his tongue.

Fuck.

"I don't know which God sent you to us, Scar, but I'm ready to be a religious man for it," Gray states, pressing kisses down my spine.

Emmett lifts me slightly, lining up my core with his cock before I slowly sink down his length. The remnants of my orgasm makes it easier around his thick and long length as I take him in, inch by glorious inch. Once I'm fully seated, he swirls his hips slightly, making me gasp, before he palms my ass and pulls out until only his tip remains.

"Your turn, Gray," Emmett murmurs, his pupils almost black as he stares at me.

Gray grabs my waist, holding me in position as I try to keep my body relaxed. My breath lodges in my throat when his cock presses against my entrance, breaching the tight muscles not wanting him to enter. I remember what Emmett said last time and I slowly push back on him, gasping as Gray stretches me further and further until he's deep inside of me.

"Fuck," I mumble, head lolling forward as I try to calm the trembles running through my veins. Emmett grabs the strap of the belt at my wrists, lifting them over his head so we're closer as I feel him inching deeper into my pussy.

Holy shit.

Slowly, Gray retreats as Emmett thrusts inside of me, alternating the movement between them both as I drift into an alternate universe of complete sexual domination. The feel of their cocks passing one another inside of me, such a thin barrier between them, makes me cry out with ecstasy.

Gray. Emmett. Gray. Emmett. Gray. Emmett.

In. Out. In. Out. In. Out.

I cry out, my body tingling as they devour my body. Ripples of pleasure take over me as I climax between them, my body self-combusting as I groan with raw fucking joy.

Their movements begin to stutter as I'm held in place between them, their cocks filling me completely and dragging out every gasp of my orgasm. Emmett's cock fills me first, his groan sending another shiver down my spine before Gray follows us both off the ledge.

He rests his head against my back, panting for breath, while I feel Emmett slowly untie my wrists. Euphoria is the most beautiful place. I know where I am and who I'm with, but I sure as shit couldn't tell you right now why I needed this feeling to begin with.

Gray lifts me from Emmett's lap, pulling me into his as he takes a seat beside his friend. I relax in his hold, my eyelids closing as I relish in the feel of his fingers trailing through my hair soothingly.

"I think I love you, Sweet Cheeks," he whispers, and I laugh.

"No, you love my cunt, Blondie," I retort, my heart racing like crazy in my chest at his words.

"Nah, that's just a bonus."

Prying my eyes open, I look up at him in confusion. "What even makes you say that?" I dare myself to ask.

He shrugs. "There's an overwhelming feeling in my chest like I've never felt before, and it's only when I'm around you or thinking about you. I feel the smallest sliver of it when I take a moment to appreciate my mom, but fuck, nothing like this, of this scale. It's consuming."

I chance a glance at Emmett, but he gives nothing away as he looks at Gray too. "I mean… it could just be trapped wind," I hedge, making him chuckle.

"Or, it's because I love you." He presses his lips to

my forehead, sealing his words to me.

My chest swells, unshed tears prickling the back of my lids as I blink up at him.

"Don't do that."

"Do what?" The confusion is clear in his tone, and I offer him the only response I can muster.

"Make me want to live forever."

# TWENTY THREE

## Emmett

I didn't think it was possible to feel closer to the woman lying beside me, but I was wrong. Looking down at her sleeping form has my heart in a vice, Gray's words to her earlier playing on repeat in my head. I want to say he's ridiculous, that he has no idea what he's talking about, but the air is different in the club, and it's not because of the shift in roles.

It's her.

I don't know how or why, but admitting it in my head makes my heart rattle faster against the prison it's locked inside.

When I stroke a loose lock of hair back off her face, she doesn't stir. Sandwiched between me and Gray, she looks peaceful. The usual tension that radiates from her no longer exists in this moment. It's almost like looking at a different woman entirely, but whichever version of herself she is, the same thing remains.

*She's mine. Ours.*

At the thought, my gaze drifts to her arm, the noticeable black ink on her skin making a grin tip the corner of my mouth.

"What are you thinking about?" Her raspy voice rings in my ears.

"Getting more of my ink on your skin," I admit, not denying the truth running through my head as she hums in response.

"Hmm, I like the sound of that." Her eyelashes flutter as she attempts to open them fully, before her bright eyes meet mine.

"You do?"

"Uh-huh." She nods slightly, sinking her teeth into her bottom lip as I bite back a groan.

This fucking woman.

"What are you two whispering about?" Gray asks groggily, adjusting the way he's lying so he's completely plastered to her back.

"Emmett wants to jab me with his prick again." The grin on her face is priceless, searing into mine as she winks at me at the same time Gray gasps.

"Fuck, man. Already? She's going to be sore as fuck, but if that's what the lady wants," he murmurs, peppering kisses along her bare shoulder.

"She means with my tattoo gun. You idiot," I grumble, swiping a hand down my face at this guy's thought process.

"Oh… in her—"

"Shut the fuck up," I interrupt, not prepared for how crazy he can really get. I reach across Scarlett and smack the side of his head while she chuckles. "Either wake the fuck up properly or roll over and go back to sleep because I can't deal with you in this state."

Scarlett's chuckle turns into a full laugh, lighting my soul as she wraps her arms around my neck.

Gray doesn't miss a beat, moving the extra inch with her. He tickles her side, making her roll to her back with a squeak as he rises up onto his elbow to peer down at her.

"So, what are we getting?" he asks, wagging his eyebrows at her.

"We?"

"Yeah, you and me. And this asshole, if he dares to let one of us tattoo him back," he clarifies with a wink.

"Like… matching?" Scarlett's eyebrows pinch as she looks between us. I know what it means in the club to have matching tattoos, but she doesn't. If she did, it would be more than the gathering of her brows that we would get in response.

I'm not opposed to the idea though. Not at all.

"Definitely matching," Gray murmurs in response.

"So, what are you thinking?" Her eyes glimmer with excitement. She goes to open her mouth, but I quickly place a hand over her lips to cut her off.

"Whatever you do, don't ask him to surprise you like you said to me, Snowflake. He'll have his name etched into your forehead and we both know it."

Her gaze slips to Gray and mine follows, and all he offers in response is a shrug. He definitely fucking considered it for sure. I stroke my fingers down her cheek, over the pulse at her neck, until I'm grazing her collarbone.

Scarlett lifts her free arm into the air, drawing all our attention to the ink already engraved in her skin. The flames on the bike lick along her skin like a dream, begging me to mark her again and again.

A knock halts our conversation as Shift sticks his head around the door. Gray quickly grabs the cover to shield Scarlett's exposed chest so his brother can't see, but Shift spins around, offering her a level of privacy no one else would get here unless they were an old lady.

"Sorry. Ryker's called a meeting."

"When?" I ask, internally groaning because I know what he's going to say before I hear the word.

"Now."

"Can't he wait until morning?" Gray grumbles, flopping his arm down on the bed like a child, and Shift chuckles.

"I'll tell him you're too preoccupied," Shift replies, glancing back over at his brother with a smirk.

"Fuck off. We'll be there in two minutes." Gray launches a pillow at his brother, but it's met with the door as he slams it shut behind him.

Fucker.

Sighing, I grab Scarlett's chin as I look at her. "Think about what you want, Snowflake. Whatever tattoo *you* want, and I'll take great pleasure in making it happen," I state, pressing a kiss to her lips before climbing from the bed.

"Dicks shouldn't be that fucking beautiful," she grumbles dreamily, too distracted by my stiff cock to respond to what I just said.

Wrapping my knuckles around my length, I offer a tug or two for her to watch, before I dress.

"Party poopers," she says with a pout when Gray and I both stand at the foot of the bed with our cuts and combat boots on.

"Think on it, Scar, we'll be back soon," Gray murmurs, blowing a kiss in her direction before stomping his foot. "Fuck, hurry up, Emmett. The quicker we get out there, the quicker we can get back in here."

He's never spoken truer words.

I collapse in the seat beside Gray, who looks as inconvenienced as I feel, but the club is our life, just as much as Scarlett seems to be becoming, and our presence is non-negotiable. We're the first here despite our reluctance, and it's fun to watch the expressions on everyone's faces as they step into the room.

Church is our sanctuary, our foundation, and a traitor has held a seat at our holy table. My hands clench, nostrils flaring as anger reignites within me.

Shift steps in with a clipped smile on his face, his brows knitted as he takes a seat across from Gray. He eyes his brother before leaning back in his seat. "I get why you guys did what you did today, but I'm not going to deny that I'm disappointed to find you didn't trust me, brother."

Gray swipes a hand down his face, sighing as he takes in his brother's words. "I get it, Shift, I do. I never doubted you, not once. Shit, even Scarlett insisted you were innocent, but—"

"Tell me how she knew and I didn't again?" he asks. His tone pisses me off, and I lean forward in my seat. He must be able to sense that he hit a fucking nerve because he quickly waves his hands in surrender. "Shit, not like that. I have her back. Always. Right now, likely before yours, Gray, I just don't understand why she was involved in the takedown of the club's mole, yet she's not here at the table now."

Well… fuck.

That's a question I wasn't expecting. I don't even know how I'm supposed to answer that. Scrubbing at my beard, I consider his words, but the moment is broken when Cash steps into Church with the prospects hot on his tail. He offers a nod in our direction, rounding the table to take his spot without saying a word. If he's as pissed as Shift then he doesn't vocalize it.

Thank God. It's the way of the club, if the order comes from above then it doesn't mean you have to be in the know. It also means there are invisible tests that we're challenged with without ever knowing. Unfortunately, this time, there was a mole to weasel out, and the task was revealed.

"Anybody up for watching the game on the big screen tonight?" Liam, the newest prospect, asks, rubbing his hands together excitedly, and I quickly back out of the conversation.

They all mumble amongst themselves about who they think is going to win this season, but my focus is on Gray as he leans in to murmur, "What tattoo do you think she will go for?"

Fuck. "Don't talk about that shit in here, man." *Not when it's going to get my dick hard.*

"Shut up, Em. I need to be thinking about this. It has to mean something," he pushes, oblivious to the rest of the room.

"You have to tell her what it actually fucking means first." I give him a pointed stare, but he doesn't seem to notice or care.

"Well, I thought if we were going to tell her, you would have said something back there, but you didn't. And let's be honest, you're the bigger man here, so if anyone was going to be open about it, I thought it would have been you."

I want to smack him around the head again. Stupid fool.

"What are you two whispering about in the corner?"

I look up to see Axel and Ryker in the doorway, the latter raising his eyebrow at us with curiosity, but I shrug in response. Blood coats their skin, their hair, their clothes. Crimson dotting them from head to toe, a reminder of what happened down in the basement.

"They were talking about Scarlett," Shift announces, earning himself a deathly glare, but he's not looking to notice. Fucker.

"About what?" Ryker adds, taking his seat. Everyone watches him, but the state of Axel is what holds everyone's attention.

"I don't know, but I do know she's not sitting here, even though she had a helping hand in finding our mole. What's that about?" Shift folds his arms over his chest, like he's mad in her honor or something, and I start to panic.

Does she want to be at the table? A woman here by choice has never happened before, I'm not above making it happen, but she didn't seem mad when we left.

Fuck.

I need to be better at this communication shit so I understand where her head is at. I know she was pissed she missed out on torturing the fucker, but that seemed like it was for more personal reasons than anything else.

My mind runs a mile a minute as Ryker takes the question in his stride. "Scarlett's not here because she hasn't asked to be."

"Do you really think she would ask? She doesn't need us, but yet again, we're relying on her, needing her more, and what are we offering her as gratitude other than an on-demand dick?"

Gray scoffs. "It's good dick though."

A few of the prospects chuckle at their interaction, but there's clearly something brewing under Shift's skin with regards to Scarlett, and I can't decide if I like it or not. Ryker must notice the same thing because he leans forward, bracing his arms on the table as he looks him dead in the eyes.

"What aren't you saying, Shift? I'm not in the mood to read between the lines."

Shift shakes his head in annoyance, before he looks back up at our Prez with a sigh. "Everyone seems to forget that I knew this woman before she fell into your lap. She's worth more than being used at your will."

Gray swore that he discussed Scarlett with Shift and he was adamant there was nothing between them. I'm going to continue to cling to that fact right now, trusting my brother, but he definitely cares for her in some way.

Axel clears his throat, breaking through the tension at the table as everyone looks in his direction. "So, Euro was a mole." He takes extra care to emphasize the *was*, glancing at his blood-stained hands as he speaks. "If anyone was working with him and still remains at this table, then talk now. This is the one moment of exemption from retaliation, otherwise forever hold your tongue and feel my wrath when the truth is revealed."

His words hang in the air, but no one speaks. Meeting the eyes of each and every person at the table, I don't see anything out of the ordinary, but I also wouldn't have believed that Euro was double-crossing us. So at this stage, I don't feel like I really want to judge.

"I can only assume that we won't have long before they realize their inside man is gone, and we need to figure shit out so we can use this to our advantage." Ryker's shoulders bunch with tension, his eyes darkening with a mixture of anger and exhaustion.

I don't think this was how he expected his rise to the throne would go, but if anyone can face it and lead us to victory, it's him.

Taking strength from him, I slap my hand down on the table and look at every single prospect in here. They wouldn't usually be in our meetings, but under the circumstances, I understand why the call was made. "Rookies, it's your time to shine. The seats you're warming now could be yours permanently if you're willing to make it happen," I declare, watching each of their eyes widen with excitement.

Opportunities for prospects to become patched members are up for grabs.

"What's our plan of action then, boss?" Liam asks, nodding, but any response from Ryker is interrupted as the doors to Church swing open in a flurry.

Scarlett stands in the open space, eyes wild as she meets Ryker's gaze.

"What is it?" he asks, understanding the urgency. If anyone knows not to interrupt a meeting, it's her. It has to be something, especially when she's wearing a t-shirt that barely covers her ass and nothing else.

"It's Kincaid. He's here."

# TWENTY FOUR

## *Gray*

My chair scrapes across the floor behind me in time with Ryker's, Axel's, Emmett's, and Shift's. The others don't move, waiting for their orders.

Irritation claws at my veins. Kincaid is a bigger dick than I expected. What motherfucker continues to show up here? A pest that's not going to go away unless you put that motherfucker down.

"I'm trying to figure out how you know that from Emmett's bed, Sweet Cheeks." I quirk a brow at her, trying to keep the mood light and allow everyone a second to focus on our unwanted guest with a clear head.

I quirk a brow at her, but she sticks her middle finger up at me. "I'm not just some sweet pussy that lies in bed all day waiting to be touched. Besides, I was hungry. And when I looked around for Maggie, I found this in the bar area instead." She waves a cell phone in the air.

"Where is Kincaid right now?" Ryker interrupts us, which earns him an eye roll from our woman.

"He's on the other side of the compound gates waiting for them to be opened."

"How the fuck do you know that?" I ask, losing my damn mind over the situation.

"Speak to him like he's a toddler, Snowflake," Emmett interjects, patting my shoulder. "He still can't piece together how you got this information."

Despite his asshole approach, he's not fucking wrong, so I reluctantly nod.

"It's Euro's cell. Sorry, I'll be more specific. It's Euro's cell phone that doesn't have a passcode, with a message from Kincaid stating that he needs him to open the gates." A ping sounds out around the room as she stops talking, making her glance down at the device in her hand. "Oh, he has no patience at all. He wants him to hurry up." She waves the cell for everyone to see, and I whirl around to Ryker.

"What's our approach?"

No one is ping-ponging their eyes between Scarlett and I now, they're all focused on our Prez. "Let him in," Ryker announces calmly, slamming the gavel down before taking a step away from the table.

"What?" Liam asks, clearly not catching up as quickly

as me, but Axel explains.

"We keep up the ruse. Check how Euro would usually respond to an order like that and do the same. Let's let these fuckers in."

Ryker twirls his finger in the air and the remainder of the members still sitting rise to their feet. We all pile out of Church without another word. It's not until we're halfway toward the double doors, Ruthless Bitches watching our every move in confusion, that Axel stops mid-step beside Ryker, raises his hand and holds his palm out in Scarlett's direction.

"Not you."

She rears her head back back like she's been slapped in the face as Emmett inches closer. Ryker looks back over his shoulder, glancing between the two of them as Scarlett folds her arms over her chest.

"What? Why?"

We each turn to Axel expectantly, and he thankfully doesn't leave everyone waiting for his response. But it's not aimed at me, the group, or even Ryker. He's looking Scarlett dead in the eyes. "He doesn't get eyes on you. Ever again if I have it my way, but at least while I'm here, that fucker doesn't have the right to see you with his own two eyes."

She gulps. Assessing him for what feels like an eternity as they communicate with their eyes only. It's a secret.

There's a reason behind this that I have no clue about. One that I very much want to know, but also fear at the same time if it invokes an outburst like this from Axel.

"Scar…" Emmett murmurs, wanting to check she's okay with this, but she doesn't look away from Axel.

"I'm not going to just sit on the sidelines, Axel. That's not who I am." There's restraint in her voice, like she's holding back whatever thoughts or feelings she has as the rest of the club stares at them.

"I know you're not. That's why you're going to run out to the garage with Gray, load up, find a good position and be our eyes in the sky. Is that ok with you, Reaper?"

She nods, then turns to me, the rest of the pack instantly starts to move, the hold the pair of them had on the group dissolving as her determined eyes settle on mine.

"Load me up, Blondie."

There's so much I could say.

So. Fucking. Much.

But instead, I take her hand in mine and run.

---

The rough stone roof of the garage bites into my skin as I lay on my front side-by-side with Scarlett. We have a clear view of the yard from the entry gates to the club doors, and the second Kincaid rolls his bikes down the path, she stiffens beside me. Her grip on the sniper rifle tightens, her eagerness to put a bullet through his brain clear.

She centers my cell phone between us, a connection linked with Emmett's so we have audio as well as the visual as everything unfolds. There's a lot I don't know here, which makes me feel helpless, so I go with my usual distraction tactic.

"I'm noticing a pattern," I say, looking down my lens to get a good view of my brothers as they slowly stroll out of the clubhouse with disgruntled looks on their faces.

"Which is what?" Scarlett asks, barely moving as she speaks.

"Every time we're alone, a gun is involved."

A smile cracks on her lips, her eyes moving away from the scope as she finally looks my way. I've broken through the surface. Despite her killer vibe being hot as fuck, I love being able to get through to her soft center.

"I mean, guns are the key to my heart. I'm not shocked." She grins at me, a carefree shimmer in her eyes.

That's my Scarlett. Not the legend that is the Grim Reaper or the defensive hard core bitch who will slay anyone on the spot. I offer her the truth. Before I can think better of it, I sigh.

"Matching tattoos would claim you as my old lady. That's why I was pushing for it before."

She doesn't move for a moment, her eyes squinting as

her tongue peeks out, assessing me. "Why didn't you say that before?"

I can't read her thought process or feelings, so I decide to continue with the honesty and lay it all out there for her. "Because I felt like the only way I could get you to agree to it was by dealing with the consequences after."

"Agree to what exactly?"

Wow. She's really going to make me spell it out. Wiping a hand down my face, I go to respond, but the voices through the cell phone interrupt me.

"Kincaid." Ryker sounds calm and collected, and we quickly move back to our weapons.

"I haven't heard very much about you paying your dues, Ryker. Should I be worried?"

He's so sure of himself, of the presence he believes he controls, but he doesn't realize he's no longer dealing with the same group of Ruthless Brothers that he was weeks ago. Scarlett taking out Banner is a sure sign that taking out a leader only offers someone else more ruthless to take their place.

Which is why Kincaid won't die today. The Devil's Brutes seem to have a reputation that offers everything to them on a platter. But that ends with us.

There are six men with him today, but they all have their backs to us so I can't tell if they're highly ranked within the club. Assholes.

"I don't recall confirming any payment, Kincaid," Ryker says with a sigh, bored with the conversation until he speaks again.

"Where's little Scarlett Reeves at?" He glances around my brothers, hoping to catch a glimpse of her. It's not Scarlett that stiffens this time though, it's Axel and me.

What does this motherfucker want with our woman?

"Are you here for anything important? Or are we done?" Emmett says, ignoring his question, but Kincaid doesn't take the bait.

"She's rather important, wouldn't you say?" I catch a glimpse of his face as he smirks, but it's dark and sinister, making my blood boil instantly.

Axel scoffs, folding his arms over his chest as he stares the Brutes down. "Club whores are just that, aren't they? We don't know where any of them are, Scarlett whatever her name is, included."

I quickly turn to look to my left, assessing Scarlett. "He doesn't mean that, Scar," I ramble, fearful she'll believe his words, but she simply shrugs in response.

"Even if he did, it wouldn't matter."

She doesn't seem angry or upset, just focused on the enemy.

I underestimate her at every turn. I should stop doing that.

"That's true, Sergeant, but you and I both know she's

339

more than that. Or is she keeping secrets?" Kincaid takes a step toward Axel who drops his arms to his side, ready to take him on, but he stops a step or two short of being toe-to-toe with our crazy man.

Axel glances at Ryker, his nose wrinkling as he shakes his head. "I have no fucking clue who he's talking about, Prez, but it's boring the fuck out of me."

Kincaid laughs, his men mimicking him as my grip on the trigger of the gun tightens.

"Maybe if you don't supply me with the guns and money, I'll take something else in payment instead."

Emmett, Ryker, and Axel try to act unfazed, but I can sense it. I know them through and through, and the subtlest of moves make it clear that his words have them on edge.

"You're not taking payment from the Ruthless Brothers in any form. The quicker you realize that, the quicker we can get on with our lives," Ryker states, moving to stand beside Axel to stare Kincaid down. "Now get the fuck off my property before I remove you."

The guy to Kincaid's left pulls a gun from his hip and aims it at Ryker instantly. Before I can even consider my own response, Scarlett pulls the trigger. Her bullet sails through the air with precision, penetrating the gun-wielding Brute's arm in the next breath. He drops the weapon with a cry, blood gushing from his wound as shouts ring out and everyone looks around.

"Hot. As. Fuck. Sweet Cheeks," I murmur, hearing a little chuckle in response.

Axel's voice rings out through the cell phone over everyone else's hollers. "That was a warning shot, please continue, we enjoy a good blood bath."

Kincaid lifts his arm in the air, and a moment later, a Ruthless Brother's prospect drops to his knees with a cry of agony. Adjusting my lens, I spot the blood pouring from his leg wound instantly, and the curse from Scarlett tells me she sees it too.

"I have eyes on you too, fucker. Please, try me. I bathe in crimson." Kincaid cuts the distance between him and Axel, a show of his own power as my brother remains unfazed. When he doesn't immediately get the response from our sergeant at arms that he wants, he starts to look around at the other members standing behind my brothers.

Dragging my scope as far as I can reach, I search for nearby spots where there could be a shooter, but I keep coming up blank. *Where the fuck are they?*

"Do you have eyes on their eagle?" I ask, and Scarlett quickly grunts in disapproval.

"Nope. Nothing. I don't understand it," she murmurs, shuffling beside me before focusing on the group again. "It's like he's searching for Euro," she adds, and I nod in agreement even though she's not looking.

"He's going to come up empty-handed unless he starts

digging a fucking hole," I grunt, earning me another huff of laughter from her lips.

"I'll be taking what's mine in forty-eight hours, Ryker. Come hell or high water, I'll enjoy watching you crumble as I take her for myself."

Scarlett stiffens beside me this time as his words process through my mind. Clarity isn't needed though, because in the next breath he turns, and faces us head-on, staring directly at the roof of the garage.

"Let me shoot him," Scarlett breathes. "I have a clear shot."

"And their eyes in the sky will shoot Ryker, Axel, or Emmett, it's too risky," I say, hating the truth on my tongue. I want to watch his demise as much as she does.

"Fuck." She dips her head down from the lens, hiding her face in her hands as the rumble of bikes sound out.

Fuck indeed.

# TWENTY FIVE

## Scarlett

My bare feet scuff on the ground as I land from the garage roof. Anger courses through my veins at that motherfucker's audacity. I could have killed him there and then. I almost fucking did until Gray reminded me that he had eyes in the sky too.

I couldn't risk Ryker, Axel, or Emmett. I couldn't. And now he likely pieced that fact together. There's someone here worth protecting, and he'll enjoy using that against us.

I head toward the crowd outside, but I barely get two steps before Gray stops me in my tracks. "Sweet Cheeks, you haven't got any panties on. You're not going back to the group without any."

There's amusement in his eyes, but the seriousness to his tone tells me he's being real as shit. "I haven't got any left since you guys keep tearing them carelessly," I state, planting my hands on my hips as I glare at him. It doesn't have the desired effect though, he grins instead of fearing me.

"Come on." He drops his arm over my shoulder as he turns me to the rear entrance to the building. I bask in his hold for a moment, taking the reprieve before we have to join the others and rehash everything that was said.

With Gray, when I'm in his arms, I'm just Scarlett. Young, carefree, and full of hope. He does that to me. That's what's been playing in my mind since he admitted what the matching tattoos would mean. The fact that he thought he could only have me completely by playing tricks blows my mind. He doesn't realize his impact.

He's not the most alpha, or the most demanding, or even the biggest asshole, because lord knows I'm attracted to that too. But he's the most naturally calm, playful, and heartwarming. Three things I didn't believe existed until I met him.

The moment has passed now though, and I don't know how to say any of it out loud, so instead I follow him to his room where he offers me a pair of his black boxers. I murmur my thanks, caught up in my thoughts as I step into them and turn the waistband.

"How do you look like a beauty queen in my boxers, your hair messy from the wind, and not an inch of make-up on?" I raise a brow at his question, unsure if it was actually meant for me or just to himself. He steps forward without missing a beat, and presses a kiss to my lips that's so gentle I feel lighthearted. "We'll take you shopping as soon as possible. I'll even buy extra so I can carry on tearing through that lace around my favorite kitty-cat," he whispers against my lips, distracting me.

"But for now, there's a prospect I need to take a look at," I add reluctantly, running my thumb over his bottom lip as I take a step back.

"Thank you," he breathes, taking my hand in his and leading the way.

Stepping into the bar area, my eyebrows quirk when I hear the commotion coming from the Ruthless Bitches, but we fight our way through the crowd to find Emmett standing at the doors leading into Church.

"There you are, Snowflake. We need your help." He points over his shoulder, indicating for me to follow, and I reluctantly release Gray's hand to step inside.

Another day, another Ruthless Brother bleeding on the Church table. The med kit and my tools from when I helped Euro are beside the newly injured prospect as I move toward him. Axel and Ryker are sitting in their chairs, solemn as I assess everything.

"What's your name?" I ask, slipping my hands into a pair of latex gloves.

"Fuck, Titan," he grunts, wincing at the pain coming from his leg.

"Well, fuck Titan, this is going to hurt like a bitch. Have you got some liquor on hand already?" I ask, getting straight to the point. There's no use lying to him. The burn of a bullet wound is real. The feel of the alcohol I'm about to pour on it is questionably worse. He nods with a huff as I inspect his wound.

"What's the plan with Kincaid?" I ask, glancing over Titan's leg to meet Ryker's gaze, but it's Axel who responds.

"I know the prospects were in here earlier but we don't usually discuss this shit in front of them. Fully-fledged members only."

It makes sense for sure, but I still snicker at his crap. "You say that like this guy didn't just take a damn bullet for this club. Do you need a deeper look yourself to confirm? He's bleeding for his brothers."

"So did Euro and look at him," Ryker bites back, and I shake my head.

"No, that fucker bled for himself." Looking up at the prospect, I pause the pain I'm about to put him through. "Are you a mole?"

His jaw goes slack, his eyes clouded with a hint of anger as he grunts, "No."

"Are you anything other than a Ruthless Brother?" I

push, cocking a brow at him.

"No."

"Why are you here?"

I'm fully aware I'm interrogating him like this is my fucking club, but someone has to do it. The mold needs changing whether they like the fact or not.

"Because this is all I have. This is my family."

"This guy is either really good at dishing out bullshit or he's on to a winner," I state, glancing at Ryker once more before returning to my task.

A few moments pass before a deep sigh echoes around the room. "I do hate it when you're right like this," Ryker grumbles, irritation and reluctance clear in his tone.

I shrug, a smirk teasing my lips. "Meh, you'll get used to it."

Gray chuckles, and the tension dwindles as I release a breath, but before I can try and ask again, a question is aimed my way.

"Do we take his threat seriously?"

I glance at Emmett, who looks at me expectantly for an answer. "The reality is you haven't taken any of them seriously so far, and look at how many lives have been lost already."

It sucks, but it's the truth, and there's no use lying about it.

"He's unpredictable and I'm unsure on how to handle

him." Ryker pushes a hand through his hair.

"He would also be dead if I could have pulled the trigger before."

"Why didn't you?" Axel asks, but I keep my eyes fixed on the bloody wound in front of me instead of making eye contact. I shrug, hoping that will be enough, but Gray explains for me.

"Because she didn't want their sniper to take out one of you guys."

Uh, now I sound like a pussy and I fucking hate it.

"Thank you," Ryker murmurs, pulling my attention to him as he looks at me sincerely.

I quickly dip my head back down and try to smother my feelings and the warm gooeyness inside at those two words. This is what I get for never living with words of praise or sincerity. It leaves me open and vulnerable to small niceties on their part which shouldn't mean as much as they do.

"So, he wants guns and money," Emmett states as if he's almost toying with the idea, but Ryker quickly shuts him down.

"He isn't getting shit."

"If he doesn't, then he comes for her." The gruff tone comes from Axel as he points a finger in my direction.

"Over my dead fucking body," Gray bites, and my core clenches at their stance on me.

That leaves us with no game plan though. Nothing to give us the edge. Sighing, I wipe the wound one last time, before lining it up to be stitched. "Then what's our move? Because right now, we sure as shit don't have one."

Someone had to say it, I'm more than willing for it to be me.

"We could try and use the Euro situation to our advantage," Emmett offers, and I nod.

"But how? Think of the bigger picture. We also have to consider the fact that he didn't see Euro in the line up earlier too."

Silence drapes over the room, before a knock sounds at the door. Emmett swings it open with a hint of irritation until he sees that it's Maggie. She waltzes in with a wide smile and her usual warmth, like the world wasn't falling apart in these four walls moments ago.

"Oh good, you're all here. I'm throwing a birthday party tonight." She beams, but I can tell by the way she plants her hands on her hips that she's preparing for an objection or two.

"For who?" I ask, entertaining her even though a party isn't really the best idea right now.

"Shift's."

Oops. I should probably wish him a happy birthday when I see him.

"Now isn't really the time though, Mom," Gray states,

and she waves him off.

"You sound just like your brother. But you little shits forget I've been around longer than you all. I know exactly when it is and isn't the time for anything and everything. And I promise you, you're going to be approaching all of this mess with fresh heads after some time to let loose."

"But—"

"No buts. None. Eight o'clock, bring a fucking smile."

---

"You shouldn't look cute like that, but here you are."

I roll my eyes at Emily's comment. I point-blank refused my usual makeover tonight. After the day's events, I don't have the energy to put on all of the make-up and the pretenses it comes with. I'm too stressed over the mess with the Brutes to even really give this my attention, but whatever Maggie says, Maggie gets.

It's almost amusing, watching grown men mumble their agreement and do as they're told. But she's a force to be reckoned with.

"Next, you're going to tell me I could wear a black plastic bag and get away with it." She chuckles at my words.

"Well, thank you for not refusing to come altogether," she teases, hip-checking me as we stand side-by-side looking at the mirror.

I'm still in Gray's boxers, with a pair of denim shorts over them and a white tank tucked in with my combat boots. French braids track down my back and there's not a speck of make-up on my face. Emily, on the other hand, looks like the epitome of sunshine. Her blonde hair is in space buns, her make-up subtle but complimenting her eyes perfectly, while she wears a daisy-patterned summer dress with a white tee underneath.

Angel vs demon.

Sun vs moon.

Yin vs yang.

Any way to describe opposites would work when looking at us, yet she is another positive impact on my life since I came here. Another complete contrast to the life I knew before. I'll start referring to myself as the holy one soon. Life before coming here; Ice Reapers. Life after; Ruthless Brothers. IR/RB. My life will now be tracked like Jesus.

"What are you thinking about?" Emily asks, stepping away to grab her purse, and I shake my head.

"What drink I should start the night with," I say, heading for the door as she waves me off.

I follow her down the hall to the bar area, the music getting louder with every step until she swings the door open and fully immerses us in the craziness that is the

Ruthless Brothers. Emily turns around as the door shuts, giving me a pointed stare with her finger aimed in my direction.

"Let your hair down, girlie," she orders, before turning toward the Prez's table where everyone is sitting.

I make my way through the dancing bodies and laughing groups, watching the table like a hawk with every step I take. Ryker sits in the center, looking every inch the Prez that he is. Emmett sits to his left, blond hair loose around his face, making my thighs clench at the extra Viking vibe he has going on. Axel is at the end, brows knitted and a scowl etched into his features like usual, but when his eyes lock with mine, he almost seems to relax. Almost. Gray is sitting to the right of Ryker, head back as he laughs at whatever Shift is saying to him, and it makes me relax just watching them.

"What do my two favorite girls want to drink?" Duffer asks as we approach the table, appearing out of nowhere and I smile.

"Vodka on the rocks."

He nods, turning his gaze to Emily, who murmurs her drink of choice before he rushes off again.

I nod for Emily to get into the booth first, sitting comfortably at the end. Even though I might want to reach out to Ryker, Emmett, Gray, and even Axel, I much prefer having an end seat. Old ways die hard, and we're under fire, so I want to be able to react accordingly.

*Hopefully, I don't crumble like last time.* I'm still expecting the deputy to retaliate after we paid him a visit, but he seems to be happy letting us simmer.

"Drinks for the ladies," Duffer announces, placing two glasses down, and I take mine, gulping back a healthy dose of liquor to calm the stress inside of me.

"Are you joining us?" I ask, moving to stand and let him in, but he shakes his head.

"Nah, the Prez's table isn't for me, Scar." It's a factual statement, he doesn't seem mad about it.

"But I've barely been able to speak to you since the doctor's, and we have a lot to catch up on," I insist.

"Do you two know each other or something?" Ryker shouts over the music, and I nod without glancing away from Duffer. A smile touches my lips, but I can't figure out how to even explain the details. Thankfully, Duffer has me covered.

"I was born into the Reapers, remember? I was taken away when my mom died; had to leave this queen behind for a little while, but she couldn't stay away in the end."

Rolling my eyes at him, I turn to glance at Ryker who nods in understanding.

"Wait, do you have some embarrassing stories about our girl here?" Gray asks, leaning forward to brace his elbows on the table.

"Fuck that. I like my head where it is, thanks," Duffer replies with a chuckle, patting my shoulder before he disappears into the crowd.

Gray pouts, disappointed he didn't get any juicy gossip, making the rest of the table laugh.

"Happy birthday."

Shift lifts his beer at me to clink, and I take another gulp of the vodka, letting it warm my veins as I relax back into my seat again.

Everyone falls into comfortable silence as I observe from the outside, watching as Emmett and Emily bicker across the table at one another. From the outside looking in, it's far too amusing, and it's a fun feeling to just sit and watch them interact. I notice Ryker glancing at me a time or two, likely concerned with how quiet I am, but I'm quite happy just watching the room.

"Happy birthday, Shiftie baby. You want to come have a dance?"

I cringe at the sound of Molly's voice as she stops at the table beside me, arms pressed against the wood as she leers at her target for the night. Emily fake-barfs beside me as Shift plasters a smile on his face.

"Thanks, but I'm good," he replies, tipping his beer bottle in her direction before guzzling it down, but that doesn't seem to deter her.

"Please don't tell me you've joined her little fucking

harem as well now, Shift," Molly hollers above the music playing, and I sigh, fixing my stare on Ryker.

"Honestly, please rethink the fact that she's still breathing. It's driving me insane."

Emily laughs beside me, making Shift choke on his beer as Ryker tries and fails to smother his own smile. "She's harmless, Rebel," he insists, and I roll my eyes.

"Let me tell you, girls like this are never harmless. Ever," I grumble, downing the rest of my vodka as Molly slams her fist down on the table in frustration.

"I'm fucking standing right here, you dumb bitch." Her eyes are wild as she glares at me. I wave my hand in her direction as I turn back to the guys, proving my case in point, and I even see Axel hide a smile behind his hand as I'm left to deal with this nut job.

The second her fingers wrap around my wrist, all of my humor is gone.

With my free hand, I enclose my fingers around her neck. Again. Will she ever learn who actually is the dumb bitch here? Because it sure as shit isn't me.

Her eyes bug out and her grip on me drops, but her attention turns to the guys at the table. Pleading for sympathy. Again.

Following her line of sight, I stand, keeping my hold on her until I lock eyes with Ryker. "The longer you let her think she's got some kind of control here, the worse she will be," I grunt, shoving her away and letting her stumble in her heels until she lands on her ass. Not bothering to offer her another second of my time, I turn my attention to Shift. "I'm so sorry, I hope you have a good night, but this isn't for me."

"Apex?" he offers, not missing a beat, and I smile.

"Please, make my day and give me the opportunity to beat both of your asses at *my* game," I say with a grin, pointing between Shift and Gray, who quickly hollers his agreement.

"We're all coming," Emmett declares, and Emily holds her hand out for me to take.

Once she's safely on her feet, I turn to look at Molly and annoyingly stick my middle finger up at her. I hate giving her a response, I hate being bitchy even more, but I really can't help it.

With my men hot on my heels, I turn for the lounge, feeling like a goddamn queen every step of the way.

# TWENTY SIX

*Scarlett*

I stir from my slumber, blinking heavily at the curtains and grumble when I don't see a hint of light peering through the edges. It's still the middle of the night. Snuggling deeper into Ryker's arms, I release a sigh as I try to get comfortable.

I'm the worst at waking up during the night, sleep eluding me, but I was hoping with his presence keeping me warm, tonight might be different.

Last night was… epic. The second we left the bar and Molly behind, everyone's energy completely changed, mine more than anyone. A night of video games, fun, and laughter was exactly what we all needed, and we definitely got it. The more I brought Shift and Gray to their knees on the firing range in Apex, the closer Ryker edged toward me. Then we decided to play some trios and destroyed team after team together, and we laughed longer and louder for everyone to hear.

Axel remained quiet for most of the night, enjoying the armchair to himself, while Emmett ribbed Gray and Shift every chance he got, completely oblivious that his sister was making eyes at the latter. How none of them have noticed the lust between Emily and Shift before now is beyond me, but it's there, I could feel it.

I expected the evening to end with me beneath one or more of them, but the second I collapsed into my bed with Ryker, I passed the fuck out. Making last night one of the most oddly satisfying nights of my life. There was no sex to help force me asleep, just a warmness in my chest and happiness in my heart.

When I stumbled into the arms of the Ruthless Brothers, I expected them to try and be ruthless with my body, but I didn't expect them to be ruthless with my heart.

Ryker's arm tightens around my waist as he presses his front to my back, and it distracts me from my thoughts as I settle against him. I feel the cusp of sleep ready to claim me when I hear a noise by the door, and I bolt upright in bed. I expect Ryker to stir beside me, but he barely flinches as my gaze lands on Axel slumped against my bedroom door with his head in his hands.

His hair is disheveled, his cut gone, and his feet bare.

"Hey, are you okay?" I ask quietly, the soft glow from

the lamp on Ryker's side of the bed offering me a view of him as he startles at my voice.

His wild eyes find mine instantly, before he exhales harshly and nods. "I'm good, Reaper."

I cock a brow, desperate to call bullshit, but I keep my mouth shut as I assess him even harder now that I can see his face. His pupils are blown, his jaw tight, and his brows knitted so tightly together it almost looks like he only has one.

Sitting up a little taller, I try to tamp down the worry rising inside of me. "Axel—"

"I'm good, Reaper. Just sleep," he grunts, his tone gruff but he's not coming across harsh as he interrupts me before I can breathe more than his name.

He seems antsy as shit though.

I clear my throat, ready for him to get pissy if I continue to push, but the thought doesn't stop me as I wait for his eyes to clash with mine before I speak again. "I can see your withdrawal symptoms from here, Axel." I try to keep my voice calm and even, but he shakes his head at me adamantly. "Please tell me I'm wrong, it'll make my night proving *you* wrong." I can't hold the sass back, and I don't know whether that's what gets through to him or not, but he glances away, defeat evident.

He needs my help right now. Just like he did the other night. Possibly more so. It may not be the anniversary of what pains him tonight, but in the dead of night when the world around you feels like it's spinning slower in the darkness, that's where the most destruction is.

Rising from the bed, I'm fully aware that I'm only in a tee and a fresh pair of boxers, but that doesn't matter to any of these guys, Axel included. I don't stop until I'm right in front of him, before crouching so we're eye level.

"Get the rope, Axel."

His eyes whip to mine in a flash, his jaw dropping as he processes my words, before he shakes his head. "No, you—"

"Get the fucking rope ready, Ax. I'll be there in a minute."

I rise, refusing to give him the chance he wants to argue back. Taking two steps back, I keep my hands at my sides instead of folding them over my chest like I want to. My eyes do all of the talking instead, and to my surprise, he pushes up to his feet.

My eyes widen as he takes a step toward me, so close I have to tilt my head back a little further to hold his gaze as I feel his breath on my forehead. Fuck. I want to reach out and touch him even though I know I shouldn't. He's intoxicating this close and I can't handle it.

His hand lifts to my face, not quite touching me as he looks from me to his hand, before taking a step back. and I gulp in a harsh breath.

"I'll get the rope," he rasps, and I nod, teeth latched onto my bottom lip as I struggle to find any words. I watch him leave the room, my body strung tight.

Spinning on the spot, I look at Ryker to find him squinting up at me. "What's going on?"

I point over my shoulder, and my mouth opens, but for a solid ten seconds, no words come out. When I can't piece together a less crass response, I settle on what I've got.

"Axel needs us."

"When I heard you murmur about rope, I assumed it was *you* he needed." Even half asleep, he gives me a pointed stare, and I wave him off, not bothering with the semantics.

"He needs me for the rope, but he needs *you* for me." A thought comes to mind as I turn for the door. "Maybe we need Gray too, for… them, and Emmett because why not get everyone involved," I ramble, barely hearing my name being called as I reach the door.

"Fuck, Rebel, slow down." I glance back at Ryker, watching him climb from the bed and run a hand through his hair. His eyes settle on mine. He's assessing me, but not in the way he's done a hundred times before. No. This time it feels different. Deeper. "You're sure?" I nod in response, words betraying me once more. "You wake Emmett, I'll grab Gray."

I don't wait for him to have a chance to change his mind

KC KEAN

as I rush out of the room and slip straight into Emmett's. My hot as fuck Viking peers up at me as I waltz through the door, the light behind me offering a glow around the room as he shakes the sleep from his body.

"What's wrong?"

"Nothing," I murmur, shaking my head. "Axel needs us."

Three words and he's climbing from the bed in just his boxers and struts around the room like a damn God, pulling his hair up into a bun, before planting a kiss on my forehead.

"Do the others know?"

"Ryker is waking Gray," I explain, and he simply nods, like it's the most casual fucking situation that ever existed. We all know it's not, but that doesn't matter.

"Are you okay?"

I grin at him, releasing another breath as I nod. "I'm whatever he needs me to be, but I'm good. More than good," I mutter, running my fingers over his chest.

"I've got you, Snowflake." He presses another kiss, to my cheek this time, before he takes my hand in his and guides me down the hall where Gray and Ryker are already waiting.

Shit. And I thought we were quick.

Gray's sleepy smile makes me weak at the knees as he throws his arm around my shoulders while Emmett doesn't release my other hand. Ryker moves into Axel's room first, the rest of us hot on his tail to find the man in need standing shirtless with a rope hanging from his right hand.

His eyes find mine first, a calmness washing over his features as the tension dissolves before my eyes. Not completely, but noticeably.

"Thank you."

I smile at him in response, stepping from between Gray and Emmett as I make my way toward him. It's not the biggest of rooms for us all, but it will do.

"Where do you want me?"

Axel's gaze travels over my shoulder first, as if seeking some kind of approval from the others.

Fuck that.

I snap my fingers, gaining his attention back as I give him a stern look and repeat the question. "Where. Do. *You*. Want. Me?"

He wets his lips, just like I desperately want to before pointing at the bed. "Same position as last time, Reaper."

I shiver at the nickname on his tongue, associating it with these moments more than anything as I do as he asks. I don't wait to be asked to strip, pulling the tee over my head before dropping the boxers to the floor.

"Am I missing something with the boxers?" Emmett asks, and Gray chuckles.

"We've torn all of her panties. She has none left. None."

Ryker snickers as Axel shakes his head. "You can get some more. Tomorrow. Black."

I gulp, wetting my parched lips as I offer a single nod in agreement.

Hot. As. Fuck.

With my back to the four of them, I kneel on the foot of the bed, getting comfortable as I relax my hands at my sides waiting for my next order. I never thought I'd appreciate them as much as I do with him. The anticipation licking over my skin is quickly becoming one of my favorite moments.

He doesn't touch me, but the way my body reacts is explosive. Add to the mix the physicality of Emmett, and now Ryker and Gray's presence too, and I know it's going to be intense in the best way possible.

"I'm going to try something a little more intricate this time, is that okay?" I nod, but I'm greeted with a huff. "Words, Reaper. Let me hear them."

"Yes, that's okay."

That earns me a hum in response. "Good girl, now hold still."

*Yes, sir.*

The first glide of the rope over my skin makes my body tingle, the second has me brimming with excitement, the third has me completely under his control. He bands the rope around my arms again, but this time he works them over my shoulders, around my waist, under my arms, before draping them around my exposed breasts. By the time he's done, my arms are secured again, but the rope around my chest is tantalizingly possessive.

A nudge, a flicker of movement, and my nipples pebble tighter and tighter with a combination of need and excitement.

"How do you feel, Reaper?" His voice is huskier now, making my thighs clench. I really need to look more into this Shibari. I want to know how far he can go with it, how far he can take me. With the way it feels against my chest, I shiver at the thought of what else he can do.

"Like I'm in heaven," I murmur honestly, earning myself another hum of approval.

"Good, now shuffle further up the bed and turn around to face us."

I take my time, not wanting to move too quickly and fall flat on my face, and when I turn toward the four of them, my heart rate kicks up. The way they're looking at me, it heats my skin without a single touch.

"What now?" Gray rasps, already pumping his cock as he eyes me.

"Whatever she wants," Axel responds, taking a step back, indicating that whatever I want, can't include him. I almost pout, but remember quickly that this isn't about me. It's about him, or even us as a whole. But just because

I can't bring him to his knees with pleasure, doesn't mean I can't watch it happen.

Running my tongue over my bottom lip, I turn my attention to Gray, my eyes displaying what I can't say out loud and he instantly cuts the distance toward me. He cups my cheek, tilting my head back before bringing his lips to mine. It's slow, delicate, and sexy as fuck, leaving me panting for breath. He offers me a wink, before turning back to Axel.

"She wants to watch, big man," he rasps, making my body tingle as Axel doesn't waste a second, dropping the zipper on his jeans as his gaze flicks between me and Gray. But when my blondie comes to a stop in front of the crazed mountain man, it's the latter that drops to his knees.

I gasp as Gray grunts, hand splayed against the wall for support as Axel takes him deep between his lips.

"Oh, she likes that a lot," Emmett states, a salacious grin on his face as he steps toward me, Ryker right beside him as they stalk me like prey. "Don't you, Snowflake?" he asks, wanting to hear it from my lips.

"Yes." I'm wound up tight and none of them have touched my pussy yet.

"I'm taking her pussy, Emmett, you can fuck her perfect little mouth," Ryker orders as the bed dips beside me. I should tell him to fuck off with his demands, but my skin heats with need, revealing how much I want this, so it's pointless trying to deny it. It only delays the inevitable.

"How wet are you, Scar?" Emmett asks, offering me his hand to shuffle me a bit closer to the foot of the bed, still giving me the perfect view of Axel and Gray as his head falls back, cock deep in Axel's mouth as he fucks his lips.

"With a view like that? Dripping," I murmur, practically salivating at the sight as Ryker chuckles. His breath runs over my skin, making me shiver as he settles behind me. I feel his fingers run over the top rope holding me in place as I suck in a breath when his cock nestles between my ass cheeks. He likes Axel's handiwork as much as I do, it seems.

"I don't think I've ever seen a more beautiful sight," he breathes, running his finger between my shoulder blades before trailing it over my neck and arms. I shouldn't be reacting so much from such a simple touch, but here I am, a puddle of wanton need.

"Thanks," Gray grunts from across the room, fingers laced in Axel's hair as he thrusts into his mouth again and again with a blissful grin on his lips.

"Fucker," Emmett grunts in response, hand encasing his cock as I peer down at his length.

I need to taste him, to feel them both, and join the ecstasy that is unraveling in the room already.

Parting my knees a little more, I lift myself up to tilt

my face down, lapping at the tip of his cock as he groans above me. The sound encourages me more, and in the next moment, his hand is wrapping around my hair as he pushes his cock further into my mouth until he's hitting the back of my throat.

Just. How. I. Like. It.

Not wanting to be left out of the action any longer, Ryker runs his fingers over the globes of my ass, before swiping over my folds. "Shit, she wasn't joking," he grunts, my desire coating his fingers as he teases my entrance, then my clit, before thrusting in my core with two fingers.

I gasp around Emmett's cock, rocking with the movement as my body clenches, desperate for more. Ryker's hands at my hips and Emmett's in my hair keep me in place as the rope glides over my skin with each move, making me hum with pleasure around Emmett's dick in my mouth.

I'm close to exploding already, my body ready to obliterate, and Ryker must sense the urgency inside of me because his fingers slip from my core without wasting a second, before he plunges his cock deep into my pussy.

He's bare. Just like Emmett has been, and it makes me choke even harder around Emmett's length as I revel in the heat consuming the apex of my thighs. My orgasm tears through me, refusing to wait a moment longer as I tremble between them. It takes everything I have to keep my eyes open to watch as Gray explodes in Axel's mouth, and he swallows every drop.

The visual only makes my core clench tighter, making Ryker groan from behind me as he pounds into me relentlessly. His movements are jagged and explosive, combined with Emmett's use of my mouth and I'm starting to get black spots in my vision as my world rocks around me.

They fuck me, use me, consume me so perfectly I think I might fucking cry with joy, but the tears that streak down my face are from Emmett's cock, or that's what I tell myself at least. His length pops from my mouth, saliva glistening on the end as Ryker pulls me up, my back to his chest, just in time as Emmett explodes all over my roped breasts.

The liquid on my heated skin, with Ryker's thrusts coming harder and faster, and the sight of Axel jacking himself off as he watches me, cum painting the floor in front of him has me falling over the edge once more. I can't tell which way is up or down as I cry out with pleasure, my head tilted back as I shatter into a million pieces along with the pulse of Ryker coming inside of me.

Fuck. Will it ever not be this intense? I don't think so. Which is what makes it more and more addicting every time.

I feel Ryker's lips at the crook of my neck, peppering

kisses as he slowly lowers me, my face against the sheets as someone starts to unwind the rope around my arms first.

If I thought last night was the perfect night, I was wrong. It is now, with this connection in this room.

This is what I crave, what I desire, what I breathe for.

It's exactly what makes me want to forever wear the title of Ruthless Rebel.

# TWENTY SEVEN

## Scarlett

My limbs ache in the most delicious way possible as I slowly stretch out, taking my time to give each muscle the attention it needs as I wake up. I feel fresher than I did when I woke during the night at least, but the grogginess clings to my body just as hard.

I don't even remember falling back asleep after the rope was untied.

Fuck.

Last night.

I want to groan with pleasure just thinking about it.

Blinking my eyes open, I frown at my surroundings for a second before I realize I'm still in Axel's room. My heart gallops in my chest, forcing me to sit up as I double check the space to confirm I'm alone in his bed.

Shit.

Is he mad?

Pushing my hair back off my face, I let the sheets fall from my body as I stand. Please don't tell me I've fucked this all up by passing out after another intense session of pure, raw need. He's going to think I'm fucking delusional now, I—

My thoughts and internal tirade fall short when I find a piece of paper folded over with one word written across the front in scratchy text.

*Reaper.*

Twisting my lips, I consider whether I want to find out what else it may say, but eventually traipse over to the card and turn it over.

*Here's a pair of boxers and a tee to cover up your sweet body.*
*There's also a stack of cash for you to take with you.*
*Emily and Duffer will be waiting to take you shopping.*
*Have fun.*
*A—*

*P.S. - Don't forget, I want to see you in black.*

Fuck.

Holy. Fuck.

It takes me an eternity to bring the sentences together,

but holy fucking shit is it worth it.

I turn the card over, expecting to find something else, but there's nothing more. Not that there needs to be anything else. Shit. A few lines of text and I'm even softer on the guy than I already was.

Grabbing the boxers and tee, I quickly dress, before running my fingers over the cash he mentioned. There's eight hundred dollars here. Not that I need it, I have my own account, but I still take it with me as I scramble to my own room and find a pair of jeans to tuck his t-shirt into.

I find a pair of socks and lace up my combat boots, before securing my hair in a bun on top of my head. Spying my sunglasses on the dresser, I grab them before moving toward the door.

There's a spring in my step that I've never felt before, a smile on my lips that just won't go away, and a warmth in my chest that I can't describe. I slow as I approach the kitchen, peeking my head around the door to find Duffer and Emily laughing about something.

"Hey," I murmur, moving to step inside, but I barely get one foot through the threshold before Emily is jumping up and waving a hand at me to stop.

"Don't touch a thing, we're having coffee and bagels on the go," she declares, moving toward me with rushed steps as Duffer slowly stands.

"We are?" I question with a cocked brow, and she

smiles wider at me.

"Uh-huh."

It seems it's settled then. She links her arm through mine as I glance to Duffer, who simply shrugs at me.

"She's the boss, I'm the bitch. I do as I'm told," he explains with a grin.

Emily whacks him in the gut as he gets close, before pointing her finger in his face. "You are *not* a bitch. Don't make me get Scarlett to put you in your place," she threatens, and he lifts his hands in surrender as I watch them both with amusement. Without skipping a beat, Emily turns to me and nods. "Ready to go?"

"Where are the guys?" I ask, not ready to answer her until I know, but her nose scrunches as she shakes her head.

"Something to do with a gun run. Other than that, I don't have a clue. I just know we've got the dollar-dollar bills to go shopping and we're wasting precious seconds right now," she grumbles, pulling me out into the hallway.

Duffer was definitely right, she most certainly is the boss. Simply because we're all fucking soft on her.

"If you get me a jalapeño cheddar bagel again, I'm in," I offer, falling into step with her.

"It's cute that you thought you had a choice. But sure, spicy cheesy bagels it is."

My bagel churns in my stomach as we ascend another level in the mall the next town over. It's overwhelming as fuck and weird as hell to realize I've never actually been in one before. That's definitely not helping the fact that I'm on high alert right now, feeling exposed as shit.

"How many more shops?" I ask as the escalator reaches the top and we step off.

"Girl, all we've done so far is buy a few cute tops. That's like technically only a sixth of an outfit if we're counting underwear too," she says, giving me a pointed look, and I roll my eyes at her in response.

I can't keep going in and out of different places, it's exhausting. I've only ever been to the thrift store on the outskirts of Jasperville. I've always grabbed what I needed out of the options available and left. Simple. Not like this. With all sorts of choices and options, I think my head might explode.

"I think she's struggling with her first mall experience, Em," Duffer murmurs, offering me a tight smile as she shakes her head.

"This isn't her..." She looks at my face and the realization washes over her. "Shit, I'm sorry. I didn't know, otherwise I wouldn't—"

I cut her off with a shh, before roping my arm through hers. "Lead me to the lingerie, and from there, we can decide if I can handle any more or not, okay?"

"You got it," she replies, beaming again.

I follow her lead as she pulls me along, Duffer keeping a step behind us as she pulls me into the huge department store that takes up half of the damn place. The greeter at the door offers us a toothy smile, slicking her blonde hair back off her face as she assesses us. I give her an impassive glance in response, but she doesn't waver. Impressive.

Emily drags me through the racks of clothes, before her steps slow at the elevator at the back of the room and I frown. "Can't we take the stairs?"

She's shaking her head at me before I've even finished. "No way. We're not all as fit as you. I can't handle all of the steps," she states, pressing the button to call the elevator, and the doors open instantly. "Get in."

I do as I'm told—a*gain*—sighing with reluctance as I step in beside her and the doors close behind Duffer. It feels like the longest ten seconds before a ding echoes around the small space, and the doors open once again.

"Wow," Duffer murmurs, his gaze scanning from left to right and back again as he takes in the array of lingerie that fills the space. "This is lingerie galore, ladies. I'm going to hang back here at the elevator. I can't imagine the guys are going to appreciate me knowing what you opt for." He scrubs the back of his neck, a mixture of nerves and embarrassment flickering through his eyes as I go to refute what he's saying, but I stop myself. He's right. I can't imagine any of the Ruthless Brothers I'm obsessed with being impressed with that fact.

I pat him on the shoulder. "I'll holler for you when I need saving, okay? You better come to my rescue," I murmur, but still loud enough for Emily to hear. She laughs, before pulling me toward the racks.

"Do you plan on trying them on?" Emily asks once we're out of ear shot, releasing her hold on me to riffle through the racks of lace bras and panties.

"Nope," I reply, the *p* popping of its own accord. "Let's just grab a handful and be done. That sounds like the best plan to me." I give her a hopeful look but she's not even glancing at me.

"I was told twenty at a minimum." Her words hang in the air a second, as casual as ever, while I stumble over them.

"Twenty?" They've got to be joking.

"I believe Gray said to also make sure they were tearable. Even multiple pairs of panties for each bra."

Dear God. Of course he did.

Spinning slowly, I take in each section, flustering over where to begin when Emily moves over to the next rack and lifts a set to show me. "How about some of these?"

The lace is delicate, no padding, just the underwire, with matching lace thongs. They're hot as fuck, in every damn color you can think of. Red, white, pink, navy, mint green, purple, and black. My stomach clenches at the black, the reminder clear in my mind as I take a step toward her.

"Can we get the same style in different colors?" I ask, excited that this may be over quicker than I thought, but the way she laughs at me tells me I'm beyond foolish.

"You wish," she snickers, before asking for my sizes. I indulge her, only to watch as she grabs the set in every color, two pairs of panties to each bra, before turning to the next rack and holding another style up to me.

Wireless lace sets turn to padded balconette styles, mixed in with a few sports bras too. It's like a rainbow exploded in the damn basket, the assistant ran over to us earlier when she could see just how carried away Emily was getting.

"What about these?" She holds up a pair of crotchless panties, wagging her eyebrows at me with her tongue sticking out of the corner of her mouth and I roll my eyes. "What? At least there would be no need to tear these off you," she adds, and I actually pause to consider her suggestion.

"Fuck it, get a few," I grumble as she giggles, piling more into the basket.

"I think we're done," she finally announces after almost an hour of traipsing up and down every rack, and I sag with relief. I instinctively glance toward Duffer by the elevator, giving him a little nod to let him know we'll be done soon and he seems to be relieved at the news as much as I am.

Trying to pay is futile as she refuses my every attempt, insisting that the guys demanded they pay. There was some bullshit about replacing the damages they caused, and in the end, I relent, deciding to argue it out with them in person later instead.

"Fuck, Emily, I'm hungry again," I complain as we make our way back toward Duffer, arms clad with bags as he shakes his head at us in disbelief.

"We can grab something to eat here or on the way home, I'll let you decide," Emily offers, and I actually refrain from rolling my eyes this time. I love her, but she is definitely bossy as shit in the best way possible. She forces me not to be a hermit, which is a great detail on paper, but in actuality, it's exhausting.

"On the way home, I'm done here," I grumble, making Duffer laugh as he takes some of the bags from us both.

"Do you want me to stop by the Mexican restaurant on the way back?" he offers, and I nod eagerly, my stomach grumbling with need at the mere thought.

"That would be a dream, please."

Emily presses the button to call the elevator and I groan. "Are you sure I can't tempt you with the stairs? It's easier going down." My hope is slim, and quickly written off as the doors open and Emily steps inside.

"Get the hell in here, Scar," she orders, and I give her the stink-eye as I follow after her.

I'm so busy glaring at her that I don't notice the rattling of a can at first, until it slams into the far wall and smoke starts to leak from it.

"What the…"

Dropping my bags, I spin around, the world turning in slow motion as the elevator doors begin to close at the same time the sound of a gun rings out. I shoulder-barge Emily to the side instinctively, as Duffer grunts and the doors close.

My pulse rings in my ears as Duffer collapses to the floor, blood staining his white tee crimson while the smoke starts to completely fill the small space.

Fuck. Fuck. Fuck.

"Oh my God," Emily screams, panic etched into her every word. My heart tears apart at the sight of Duffer's lifeless body on the floor.

Ten seconds it took to get up here, which means I have seven at best before we either hit the ground floor or the gas takes us out.

*Think, Scarlett. Fucking think.*

It's not about me and it's not about Duffer right now. Priority number one is protecting Emily. Whirling around, I face her, grabbing her shoulders tight as I stand eye to eye with her. "I need you to listen to me." She's shaking uncontrollably, but I need her to be present and focused. "Get on the floor, Emily." I push a little on her shoulders and she drops to her knees at first, before I nudge her to lie down beside Duffer's body. "It's okay, you're going to be okay, Em. I swear it. But there's no time. I need you to play dead alright? Whatever happens from here, I need you to run. That might be in five seconds or thirty fucking minutes but either way you run as soon as you get the chance, and you don't stop until you're at the clubhouse. Do you hear me?" She blinks up at me with wild eyes, and I shake her. "Do. You. Hear. Me?"

"Y-yes, but Scar, I—"

I squeeze her shoulders in comfort, pressing a kiss of reassurance on her forehead, before doing the unthinkable and dragging Duffer's dead body closer, half draping him over her as I smear some of his blood across her clothes and face.

"Close your eyes, everything's going to be okay, just close your eyes," I breathe, watching her bottom lip tremble as she does as I ask.

I hate to step away from her, but there's no time. A second or two at most.

I can barely see in front of my own face, but that doesn't stop me from pulling my cell phone from my pocket. Blindly, I attempt to hopefully open the messaging app as I splutter with the gas I'm inhaling. Lightheaded, I feel like I'm going to pass out as the doors to the elevator finally open and the gas alleviates a little, but the sight that greets me is no better.

My cell phone clatters to the floor before I'm even close to hitting send as my eyes settle on Kincaid's.

Satisfaction shimmers in his eyes as my legs turn to jelly, but before I can hit the deck, someone catches my fall.

"There you are, I've been searching all over for you. I had to wait patiently while you chose some lingerie for me though," he announces with a wicked grin.

I sneer, unable to stop the hands from carrying me toward him. I can't even focus on where the person is that's doing it, but that doesn't matter. "You killed them. You killed them both, you're going to fucking pay for that," I hiss, nostrils flaring as I struggle to keep my eyes open.

My threat earns me a punch to the face, pain ricocheting from my cheek as I sag in the arms of the men holding me. I assume men, I don't even fucking know. All I know is panic, fear, and pain.

"Bring the panties, I'm going to have fun parading you around in them," Kincaid responds, ignoring my words as I'm slowly carried along after him. My eyes fall to half-mast, unable to comprehend what's going on. How is he doing this in the middle of a fucking mall?

"What about these two, Boss?" someone hollers, my

heart stilling in my chest until Kincaid grunts a reply.

"You heard her, they're both dead. Leave them. We can send in a clean-up crew once we've paid off the staff."

Relief consumes me as my body shuts down from the gas I've inhaled. The knowledge that they're not going to touch Emily is all I need to know before my world goes black.

RUTHLESS BROTHERS MC

# TWENTY EIGHT

## Axel

Paisley laughs as he offers out his hand and I shake it firmly, relieved the Iron Scorpions are still in business for guns. They've been on the block long enough to not get involved in other MC business, but something still niggled in my gut on the way over here.

We've had a successful drop, with no interruption from the Brutes and it's fucking refreshing.

"Something is different about you, Axel. I can sense it," he states, his laughter dying down as he observes me with a quirked brow.

I fucking feel different. I don't say that though, instead I just shrug like I have no idea what he's talking about. My life might be unraveling before my very eyes, but he doesn't need to know that.

"I don't know what you're talking about, old man,"

I say with a wry smile on my face and he chuckles once again.

"Whatever you say, but I know that twinkle in your eyes. I've even felt it myself before." He releases my hand and thankfully drops it, before turning to wind things down with Ryker. Eager to put some much needed distance between us, I head back toward my motorcycle where Shift is standing.

"Are you free a minute, Ax? While it's just the two of us?" he asks, peaking my interest as I jut my chin in acknowledgment. He glances behind me first, likely checking for Emmett and Gray, who are taking the last two crates into the Iron Scorpion's storage unit, before he focuses his gaze back on me.

Taking out his cell phone, he swipes over it a few times before he turns it in my direction. "Is this her?"

My heart stops in my chest as the red wavy hair greets me, the familiar green eyes glaring back at me. Fuck. Wiping a hand down my face, I finally manage to rasp a response at him. "Yeah."

Despite the circumstances and her role in my life, a smile creeps over his face. "She's the last one, Ax." My stomach churns, the reality of his words settling over me as I play them on repeat.

She's the last fucking one.

The last woman from my past that still walks, talks,

and breathes the same air as unsuspecting victims, as me. But not for much longer. "Where is she?" I ask, ready to get on my bike now and tear off in that direction.

"Florida."

I wet my bottom lip, deciding whether to leave now or later, but the thought of taking off for a few days without seeing Scarlett before I go clenches my chest. I can detour by the clubhouse on the way, it'll be worth it.

"Thanks, man. Send me the location?" I ask, patting him on the shoulder in thanks as he beams back at me.

"Of course."

I grab my helmet from the handlebars of my bike and secure it on my head as I get comfortable on my seat. If Paisley thought there was a bounce in my step before, that's nothing in comparison to now.

He finishes up his conversation with Ryker, who makes his way back to us once they're done, and we're all set to go. Thankfully, nobody lingers and we're back on the road in no time. For the first time since being assigned the sergeant at arms role for the club, I hate the fact that my job requires me to guard the back of the pack. I'm desperate to floor the accelerator, but from this position, I can't.

As the town drifts by us, I can't help but wonder how I will feel when all is said and done and the final woman who haunts my nightmares is gone. Does it still matter to me now? Even with Scarlett's crazily calming presence around me? Fuck yeah, it does. If anything, it matters now more than ever.

Maybe seeing the end of her will bring my troubles to an end too. I know that's not realistically likely, but it's the first time I have a positive mindset about it, so that feels like progress at least.

Ready to lay my past to rest, I drive the rest of the way home with excitement buzzing in my chest. Even when I roll my bike to a stop outside of the compound and switch off the engine, I still feel like I'm vibrating.

I leave my key in the ignition, before taking off my helmet and standing. It's only when I'm halfway to the double doors that I remember Scarlett left for the mall with Duffer and Emily. Fuck. I can wait a little if needed. It won't put me behind.

Stepping through the double doors, I spy Maggie behind the bar and a few of the Ruthless Bitches along with some prospects playing a game of cards in the corner.

"Beer?" Maggie calls out, and I shake my head as Shift hollers from behind me that he'll have one.

Spinning, I search for Emmett and catch him stepping inside with Gray and Ryker. I try to keep my voice low, not wanting to reveal my fucking kryptonite to the whole place as I lean in. "Have you heard anything from the girls? I'm guessing they're not back yet."

Ryker offers me a knowing smile. The same fucking

one he's had on his face since last night, so I continue to ignore him.

Emmett checks his cell phone and shakes his head. "I'm guessing they're still shopping because I haven't heard anything."

I nod, twisting my lips as I consider what I should do with myself until then.

"Are you joining us for a bit before we clean up the bikes in the garage?" Ryker asks, and I shake my head.

"Shift has a lead for me," I murmur, watching as his eyes widen in surprise. As much as he knows how I've been going about my business with regards to my past, I've never outwardly spoken to him about it. "I was just hoping to check in on Scarlett before I leave," I admit. But in my defense, last night escalated, and my conscience needs to see her before I can confirm she's still okay.

"Ax, man, that's—"

Ryker's words die off as the double doors slam behind him, ricocheting off the walls and echoing around the room as we all turn to look.

"What the fuck?" Emmett gasps, horror etching into his features as he stares at the same person I do. "What the fuck happened to you?" he breathes, eyes darkening as he takes off toward the door where his sister stands.

Blood stains her clothes and is smeared all over her face as she sobs and trembles uncontrollably. Her bottom lip wobbles as she gapes at her brother, before uttering his name on a soft cry and the world erupts with panic.

Emmett lifts her off the floor, sweeping her into his arms as he holds her tightly and heads for Church. Ryker, Gray, and I are hot on his heels because when she left the compound this morning, she had Duffer and Scarlett with her, and now… she's alone.

What the hell happened while they were gone?

"Where are you bleeding from?" Emmett murmurs as he slowly places her down on the table inside Church, and I kick the door shut behind me.

"I-it's n-not my b-blood," she sobs, twisting the pain inside me.

"Whose is it, Emily?" Gray asks, his voice clipped as his hands flex at his sides. He's just as worried as I am.

"It's D-duffers." She cups her face with her hands, sobbing even harder as Emmett soothes her the best he can.

The door swings open behind me, and I'm ready to give someone a piece of my fucking mind, when I see it's Maggie with a bottle of bourbon in her hand. "She's going to need this," she mutters, offering it to her, but it's Emmett who grabs it.

"I don't think so," he grunts, which earns him a scoff from Gray's mom.

"Look at the state of her, Emmett. A soda isn't going

to take the edge off and that girl is in shock. Trust me, give her the fucking bottle, we're all here to take care of her. She's not alone."

He glares down at the bottle for what feels like an eternity before sighing and untwisting the cap before extending it toward his sister. She takes it with shaky fingers, bringing the liquor to her lips as more and more tears stream down her face.

Fuck.

I'm not good at this. She clearly needs coddling and taking care of, but all I want to know is where the fuck Scarlett is.

Maggie takes a seat beside Emily, holding her free hand when she finally lowers the bottle from her lips. Emily's eyes fill with more tears ready to pour over the surface as I start to pace back and forth in front of the door.

"Duffer is d-dead, and Scarlett, she... fuck," she gasps, taking another swig of the bourbon as everyone waits with bated breath as she tries to fucking finish that sentence.

"Start from the beginning, girlie, so we can understand," Maggie soothes, and I exhale harshly as my lack of patience threatens to get the better of me. That earns me a glare from Emmett, but I don't pay him any attention as I stare his sister down.

"We had just finished buying all of the lingerie, and Scarlett was complaining again that we were taking the elevator." Another sob bursts from her lips as she sniffs, trying to take another calming breath. "I should have listened to her, I'm so sorry," she rambles, but no one utters a word as we wait for her to continue. "It all happened so fast. We stepped into the elevator and before the doors shut, a gas canister rolled in and started filling the space with smoke and then a gunshot rang out. S-Scarlett shoved me to the side, but it was Duffer who took the hit." Her words go quiet at the end as she squeezes her eyes closed, watching the scene play out on the back of her eyelids.

"It's okay, Emily. We're here. What happened after that?" Emmett asks, and she blinks her eyes back open slowly.

"Scarlett made me l-lie down on the f-floor a-and asked m-me to pretend to be d-dead. T-then she laid Duffer over me and covered me with blood..." Her hand cups her mouth as she sobs again, and my chest tightens with the pain I'm feeling just from hearing this fucked up shit unfold.

"Then what?" Maggie pushes, stroking a hand through her hair comfortingly.

"Then the elevator doors opened and the Devil's Brutes were there, and Scarlett started saying you killed them, you'll pay for this, then t-they knocked her out and t-took her."

Her cries become wails once more as we all freeze in

place. The Devil's Brutes have her. Kincaid fucking has my woman.

Mine.

*OURS.*

I vowed to her that she would never be in his presence again.

"How did you get here?" Maggie asks.

"The gas knocked me out, I don't know how long for, but Scarlett made me promise that the second I could leave and the coast was clear, I would run. She said don't stop until you get home, and I didn't, I promise I didn't." Sobs rack her entire body as Maggie drapes an arm around her shoulders. "They took her, they took her and it's my fault. All she was worried about was protecting me and hiding me instead of worrying about herself."

"That's just Scarlett. She has a way of putting everyone before herself, which means now more than ever we have to make her our priority," Ryker declares, anger burning in his eyes as he looks to each of us, waiting for a nod in agreement.

"Where's your cell phone, Em?" Emmett asks, tugging at his hair, and she throws her hands up in defeat.

"I don't know. It could be on the floor in the elevator still, I'm not sure. I just got up and ran like she told me. Duffer is still there though, and before I passed out, I heard them talking about sending in a clean-up crew. He's dead and alone and they're going to dispose of him." She shakes her head in disbelief, her emotions overwhelming her once again.

My heart thunders in my chest, my pulse ringing in my ears as my earlier plans fall to the wayside and my sole focus becomes Scarlett.

"How do we respond to this? How do we get her back? We don't even fucking know where they may have taken her," Gray grunts, jaw tight and nostrils flaring with anger as he bounces with anticipation.

"We can't sit back and do nothing anymore. We need to move, and we need to do it now, but we also need a show of numbers. If we want to dominate them, then we need men on our side."

"We need to save Scarlett and retrieve Duffer's body," Emily declares, and Ryker sighs.

"Emily, saving Scarlett is priority number one, but Duf—"

"No, Ryker. Please, you need to listen to me. He was important to Scarlett too." Her face scrunches with pain as Gray brushes past me to open the doors and hollers his brother's name. He must have been standing on the other side of the doors because he's stepping into Church in the next breath, eyes focused on Emily as concern narrows his eyes.

"Tell me what's going on," Shift orders, moving around

me to get a better visual of the state Emily is in before turning to face our Prez, our leader, the one who needs to get us the fuck out of this mess, with our aid.

Ryker doesn't skip a beat as he cracks his neck and snarls. "We need to call in the other chapter, so we can take down these fuckers once and for all."

"If they have so much as touched a hair on her head," I grunt, fists balled at my sides as I realize I never even fucking did that. All I've ever done is braid her hair and tie her up in rope of my choosing. I never got to touch her because of my stupid fucking trauma, and now she's gone.

This isn't how this ends for us, I refuse. Rolling my shoulders back, I stare at each of my brothers as adrenaline courses through my veins. "We bring our girl home, no matter the cost."

# TWENTY NINE

## Scarlett

My tongue feels like lead in my mouth, my eyelids are cemented shut as my mind awakens. Confusion laces my veins as I fight past the grogginess tempting me to fall back asleep, until the memory of the events leading up to this moment consume my mind. My heart begins to race, my mind waking more as my body slowly attempts to catch up.

I can feel the leather beneath my palms, the vibrations of a moving vehicle, and the low hum of the radio playing in the distance.

It takes every ounce of strength I have to pry my eyes open, then an eternity before my gaze settles without a wave of nausea hitting me. Exhaustion roots me to the spot as I slowly take in my immediate surroundings.

I'm in the back of a moving SUV, with two men up

front. Both of them wear the telltale cuts of the Devil's Brutes, and my spine stiffens, but I know I have the upper hand right now, especially without Kincaid's presence.

Running my tongue over my dry lips, I squint at the sun peeking through the windows as I try to see what time it is, but I don't have a good view of the dash from here. Twisting my wrists and ankles, I inhale through my nose and exhale slowly through my mouth a few times as I work the heaviness from my limbs.

A quick glance out of the window offers me no real clue as to where we are, which is completely useless, but I focus on the men instead of getting stressed over the lack of knowledge I have right now.

"Where's Kincaid?" I ask, my voice raspy as the remnants of the toxic gas I consumed lingers within me.

"Oh, she's decided to join us, how nice," the guy in the passenger seat says with a chuckle, giving me a pointed glare over his shoulder as the driver snickers at him.

I don't have time for their bullshit. Sighing, I repeat myself, "Where. Is. Kincaid?"

It's the driver's turn to glance back at me this time with a response. "Don't worry, princess, he'll be waiting for you."

Fuck, that still really doesn't answer my question. Not even a little bit, fuckers.

Pressing my palms into the leather beneath me, I sit

taller in my seat as I reconfirm that there are no restraints on my body. It's almost amusing that they underestimate me so damn much. Being a woman comes with its fair share of trials and tribulations, but fuck does it come in handy when you want people to believe you're defenseless.

As the two men go back to discussing some baseball game amongst themselves, I catalog every inch of them to memory. The passenger has a shaved head, hazel eyes, and broad shoulders. I noticed the sparkle of a gold tooth earlier too. The driver, on the other hand, is slim and tall, with a crooked nose and jet-black hair. Realistically, their characteristics don't matter, because by the time I'm done here, they'll both be dead.

I weigh up my options as I glare at the back of their heads. I can either get comfortable in my seat and ride it out with them so I can finally know where their compound is, or I can escape now and save myself some trouble.

It's a no-brainer what the easier option is, but let's face it, I've never been offered the easy path a day in my life. What's the point in considering it now?

"How far away are we?" I ask, pushing my luck as we seem to turn off the highway and head down a country lane.

"Five minutes. Now shut the fuck up before I do it for you," the passenger grunts, and I bite back a grin as I force myself not to respond.

I've got five minutes to get my shit together and have something that resembles a game plan in place. But I have no idea who or what I'm walking into, so it's definitely easier said than done. Five minutes is more than I had in the elevator, and I can only pray that nothing happened after I passed out.

With the determination and need to see Emily and the Ruthless Brothers as soon as possible, I scan around where I'm sitting for any kind of makeshift weapon, but I come up short. Sighing, I know exactly what I need to do.

Unclasping my bra, I pull the straps down my arms as discreetly as possible, before pulling the cups down under my tee. With a little force, I manage to stab the wires out and tuck them into the pocket of my jeans. I save them for later, and tighten my grip on the non-padded lace remains of my bra.

I try to relax my limbs, but it's pointless as my spine remains as stiff as it was the second I opened my eyes. The SUV starts to slow, and I notice a perimeter fence straight ahead. A metal gate opens when the passenger aims a fob at it and presses a button.

This is it.

Lurching forward, I lift the bra in my hands and quickly wrap it around the passenger's throat, catching him completely off-guard as he instantly gargles and chokes at my assault.

"What the fuck?" the driver shouts, slamming his foot on the break so I lurch forward, but I make sure to double down my efforts on the passenger. My grip on the lace burns as I lean further back, putting weight behind it as my victim flails his arms and legs with panic. "Fucking bitch," the driver spits, unbuckling his seatbelt to reach for my hand closest to him, but I twist my angle at the last second and move out of his grasp.

He grunts under his breath again before climbing out of the vehicle, and I know I have a split second to kill the fucker in my grasp. Pulling both bra straps into one hand, I reach into my pocket with the other, searching for the wire. Once it's in my hand, I zero in on my target, before plunging the metal into the Brute's throat.

I know I've pierced an artery the second I stop, blood spluttering from his neck like my favorite waterfall, cascading over my skin and the seat between us as the fucker goes limp in my hold. I barely release my hold on the lace when the door to my right swings open and the driver grabs my leg.

Before I can kick him off, he's dragging me from the SUV. I grunt as my back smacks against the ground, but I manage to stop my head from receiving an injury. The driver sneers at me, shoving my leg away from him, but that's another mistake on his end, the first was thinking he could take me to begin with.

Kicking out, I connect with his calves, but he doesn't fall to the ground.

*Asshole.*

He leans toward me, attempting to grab the collar of my tee, but I punch him in the face before he can get a hold of me. That doesn't stop him from returning the favor in the next second as he smashes his fist into my face, another shiner to match the one from Kincaid earlier, making me wince as I instantly feel blood trickle down over my lip.

This time, he manages to get a grip on my collar, lifting me up slightly as I scramble to fight back. Another blow to my face, another drop of blood on my t-shirt, another flame to my fire, as I yell an almighty battle cry from my stomach.

Swinging my arms, I aim for his chest, and he grunts. He sways with the force, and I use the move to my advantage, swiping my leg at his calves once again. This time, he topples to the ground, and I quickly stagger to my feet. The second I have my balance, this motherfucker returns the same action my way, and I'm falling backward against my will before I hit the ground. Again. Only this time, my head takes the majority of the blow instead of my back.

Familiar black speckles taint my vision as my head throbs, pain emanating throughout my body as my pulse rings in my ears.

Fuck.

Stones press into my palms as I try to lift myself up, but the knock hits me harder than I care to admit. A boot slams into my stomach from the side as I roll with the movement, pain adding to more pain as he beats down on me.

Tensing my body, I cocoon myself to the count of ten.

One. Two. Blow. Three. Four. Kick. Five. Six. Fist. Seven. Eight.

Fuck it.

With all my strength, I roll my body toward him. One hand reaching into my pocket as the other grips his ankle. Before he can hit me one more time, I thrust the bra wire at his ankle, severing his achilles tendon with one move. The wire clatters to the ground beside me and I exhale.

He crumbles to the floor, and I use the reprieve to catch my breath, my lungs burning as I roll myself up onto my hands and knees. Gulping in a few breaths, I push through the pain and lightheaded feeling consuming me to make it to my feet.

Eyes fixed on the Brute beside me, I edge back toward the SUV slightly, leaning against the rear bumper for support. This idiot isn't done though. He crawls toward me, unable to put any pressure on his foot. I don't move, letting him use his energy to get to me, until he braces his hand on the bottom of the door frame to try and prop himself up. That's when I move.

Reaching for the exterior door handle, I don't think twice as I slam the door shut on him. A crunch echoes around me, vibrating through the door as one or more of his bones crush. It's not enough though. I do it again and again, panting and yelling with every blow as blood splatters around me, painting the SUV and me in more deep red smears.

When my arms are burning and I can't make another swing, I push the door open, slumping back against the vehicle as exhaustion threatens to take over my limbs. Looking at the Brute now at my feet, his skull crushed, brain matter exposed, I try to catch my breath.

Giving myself a moment, I consider what the best course of action is with him, and before I can decide better of it, I place my hands under his arms and hoist him into the SUV with a grunt. Every limb aches, but I manage to clamber him inside, slamming the door shut with a sigh as I finally take stock of where we are.

The gate is still open behind me, and a clubhouse sits in the far distance. If anyone knows we're here, no one seems to be paying us any attention. I know I need to move. Now.

With trembling hands, I slowly walk around the SUV to the driver's seat, only to remember the very dead passenger is still in the car. What a fucking state I'll look like with this kind of baggage. Maybe I can joke about it in the future.

Maybe.

Slipping into the driver's seat, I stare down the house ahead, considering whether I should take them on now, but the reality of the matter is I have no weapons, no defenses, no army, and I'm already injured.

I don't have the Ruthless Brothers. And that's exactly what I need. Now more than ever.

# THIRTY

*Scarlett*

Driving at the speed limit is harder than I expected. My vision is ruined. I'm sure I have a concussion, but that doesn't stop me trying to find my way home.

That's where I'm heading. Home. Wherever the Ruthless Brothers are is where I need to be.

I get lost too many fucking times after I get myself back to where I came around in the back of the SUV. But then the highway appears up ahead, and I'm putting my foot down the best I can to cut the remainder of the distance.

Frustration and pain has my eyes lined with unshed tears. Drops I refuse to let loose because I'm fucking stronger than this.

The sun is slowly setting in the distance, guiding me home, until I'm winding my way through the roads leading to the compound. Excitement buzzes in my chest, exhaustion clawing at me, setting harder into my veins with every inch of comfort that comes with the close proximity now.

As the familiar gates appear in the distance, a sob breaks past my lips, and I'm relieved there's no one here to actually hear it. My eyebrows pinch together though when I notice a van pulling into the compound ahead of me.

What the fuck is going on?

I press my foot down a little more, eager to understand, when I notice the metal gate to the compound start to slow behind the retreating gray van. No. Fucking. Way. Despite my vision blurring, I stomp my foot down, sailing down the road until I cut through the remaining gap in the fence, the metal scraping against the side of the SUV.

Just as quickly as I accelerated, I hit the brakes, screeching to a stop and wincing when I hear the dead body in the back bump around.

My knuckles are wrapped tightly around the steering wheel as I squeeze my eyes shut and try to catch my breath, for what feels like the hundredth time in the past hour. Blinking my eyes open slowly, I manage to stabilize my vision for a few seconds as I watch a handful of prospects round the back of the van and open it to reveal a gurney with a plastic bag shielding a dead body.

Fuck.

No. No. No. No. No.

Swinging the door open, I lurch before I remember to unclip myself, before I drop down to the ground and rush toward the body.

"Who is in there?" I ask, watching as their eyes go wide at the sight of me.

"Fuck, Scarlett. Are you—"

"Who the fuck is in there?" I grind out, interrupting him as I point at the bag with a trembling hand.

The prospect before me swipes a hand down his face, a solemn look on his face and my heart burns with every beat in my chest. "It's Duffer. He didn't make it."

Pain and relief collides inside of me at once. I knew he was gone earlier, I had opted to compartmentalize that information for later when I was ready to deal with it. I'm just thankful it's not—

"Where's Emily?"

Any response is lost when the doors to the compound swing open with a thunderous slam. "Who the fuck is... Scarlett?"

My eyelids fall closed again at the sound of my name on his tongue, hope and relief blossoming in my chest as my heart all but bursts from my body. Wetting my parched lips, I lift my eyelashes once again to reveal Axel taking slow measured steps toward me.

"Axel." His name is a prayer on my lips as I fight back the need to fucking cry at his mere presence.

"It's you. You're here," he states, more to himself than anyone else as he continues toward me, and I offer a feeble nod in response.

His steps pick up, and I realize too late that he's not going to slow down, and on my next breath, I'm lifted into the air with a gasp. Axel's arms band around me, pinning me to his chest as a tiny sob escapes my lips, more with the shock of what he's doing than the current situation.

Tentatively, I wrap my arms around his neck, clinging to him just as hard as he does to me. I want to drop my face into the crook of his neck, but I don't want to push him further than he's expecting.

Another slam from the clubhouse has me glancing back over his shoulder to see Emmett, Ryker, and Gray rushing toward us. They're just as shocked as I am, but nowhere near as devastated as I am when Axel slowly lowers me to the ground.

Once my feet are balanced on the hard surface, I expect him to realize what the hell he's doing and put some much-needed distance between us, but instead, he tilts my face up so we're eye to eye. Locked in his intoxicating gaze, I gape when he lowers himself an inch at a time, until he presses his lips against my forehead.

I'm dead. I must be. This is what heaven looks and feels like, surely.

"Are you okay?" he asks, his thumb stroking back and

forth over my chin as I manage a nod. "Words, Scarlett," he adds, quirking a brow at me.

"Yeah," I rasp, my voice hoarse as he takes in a deep breath. "Where's Emily?"

Axel grins down at me like he knew that was exactly what I would say next. "She's inside sleeping. She drank enough bourbon to knock me on my ass, so she might be out for a while."

"But she's okay?" I clarify, needing to hear it.

"She's perfect, Reaper, and that's all because of you."

I start to deny the fact when the rumble of bikes gets louder and louder and I turn toward the gate. Bike after bike filter into the compound as Ryker, Emmett, and Gray edge closer to us until we're standing in a line.

"Who is that?" I ask, pushing my blood-stained hair back off my face as I watch them all.

"It's our other chapter, Sweet Cheeks," Gray murmurs, sweeping me off my feet, not caring that the men are arriving. I melt into his hold, tucking my face into his neck like I desperately wanted to do to Axel a moment ago. "Emmett and Ryker won't reveal that you matter to them, Scar. Not in front of them, not just yet. Trust me, it's for the best," he breathes against my ear.

"Why?" I ask, confused as fuck. "Why are they here to begin with?"

"Because Kincaid took you and we needed backup."

Before I can ask him anything else, I'm being placed back down on my feet against my wishes. Three of the bikers move forward on their own first, the remainder waiting by their bikes.

It's like life moves in slow motion for the second time today as the three in front of us take their helmets off, revealing their faces. Just like that, my world collides. Again.

"Are my eyes deceiving me, or is that little Scarlett Reeves."

I don't have any energy left to keep fighting right now, never mind dealing with this motherfucker in front of me.

"You two know each other?" Gray asks as Axel moves to cover me ever so slightly.

"Know each other? It's more than that, isn't it, Scar." His voice goes through me, but I can handle it more than his father's, who stands to his right. I can sense his beady eyes all over me and I want to be sick.

"Explain," Axel grunts, looking at me for the truth instead of the club president standing across from us.

With all the strength I can muster, I roll my shoulders back and point at the leader first. "Axel, I'm assuming you know Declan, he was my first. Not by choice, I might add, and his father, Graham," I add, refusing to look at him as I point in his direction. "Taught me everything I know."

Rage radiates off Axel before he leans in close to

murmur against my ear so only I can hear. "Are you telling me that we called in *your* enemy to help rescue you from *our* enemy?"

I gulp, hating that my feelings and emotions are getting the better of me time and time again. Especially when I think I've overcome one hurdle, only to be hit with ten more. But this is different now; I'm not at my father's or the Reapers' disposal any longer.

No. I have the Ruthless Brothers behind me, a foundation I'm going to use to prop me up as I act unfazed by their presence despite the nausea rising inside of me.

"Yes. Yes, you did."

# TO BE CONTINUED...

# THANK YOU

Michael 'the boss man' husband, you've held my hand, you've squeezed me tight, and you've been my entire rock throughout this series. It's been like nothing else, and you'll forever be my king for remaining close, while spreading my wings for me to fly too.

Thank you to my Queen Bee's; Tanya, Nicole, and Jen. Like for real, how you motivate me to keep going, and to write the scenes you want haha is beyond me. You keep me sane and give me strength simply by being at the other end of the chat. Thank you.

A million thank yous to my beta's; Monica, Keira, Lorna, Kerrie, Marisa, and Krystal! You rock! Honestly, I was worried this book was a sack of poop but your comments gave me all the vibes and strength. Thank you.

Kirsty. My bad-ass famalam. Thank God for your ability to run my life with a notebook haha I appreciate you. Thank you.

Laura and Katie. I'm obsessed with this beauty so much. It means the world to me the amount of effort we put into this. Stunning. Thank you!

Sarah you rocked those proof vibes as always and you are forever the queen sassi in my life.

Zainab, thank you for making this baby so beautiful.

I love every single word.

# ABOUT KC KEAN

KC Kean began her writing journey in 2020 amidst the pandemic and homeschooling… yay! After reading all of the steam, from fade to black, to steamy reads, MM, and reverse harem, she decided to immerse herself in her own worlds too.

When KC isn't hiding away in the writing cave, she is playing Dreamlight Valley, enjoying the limited UK sunshine with her husband, children, and furbabies, or collecting vinyls like it's a competition.

# ALSO BY KC KEAN

### Ruthless Brothers MC
*(Reverse Harem MC Romance)*
Ruthless Rage
Ruthless Rebel
Ruthless Riot

### Featherstone Academy
*(Reverse Harem Contemporary Romance)*
My Bloodline
Your Bloodline
Our Bloodline
Red
Freedom
Redemption

### All-Star Series
*(Reverse Harem Contemporary Romance)*
Toxic Creek
Tainted Creek
Twisted Creek

*(Standalone MF)*

Burn to Ash

**Emerson U Series**

*(Reverse Harem Contemporary Romance)*

Watch Me Fall

Watch Me Rise

Watch Me Reign


**Saints Academy**

*(Reverse Harem Paranormal Romance)*

Reckless Souls

Damaged Souls

Vicious Souls

Fearless Souls

Heartless Souls


**Silvercrest Academy**

*(Reverse Harem Paranormal Romance)*

Falling Shadows

Made in United States
North Haven, CT
06 December 2024

61739356R00257